Once Upon a Rose

Once Upon a Rose

by LAURA FLORAND

Chapter 1

When the car stalled, Layla started to wonder if she hadn't made a big mistake.

Sure, it was a nice fantasy, escaping to a forgotten heritage in Provence, abandoning the world after first playing in a Paris fountain with your phone in your pocket. No *way* a producer could email or text a fugitive musician about where her next songs were when her phone was sitting in a box of rice.

But right about now, it would have been nice to have Google Maps.

She climbed out of the little van, scrubbing her face. Peace greeted her. Just this soft hush of it, as if all sound had been velveted by rose petals. She leaned back against her van, staring up at the stars. Wow, they were gorgeous here, with so little light to compete with them. Pure and beautiful, a silent song of stars.

She used to feel that way—as if she was pure song. As if everything she did, everything she was existed to pour out music.

Her hand slipped into her pocket, and she worked her fingers over her hand exerciser nervously, in lieu of the guitar she hadn't touched in days. Not since her last gig, and it had been months before that since she'd written anything new. She'd played her old songs over and over, a new town every night, bombarded by kudos and critics, but the well of creativity those songs had once been drawn from seemed to have gone completely dry.

If you were a singer-songwriter, if that was who you *were*, and you didn't write music...who were you?

Maybe she should get some rest. She'd driven straight down from Paris in one go, a drive of ten hours, and then she'd gotten lost for hours more on these impossible back roads.

All to check out some house in the south of France that had found its way down to her years after her erratic father's passing. Did she have time for this? No. *She had an album to write.*

Maybe she could hole up in the house and write the damn thing. If she could ever find it. At this point, she was so tired and so sick of driving around lost, she was about ready to sleep in this field of...of...

Flowers? The road was built up higher than the fields around it, so that she could stare over...were those roses?

She straightened from the van, taking a step toward them. Like...a whole field of rose bushes, stretching...how far did they stretch? Moonlight gilded the petals, making leaves stand out sharply as far as the black form of the hills.

She climbed down the bank to touch petals softer than silk, then bent to breathe in. A soft sweetness filled her lungs, as if all those crisp scents of thyme and rosemary and pine that had filled the air in these Provençal hills for the past few hours had decided to lay themselves down in a bed of roses for the night and go to sleep.

Roses.

The little house that she'd inherited was on a road called Rue des Rosiers. Road of the rose bushes. It was supposed to be on the edge of fields of roses, nestled in a valley.

Hills rose around her in the distance, great shapes against the stars, with a handful of lights here and there against their darkness. Meaning she was in a valley, right?

Maybe, at long last, she was getting close to her destination.

She eyed the lights glowing from a house deeper in the valley. A mile off maybe? The house must belong to whoever grew these roses.

Seriously, how bad could someone who grew roses for a living be? She'd once busked her way through Europe when she was still a student, and she'd certainly crashed many a night, while on the music circuit, with near strangers she'd met at whatever festival she was playing. She could handle this. She headed through the field toward the lights.

Walking through the dark rows of roses was the oddest blend of peace and stress. Alarm and pleasure mixed in the strangest way. Stranded alone at night in a foreign country...the sweet scent of roses wafting off an endless field...walking through the darkness, which everyone knew from films was always full of monsters...stars brilliant overhead, a balmy Provençal May night...

Look, don't let all this fool you! A woman didn't survive summers busking her way through Europe without learning better than to let the beauty of her surroundings lure her into a false sense of safety. *That's why tourists are always getting in trouble. They think they've fallen into a fairy tale and forget fairy tales have ogres.*

The noise from the house got louder. She followed a packed dirt road off the main one, and then a long gravel drive, lined with cars. Loud music spilled from open windows, nearly overwhelmed by the drunk voices joining in to sing *Allez, allez, allez!*

Her body shifted into the rhythm without thought, shoulders and hips dancing a tiny bit to that happy, triumphant rhythm. It was the kind of music that invited a music-lover to throw off tiredness, to bounce into that farmhouse and join the party.

She stopped in front of the door. From inside the house came sounds of people either throwing tables at each other or possibly trying to dance on top of them. Her kind of place, in fact. Well, it wouldn't be the first

3

time she'd turned up at a stranger's house in the middle of the night. Not even the first time she turned up to find the strangers throwing tables. Sometimes, the chance-met hosts at a festival who seemed so nice and friendly during the day turned out to have over-indulged in mushrooms while waiting for her to wrap up, post-performance.

Still. It was either this or walk back to her van. Might as well check it out.

She took a deep breath and knocked. Then knocked harder. Then knocked really, really hard. Then finally turned the doorknob and eased the door open a bit.

And that moment when the friend with the Great Dane opens the door and the whole scrabbling force of claws and long tongue that door had been holding back gets freed and leaps for your shoulders? It was kind of like that.

Chapter 2

To this valley! Matt growled, lifting his glass high. No one paid any attention, even though it was *his* thirtieth birthday, and *he* was the family patriarchal heir, no matter what Raoul and Damien wanted themselves to be.

He toasted himself while he was at it. Matthieu Rosier, Jean-Jacques Rosier's heir, owner of all he surveyed. Every petal of a rose. Every worm in the dirt trying to eat those roses. All of it.

It was all on his shoulders, but it was also all his. *J'y suis, j'y reste*, as his ancestor Niccolò Rosario had mandated over four centuries ago. *I am here and here I'll stay.*

Just for a second, that old claustrophobic feeling tried to descend on him again—that thing that had driven him to the Paris offices and into the not-so-tender embrace of a supermodel the year before, in hopes of proving that his life existed outside this valley. He drowned it in another swallow.

No, this is my place. This is where I'm *meant to be.* Here, he could handle anything the weather or people or time threw at him, do anything that needed doing. *I'm Matthieu Rosier. I know it now, and my next thirty years are going to be awesome!*

Awesome. Definitely. Grinning suddenly, he grabbed his cousin Raoul's girlfriend Allegra as she headed past him, placed her firmly behind him with her hands on his waist, and started a chain dance.

Which kind of had a bad effect on the tables, but it wasn't his fault he had so many big male cousins who danced like elephants. They'd all been trained to dance properly, too—you'd think it would come across somewhat even when they were chain dancing. *No more tuxedoes and waltzes for me, thank God. I'm never putting on a tuxedo for a woman again. From now on, I'm sticking with women who like to see a man in jeans.* He bumped into another table.

One of his aunts protested, the whole chain abandoned him and wound itself the other way, and he lurched off the table, grinning and feeling a smidge dizzy. Maybe he needed to get some air. He could probably come back in and hold still more wine afterward.

Which sounded like a great idea, because he had had *excellent* taste when he set that wine aside at twenty for his thirtieth birthday.

He turned to the door and ran straight into a guest trying to slip inside the house. Her face smashed into his chest, and he looked down at a wild mass of bronze-tipped curls and then a heart-shaped face tilting back to look up at him as she bounced backward.

"Well, *hello*," he exclaimed, delighted, picking her straight up off the floor before she fell. Then he wasn't quite sure what to do with her—maybe it had been a *tad* excessive, picking her up completely to stop her from falling? Still, he could hardly drop her now.

She was gaping at him, for one thing. And since she had the most adorable rosebud mouth, a gape was a *very* hot look on her. Her skin was this luscious sun-warmed color, as if she'd escaped from an island, and she had corkscrew honey-brown curls springing out at all angles. Even with a few of them smashed into a ponytail like that, the rest were making her head look a foot wide.

"Umm...*bonsoir*," she said carefully, wiggling her dangling toes.

Oh, and she had an *accent*. Oh, that was *hot*. "You're late," he said cheerfully. "You should have got here before I was quite this drunk."

Those rosebud lips parted again. She really shouldn't leave that mouth of hers open as if she was going to let someone else figure out what to do with it. Not when the someone else was him, anyway. Although...it *was* his birthday. He wished he could remember her name. Be shitty if she was dating one of his cousins.

He looked around, still not quite sure where to put her. At last, he crossed the great room, still carrying her by the hips, shoved some bottles out of the way on the bar, and set her butt firmly there. Nobody had hit him yet, so she probably wasn't dating one of his cousins.

Then he frowned a little bit at the bar, because it seemed a shame he'd pressed her butt against it before he had remembered to check it out. On the plus side, this set her at a level where he could just *tilt* a bit forward and end up with his face in her breasts. And he *was* feeling dizzy, and it *was* his birthday, and also, those were cute breasts. Hiding under a shirt like that. Seemed a shame. He remained upright with a valiant effort of what remained of his will. "You can talk some more," he told her, patting her on the knee. Nice muscles to her leg, there. Promising sign for her butt. "I like your accent."

"*Merci*," she said faintly, and her trouble with the R just *tickled* over his body. "Umm...do you know my name?"

Oh, damn, no. *What* was it? Shit. She was bound to get offended if he couldn't remember where they had met last. Where *had* they met last? Why didn't he remember her? She was at his birthday party, for God's sake. True, half the people around Grasse were, but you'd think he would remember the cute ones.

Some of the younger cousins tumbled against his legs while he was trying to think, and he bent down to right the littlest boy absently. The little Delange girl chasing them with confetti paused long enough to throw more of it over him and the new arrival, so that it ended up caught in that curly hair. He smiled at the little terror approvingly and felt his own hair. Yeah, there was so much confetti in it at this point that it was probably hopeless.

His aunt Annick passed by with a big tray of mostly empty glasses, persisting once again in cleaning up while the party was still going on. His grandfather and his

Tante Colette had long since retired but everyone else was in full swing. And look at that, someone was wasting his good wine. He snagged the half-full glass off the tray and offered it to Curls.

"No," she said faintly, and then reached out and covered the top of it with her hand, removing it from his grasp. "And you've had enough," she said firmly.

Matt grinned. He'd been starting to have a niggle of a doubt, but that was definitely a girlfriend thing to do. Off in that surreal world where girlfriends actually cared about you enough to boss you around, like Allegra did Raoul.

"Matt. Who is this?" Aunt Annick paused long enough to ask, her eyes bright with joy at being the first to discover whom one of the cousins was dating.

"My girlfriend," he said cheerfully. He looked at his girlfriend expectantly. *Hint, hint. You can go ahead and say your name now.*

She gaped at him again. Damn, that was such a good look on her.

"Your—girlfriend?" Aunt Annick looked pretty surprised, since the aunts thought the cousins incapable of going out with someone more than once without one of them finding out about it and telling all the others. Matt grinned at her smugly. *Fooled you, didn't I?* She'd probably thought he was still brooding over Nathalie. Date just one damn supermodel in your life and no one ever thought you could get over her.

"I like to call her Bouclettes," he said grandly. It seemed plausible as a nickname. All those curls.

Aunt Annick frowned a little bit. "Half a second," she told Bouclettes. "Let me put this down. I'll be right back."

But en route instead, she crossed paths with Raoul, and Matt saw her give him the go-check-on-your-cousin poke. Damn.

"Matt," Raoul said, surging up into their space. "What the hell are you doing? Who is this?"

8

Oh, fine, put him on the spot. He gave Raoul a dirty look, hopefully dirty enough to encourage him to go back to Africa. And *not* laugh at him. Was Raoul laughing at him? Matt was picking up on far too much amusement. Also deep aggravation.

"A friend," he told Raoul coolly. "Back off. Go play with Allegra."

"Do you want to be his friend?" Raoul asked his guest instead, unforgivably.

Matt scowled at him. Raoul *had* a girlfriend already. What was Raoul doing trying to steal *his* girl? "He's got a girlfriend," he informed Bouclettes just to make sure she didn't get distracted. "Ignore him."

"Umm, actually..." Bouclettes began, sounding hopeful, "is your girlfriend *here*? And sober?"

"Probably not sober," Raoul said. "But better off than him. He just turned thirty."

Matt gave him an indignant look. Was it necessary to mention that? This girl looked mid-twenties, tops.

"Matt. Who is this?" his cousin Damien appeared to ask. "And why are you picking her up and carrying her around your birthday party?"

Damn it, he *knew* he only had seconds with her before all his cousins started flocking in. "Go find your own girlfriend!" he snapped at Damien. *Merde*, now Tristan was circling in, too. Tristan and Damien *liked* putting on tuxedoes. And probably liked women with corkscrew curls, too. Whose tastes *wouldn't* include those corkscrew curls? Matt wanted to squoosh those curls between his hands so bad.

"The thing is, Matt, what if she's not your girlfriend?" Raoul asked. Raoul was just being a bastard tonight, wasn't he? "You've never introduced her to us before."

"Yes, well, who wants to introduce a girl to you vultures," he retorted, sliding an arm possessively around her waist, where she still sat on the bar. It made her curls tickle his shoulder. He grinned, delighted with them. "Don't listen to them," he told her. "They're just jealous."

Damn, did he want her to know they were jealous and therefore let her realize they would be interested in her? One problem with having so many cousins nearly his size and nearly his age and sometimes with even more money was that it made for one hell of a lot of competition.

"About that girlfriend of yours," Bouclettes said to Raoul, rather desperately. She tried to sidle away from Matt's arm, but she ran into some more wine bottles packing the bar, so he tightened his arm to protect her from them.

"Right." Raoul turned, looked around the crowd of laughing, drunk dancers, and then proved he was more than a bit drunk himself by finally tilting his head back, opening his mouth, and loosening a boom that shook the rafters: "Allegra!!"

Allegra turned her dark head and shook herself free of what remained of the chain dance with some difficulty—several people kept pulling her back to dance—and appeared beside Raoul, fixing him with a minatory gaze that made Matt's heart tighten in jealousy. That chiding look was so, so...*cozy*. As if Raoul could be as annoying as he pleased and still be loved for it. Matt was annoying, too, and all he'd gotten for it so far was an astoundingly bad dating history.

He snuck a glance at Bouclettes hopefully. No time like the present for changing a man's luck with women.

"I'm not a dog," Allegra told Raoul severely.

Raoul grinned and shook his shaggy rust-and-charcoal head, instantly pseudo-meek, lifting up both her hands to kiss them. "*Pardon, bonheur.* I thought you might help us not scare Matt's new girlfriend to death."

"Or you could try backing off," Matt told him resentfully. "I was doing just fine until the three of you started crowding her." Of *course* that would be too much. Four big guys like that. He and his cousins had been

10

pretty stubborn about trying to outgrow each other as kids. He tried, with considerable difficulty, to imagine what it might be like to be surrounded by a group of guys when your head didn't reach their shoulders, but he couldn't manage to get the angle right. In his head, he was always looking down, not up. Still, it had to be crappy, to have so many people towering over you, so he squeezed Bouclettes's waist reassuringly.

"I'll take care of you," he whispered to her. Very intriguing green eyes started to crinkle, as if she was about to laugh, which was a good sign. A man didn't get to thirty without knowing the value of making a woman laugh, so he pursued that line of attack: "Don't worry about them. Do you want me to hit one of them?"

Her eyes widened again, the laughter retreating.

"His aunts are here," Allegra told Bouclettes.

"Where are they?" Bouclettes asked rather desperately.

Allegra waved a hand to the dance floor, where Damien's mom, Tata Véro, was chopping her arms up and down in an exuberant robot dance, grinning up at his uncle Louis as she got him to try to imitate her.

"Is *she* still sober?" Bouclettes asked doubtfully. She had a really weird idea of his hospitality, if she thought his guests might still be sober at this hour of the night. What did she think he was serving people, water?

"I'm sober!" Allegra said indignantly, settling her weight against Raoul's side as if her bones might not support her by themselves. "I've only had a couple of glasses. I think." She looked up at Raoul, as if he might have kept track, but Raoul shrugged in clear indifference.

"Thanks for coming." Even if Bouclettes had gotten there a little late. They'd already sung "Joyeux Anniversaire" and everything. Matt frowned suddenly. "Are there any *choux* left? She didn't get any! Here."

He hauled Bouclettes off the bar, holding her pressed to his side as he worked his way through the

11

crowd to a long folding table that had been pushed against a wall and was littered with remnants of the cakes that had been on it.

"Look. There are still some left." He picked one of the pastry puffs from the giant *pièce montée* they had once formed—it was about like his family to offer him a Ferrari made out of pastry puffs instead of the real thing—and proffered it right to her rosebud lips.

Well, they were gaping at him again as if she wanted him to take control of them, and even he wasn't so drunk he was actually going to do all the *other* things he kept thinking about doing to them right there with all his cousins watching. A pastry puff was a good way to sublimate.

She must have thought so, too, because those green eyes held his a moment— the pastry puff pressed against her teeth—and then she finally sighed and bit into it. Cream clung to her lips. Matt just grinned. It was probably good he was too drunk to properly articulate exactly what a good look that was on her.

She licked the cream off.

Oh, yeah. Yeah, this was a nice birthday. He bent down and kissed her to say thanks for it before he remembered he wasn't going to do *any* of the fantasies, not even the kiss one, in front of his cousins.

Her mouth was warm and—rather surprised. She pulled away from him, set her hands on his chest, and shoved.

What? He loosened his arm, deeply wounded. "What's the matter with you? Don't you like me anymore?"

"I need help," she said firmly, words that ran right through his bloodstream and made every cell in it perk up and beg to be a hero. She looked around again. As if she was trying to find some *other* knight.

He looped her straight back into him, pressing her against his chest as much as she would let him, since she was arching her upper body back. "I'll help you."

Come on, please? I want to be the one who does it. Whatever it is. Storm a castle, maybe? Climb to the top of a glass mountain?

"Matt." Allegra reappeared and poked at him. "Do you actually know her at all?"

Would people quit asking him questions like that? It was getting annoying. She was at his birthday party, wasn't she?

"No," Bouclettes said, wounding him to the heart. "He doesn't. My car broke down, and this was the nearest house."

"Oh, my God." Allegra clapped her hands to her mouth. "Matt, *let go of her.*"

"You need me to fix your car?" Matt asked, his tongue feeling fuzzy. He could do that. He could fix just about anything. Seemed odd in the middle of the night when he was trying to celebrate his birthday, but then again...if one of the damn machines on this place wanted to break down, it *never* did it at a convenient moment. "All right." He looked around, trying to remember where he had put his tools. "The *atelier d'extraction*," he remembered. "They're probably in the extraction plant. I'll be right back."

He started to haul Bouclettes with him, because he was not at all fond of the idea of leaving her alone with Damien and Tristan, but Allegra reached in and grabbed his waist. He gave Raoul an appalled look. *Hey, that's not my fault. She started it. I never touched her.*

Raoul grabbed his other arm, which made Matt wince, because he was sure as hell too drunk to stop the punch that was coming. "Matt," Raoul said, instead of hitting him. "You cannot fix a car in the dark while you're this drunk. You'll undo her brake cable or something by accident, and she'll run off a cliff. I don't think any of us are in a state to work on it, really. You'll have to wait until morning," he told Bouclettes.

Morning. "You want to go to bed?" Matt asked her helpfully.

She wrenched out of what was left of his hold.

"Matt!" Allegra wedged her body with great determination between him and Bouclettes, and Raoul *still* didn't hit him. Raoul must be drunk, was all Matt could figure. "He's harmless," she told Bouclettes. "Or he's trying to be. But seriously—you can see everyone is wasted. They have mattresses filling the old attic for all the people who can't drive home tonight. Why don't you sleep on one of those, and in the morning we'll get you going again. Matt can fix your car in minutes, when he's not this drunk."

"Depends," Matt corrected conscientiously. "Is it a Ferrari?" The Ferrari he didn't get for his birthday? "I wouldn't want to rush it, if so."

Bouclettes looked at him, looked at Allegra so rudely wedging her body between Matt's and hers, looked around at the party, and finally spread her fingers across her face and began to laugh. She laughed so hard Matt started to worry she might be too drunk to drive, too. "Best to sleep it off," he told her, which brought another wave of semi-hysterical laughter.

"You need food," Allegra decided. "Also something to drink."

"*Not* wine," Bouclettes said firmly.

"It's good wine," Matt told her. "Been in our *cave* for ten years, this one, I think. One of the first wines I ever stocked in the *cave* myself."

"No, no, no," Allegra agreed with Bouclettes. "We must have fizzy water somewhere. Would a sealed bottle make you feel more comfortable?"

"A little bit, at this point," Bouclettes said, for no reason Matt could figure out.

But Allegra grinned in wry sympathy, as if women had some secret language concerning sealed bottles of water. Which would just figure, with women. And she indicated the much-diminished cheese platters. "Here, have some cheese. Raoul, can you haul Matt into one of the bathrooms and put him under the shower?"

14

"It's my birthday!" Matt protested.

"Hose would be easier," Raoul said. "But that's a myth, you know. It won't really do any good, just make him wet."

"I'll take care of it," said Damien, who *always* had to prove he could fulfill people's wishes better than anyone else. He grabbed Matt. Matt decided not to hit him, so as not to make a bad impression on Bouclettes. Also, Damien might duck, and then you never knew which of the people packed around him his fist might hit instead. If it was Allegra or Bouclettes, his cousins probably wouldn't let him live to see his thirty-first year, and who would want to, with that on his conscience?

"Allow me." His cousin Léa appeared beside them, blonde hair caught back in one of her matter-of-fact ponytails, and Matt looked at her with some relief because she always showed good sense. Actually a second cousin and one of the few girls to play with the five male first cousins growing up, she'd kind of been forced into that sensible role. "Come on, Matt, here." She took his arm from Damien and slipped it around her own waist.

What *was* it with the women tonight? Was it because it was his birthday? Léa's husband Daniel gave him a look of rather steely patience, but also didn't hit him. Somebody should have told him the guys would let him hug their women on his birthday. He would have been taking greater advantage.

"But—don't you want to come?" he asked Bouclettes wistfully as he let Léa lead him away. He might not be quite the putty Daniel was in Léa's hands, but Léa was hard to say no to.

"I'm good right here," Bouclettes said firmly, holding up a hand. He really wanted to kiss her right in the center of that adamant palm and see what she did with that.

But he let Léa boss him, because it was Léa. And when he got back, Bouclettes was gone.

Gone.

Just plain gone. Like he had imagined her or something.

What the fuck? It was his *birthday*. He didn't get to keep her?

That was so damn lousy he had to open up the bottles he had put aside on his twenty-first birthday and which he was supposed to be saving for next year.

Chapter 3

A horde of bears clawed Matt awake, stuffing their furry fat paws down his throat and somehow twisting them around and raking his eyes and head from the inside. One of them kept pounding its fat paw into his ribs, too. Hell.

He rolled over onto his back and managed to pry his eyes open enough to see Raoul standing over him, foot still raised to kick his ribs. Matt himself seemed to be lying on a mattress on the floor, which gave Raoul close to two meters to loom over him, and that was *not* a good position for the man on the floor. He was not entirely sure he could get up without being sick all over Raoul's toes, though, and he couldn't make up his mind about whether that would be more humiliating for him or for Raoul.

"Get up, Matt." Raoul sounded merciless, and amused about his position of power, too, which just proved he hadn't changed in the fourteen years since he'd abandoned his family. Raoul was the oldest of the cousins, but Matt, as the son of Jean-Jacques Rosier's firstborn son, was heir to the valley, which had always made the relationship between Matt and Raoul particularly complex. They both thought they were born to dominate. Matt had been sixteen, just starting to think he might actually get as big as his cousin one day, when Raoul had just up and left him before he could. "Or did you want me to take charge of the rose harvest for you?"

Oh, God, would you? Matt fought to suppress a whimper. *For my birthday?*

But it was his valley. Raoul got to run off to Africa. Matt stayed here and handled everything this valley could throw at him. That was why it was his valley. Raoul, Lucien, Damien, Tristan—they could all go out to have adventures, live a glamorous life, date actresses and supermodels and live to tell about it. Matt—Matt was the heir. The steward. The man who would always be the valley. When *he* dated someone glamorous and famous, it was a fucking disaster.

"I'll run the harvest," he growled, rolling onto all fours. His stomach lurched. A sledgehammer tried to beat his head down to the floor. *Pépé resisted the Gestapo,* he reminded himself. *This is just a damn hangover.* A vision of his grandfather's blue eyes filled his head, looking his heir over critically. *Get up.* He got up. Then he had to reach out and grab Raoul's shoulder to keep himself upright, an instinctive seeking of support from his cousin that seriously pissed him off.

Raoul simply let Matt brace himself against him, though. Watching him like a wolf keeping an eye out for the jugular, but steady as a rock. "Remember anything from the end of last night?" Raoul asked.

A pair of rosebud lips and a wild mass of hair flashed through Matt's mind, and he clapped his hands to his face to try to shut it out, along with the ghastly sunlight filtering into what had once been the attic from the tiny windows. Oh, *bon sang. Merde. Merde. Merde.*

Who the hell was she?

Oh, good God, she had said something about her car being broken down.

Oh, *fuck,* he had acted like that with a completely strange woman who had come to ask him for help.

Who had curls. Who had the cutest mouth. Who had—

Bordel de merde. Why hadn't anyone stopped him? What the hell point was there in having so many cousins if none of them could have stopped him from making an idiot of himself?

Damn it. *Putain de bordel de merde de, de*—It wasn't like he got drunk regularly! Why did she have to show up on his birthday of all days? At midnight, too. Talk about setting a man up. Couldn't she have come at six or something, before the drinking started, and given him one damn chance to make a good impression?

"Oh, you *do*," Raoul said sadistically. "Way to impress the girls, Matt."

"Leave me the fuck alone, Raoul."

Probably Raoul had fixed her car. Someone like that. While Matt had made a fool out of himself.

Merde, he hoped someone had fixed her car and gotten her out of the house, because he could not face her sober. How had he managed to get that drunk?

"We must have scared the shit out of her. I wish I'd realized faster that she didn't actually know you," Raoul said.

Putain de merde. Matt stalked off to the bathroom, where he was desperately ill and then tried not to look at himself in the mirror while he used one of the stock of new toothbrushes they kept in the old attic room to brush his teeth. Hell, he couldn't believe he had slobbered all over that poor girl.

Damn it.

He stomped back out of the bathroom, trying not to show that each impact of his foot drove its way right through his stomach and up his throat, nearly taking the contents with it. "So what happened to her?" he growled.

"I think she's barricaded in what was supposed to be Tata Annick's room. Tata slept on one of the mattresses up here. If we'd tried to get that girl to sleep up here in a room full of mattresses with people like you on them after the way you acted, she would have run off into the night. *Merde*, Matt."

"You could have hit me over the head!" It wasn't as if Raoul had ever hesitated when they were kids.

"I'm trying to give that up," Raoul said. "So are you going to fix her car or do I need to?" Back in the days when they used to do junior rallies, Matt had always been the best mechanic, but everyone who drove or co-drove in rallies knew his way around a car.

"I'll fix it." He still had a chance to *fix* something for her? "You stay the hell away from her car, Raoul." His damn greedy cousins were always trying to swoop in and steal his things.

***

Layla woke in startled panic. Her celebrity duo of producers had tracked her down and were pounding on the door, demanding the damn songs. And when she failed to turn them over, they hauled her up out of bed and marched her out in front of her fans stark naked except for a banner that said, "Album delayed". The fans started pelting her with rotten...rotten roses? One hit her in the face, and her eyes flared open as she sat up in bed.

Where the heck was she?

Unfamiliar curtains with a pattern of blue flowers on white, her fingers resting on soft, old sheets embroidered with small roses. The scent of lavender teased her from the sheets.

And someone was indeed knocking on the door. She turned her head to spy the chair lodged under the door handle, and blinked finally into reality.

She was in a valley of roses.

Her tour was over. Her phone was out of commission. Nobody could text her. Nobody could email her. Nobody besides her mother even knew where she was. Actually, Layla wasn't even sure she herself knew where she was.

God, she was *free.*

Kind of *The Fugitive* style free, but still.

Energy shot through her, all exhaustion forgotten.

"Coming!" she called. "Just a second." She pushed out of bed, double-checking herself. She'd been offered a T-shirt, in lieu of going back to her car to get her things, but she'd opted to sleep in her clothes. All that time on the road, playing in bars and at festivals, had taught her a few things. How to judge when she was really in danger, for one. But never to get so sure of a completely strange place and situation that she didn't take a few precautions, like putting a chair under the door handle or sleeping dressed and ready to handle anything.

A drunk bear of a stranger who hauled her around a party might not seem like the most reliable host, after all. Even if he did stop to ruffle kids' hair.

She bit back a grin. The Bear really had been cute, though. All that delighted approval from such a big, hot guy. He had been so—him. Natural. Enthusiastic. Her mouth curved more. Very enthusiastic. Granted, he had been drunk out of his mind, but she could at least pretend that his delight in her had been genuine, right? Right?

No one ever said a woman couldn't indulge in a little light, pretend flirtation in her head to distract herself from her real problems.

She touched her hair, the impossible curls all stale and tangled from travel and sleep, and sighed. *He was dead drunk. Let's just face it. He probably would have been utterly charmed by his best friend's grandmother at that point.*

She pulled the door open. "Hi." Allegra stood on the other side of it—the little American girlfriend of one of the big guys in this family. She and a chic woman who claimed, with some exasperation, to be the Bear's aunt, had set Layla up in this bedroom the night before. Despite the many times Layla had crashed with strangers, she always felt self-conscious about her intrusion the morning after.

"Morning!" Allegra said. With glossy dark hair and vivid dark brown eyes, she looked vibrant and pretty and entirely eager to take on her day. "Listen, we're all heading out to the rose harvest. Almost everyone has already left, but I didn't want you to wake up scared in a strange house."

Okay, clearly these people didn't keep musicians' hours. "Rose harvest?" Layla tried to reach for her phone to check the time and then remembered the whole incident with the fountain.

"Yeah, it's the harvest. You know? For the perfume industry?"

Layla looked at her blankly.

"I guess you couldn't see anything last night, but this whole valley is full of roses. One of the last valleys like this in France. Most of the regional production has gone to Bulgaria or cheaper areas. But Chanel No. 5 and Abbaye have always used the *roses de mai* here, and they claim they always will, that their noses—their perfumers' noses, you know, *the* Noses like Tristan, not ordinary noses like yours and mine—can tell the difference in the scent."

The language was so different from Layla's habitual one of chord progressions, guitar licks, filigrees, and pop signifiers that the synapses in her brain almost didn't have paths for the words. She took a deep breath, shaking her head to put it on this other track, this one of perfumes and flowers.

"A whole valley of roses," she said softly, remembering the walk in the moonlight, the soft light gilding over softer petals. So she was in the right place. Somewhere around here was that mysterious house she had received, from somewhere back in the roots of her family's biological history, some heritage from a great-grandmother long lost through the adoption and war that had rerouted her family genealogy through two generations. Layla had thought those wars, adoptions, divorces, and migrations had left her no roots whatsoever, and then...this odd thing had sprouted up out of the blue, like a seed that had blown over from the field of someone with a past.

"Go brush your teeth, and I'll show it to you." Allegra thrust a stack of items into her hands that included a towel, washcloth, and an unopened toothbrush. "Matt says he fixed your van." She paused in the act of turning away and grinned back over her shoulder. "Well, actually, he says that it would take a month to fix everything that's wrong with that van, and he wants to know why the hell you are driving that thing—he's got a hangover. But it does at least crank again now." Allegra winked at her and pushed a couple of doors open to show her toilet and shower rooms, then headed on down the hall while Layla got ready.

The farmhouse felt centuries old. Heavy, exposed stone walls surrounded Layla as she took a two-minute shower. (A girl who had often depended on the kindness of strangers on the road learned fast that in Europe, water and electricity cost her hosts a lot of money.)

Outside the house, an empty, faded teak table sat in the shade of a massive plane tree. Newer outbuildings stood a little distance from the farmhouse, across a wide gravel yard. As Layla and Allegra headed around one outbuilding, Layla caught glimpses of metal and blue barrels through the factory doors, a chemical scent washing over her. Someone was unloading burlap sacks from a truck onto a conveyor belt that carried those up to a man on an upper level.

She and Allegra rounded the building and—

Layla stopped dead, all the muscles in her body relaxing in pleasure.

The roses stretched out for what seemed like miles, their glory revealed in the morning light. Row after row of pink, stretching all the way to a village at the end of the valley, a stone church steeple rising past the fields. Morning dew still gleamed over the petals—not the formal, sculpted buds of the cut roses used in bouquets but softer, more open blooms, thickly ruffled with pink petals. The sun lifting past the horizon angled rays the whole length of the valley until the entire vision sparkled in her eyes. Scents wafted over her, and her hand slid away from the grip exerciser in her pocket. For a moment, her mind was blank even of music. All she wanted to do was breathe.

Allegra smiled at her. "Beautiful, isn't it?"

"It's incredible."

"Isn't it amazing?" Allegra hugged herself with pleasure. "I saw some of the rose harvest last year, when I first got here, but this time I'm *part* of it." She spread her arms wide to embrace everything around her, a sparkling, vivacious, happy woman who turned a ready friendliness on Layla. She was exactly that never-met-a-stranger kind of person who, if a music fan, was likely to offer Layla a room for the night while out on the road. "I bet you could stay a little bit and see what the harvest is like, if you want. They won't mind." Suppressed amusement. "Matt definitely won't. Although he was even grumpier than usual this morning, with that hangover."

"Is Matt the hot one?" A vision flashed through Layla's mind of the other men who had appeared to try, in their alcohol-fuddled way, to make sure she was fine the night before. Okay, maybe they were all hot, but—

Allegra grinned as she headed through the rows of roses. "Oh, man, can I tell Matt you said he was *the* hot one like that? Out of all his cousins? Because that would make him so happy."

"No," Layla said indignantly. "You cannot! What's wrong with you?"

"No, seriously, he'll probably blush. He'd *love* it."

"Allegra!"

"Are you going to be staying here long, or are you just on vacation? Because he's single, I'm just saying."

Layla's eyebrows rose. "How did he manage that?" Because, seriously...very hot guy.

"Trust me, if I could figure out how those guys manage to get in such screwed-up relationships with women, I would solve the mystery of the universe. The perfume industry is *not* the healthiest dating environment, let's put it that way. Too many models and actors and people obsessed with image and what others think of them, constantly pretending perfection. Always performing who they are instead of being it."

Performing. Layla rubbed her fingers against her jeans uneasily. The calluses on the fingertips of her left hand scraped gently against the denim.

"So how long are you staying in the area?" Allegra asked.

Layla smiled wryly. "A long time, if I can't get my car fixed."

"Oh, don't worry about that. If Matt said he fixed it, he fixed it. He can fix anything."

Could he, now. That Birthday Bear got sexier all the time.

"Anyway, I don't even know where *here* is," Layla said. "And I'm still trying to find where I'm going." And how to get past the incredible mental roadblock she seemed to have set up between her and getting there.

She stroked the petals of the roses as they passed. Softer than silk, their scent rising around her. Could her destination really be somewhere around here?

"Ask the guys. They know everywhere within a three-hundred-kilometer radius, I swear," Allegra said. Her eyes sparkled. "So you really thought Matt was hot? Even the way he was acting?"

He'd made her feel alive. Not scrambling desperately for more music, not worried about the performance of herself, just full of *being* herself. Granted, he'd been dead drunk and completely out of line, but still...all that buoyant enthusiasm for her had been pretty darn charming.

Plus—she liked his hair. It was black and glossy, and a little long, with all these half-curls that curved up and ended before they could do a full spiral. A woman wanted to run her hands through that hair and see if those little half-curls tickled her palms. Layla bet they would be smooth, like silk.

But all of that seemed far too intimate to say to a woman she barely knew. Well, unless she had a guitar in her hands, in which case she could get up on a stage and sing about it to ten thousand people...then complain in the post-performance let-down how worn out and over-exposed she felt. She was tired of over-exposing herself. So she stuck with the primitive, the thing they could all agree on without revealing too much of their hearts: "He's got a really good body."

Big shoulders, muscled arms, strong wrists. He sure had picked her up and hauled her around that party as if she weighed a feather. Despite her brain's insistence that this was completely unacceptable behavior, her instincts kept finding it rather—hot. *How long can you keep carrying me this way before your arms get tired, hot stuff?* Indefinitely, it had seemed.

"Seriously?" Allegra begged. "Can I *please* tell him you said that? He wouldn't even know what to do with himself, he'd be so happy. All that grouchiness would get tangled up in this fuzzy blanket, and he would just, like—it would be so *cute*."

Layla hesitated, enticed by a vision of that size and hotness getting all fuddled and thrilled. Was there any chance he might keep that enthusiasm for her when he wasn't drunk? A quirky-looking girl, who only managed to fit in among eccentric, rolling-stone musicians, and didn't really impress people until she opened her mouth and started to sing?

"Don't tell him in front of me, okay? And don't let him know I said it was okay to tell you." Down at the far end of the field, trucks parked, a sprawl of people moving through rows, and she caught a glimpse of a particular dark head and imposing set of shoulders. "Wait—grouchiness?"

"Ah." Allegra cleared her throat, cast her a sidelong glance, and gazed skyward a moment. "He, ah, might have a few little issues with grumpiness. And bossiness. And stubbornness. But I'm sure it won't come out with someone who's busy telling him he's hot."

Layla tried to imagine a scenario where she would tell Hot Stuff that he was hot straight to his face. A vision of a broad, hard naked chest rose up, her hand resting on it and—ahem. She focused on the van.

"I mean, he's such a nice guy, really," Allegra said. "Really. He really is."

Allegra was kind of protesting a lot there, wasn't she? Layla stopped at her little blue van, eyeing the other woman. Beyond and below Allegra, the field of pink and green stretched all the way to the dryer green of the hills, a sea of roses that seemed to fill the world.

And yet that pink had predators. The roses were disappearing as if attacked by locusts. Women and men moved down the rows of it, eating away the pink with their hands faster than Layla could have even walked the row, snapping flowers off and dumping them into an apron-like pocket that hung against their thighs. Most of the women wore long, colorful skirts that came down to their feet, shirts that covered every inch of their skin, broad-brimmed straw hats, sometimes even their faces covered.

Layla's stomach tightened in reaction as all the blooms were stripped away, leaving those poor bushes with nothing. All that beauty, all that eagerness to share it with the world, and just like that, it was gone. The world had taken the roses up on their offer and stripped them of everything they had, leaving them innocuous green bushes, nothing special about them at all.

Get a grip, Layla. They're roses, not your personal metaphor.

"Who are the harvesters?" Layla asked.

"Seasonal, mostly migrant workers," Allegra said. "They're able to keep a core of a couple dozen all year round, but they have to hire temporary workers to help with the main harvests—roses in May and jasmine in August. You can spot a few teenagers or locals looking to make a little extra money among them. And the family will pick sometimes, like today, but mostly for nostalgia's sake. Rosier SA has gotten so big. But the bulk of the harvesters are from Morocco these days. It used to be Spain, and before that Italy. That's what I'm doing my dissertation on, actually. The effect of the fragrance industry on population shifts. From as far back as you can look into history, it's had an incredible impact."

At the end of the rows, men waited, some shirtless, filling big burlap sacks with the contents of the kangaroo pouches. Wherever the harvesters passed, in their easy, fast rhythm, the fully-bloomed roses disappeared in their supple hands, until only a few tightly closed buds remained among the green leaves. Layla wanted to bury her hands in the contents of one of those burlap sacks and come up with her arms full of rose petals.

A big, dark-haired man lifted his head and looked at her, and her skin prickled.

"Key's in the glove compartment," Allegra said, waving her text screen at Layla.

Layla slid a glance back down at that dark-haired man in the field of roses. Her fingers stroked lightly over the callus builders on the grip exerciser in her pocket. "I should go tell him thanks, shouldn't I?"

Allegra's brown eyes sparkled at her with approval. "You *definitely* should say thanks. Also, happy birthday. It's only polite, considering he thought you were his birthday present." Allegra bit back a grin. "Plus, you need to drop me off down there so I don't have to walk. And you need directions to wherever your house is. And didn't you want to see what the rose harvest was like up close? I mean, there are *so many reasons* you need to go talk to Matt, don't you think?"

Layla tried to give her a withering look, but she was having a hard time biting back a laugh. Well, what? There *were* so many reasons.

Not least of which was that he made her pulse race with anticipation at the thought of walking up to him.

Not least of which was that he had no idea who she was and, ironically, he made her feel really intrigued to just be...her.

***

Burlap slid against Matt's shoulder, rough and clinging to the dampness of his skin as he dumped the sack onto the truck bed. The rose scent puffed up thickly, like a silk sheet thrown over his face. He took a step back from the truck, flexing, trying to clear his pounding head and sick stomach.

The sounds of the workers and of his cousins and grandfather rode against his skin, easing him. Raoul was back. That meant they were all here but Lucien, and Pépé was still stubborn and strong enough to insist on overseeing part of the harvest himself before he went to sit under a tree. Meaning Matt still had a few more years before he had to be the family patriarch all by himself, thank God. He'd copied every technique in his grandfather's book, then layered on his own when those failed him, but that whole job of taking charge of his cousins and getting them to listen to him was *still* not working out for him.

But his grandfather was still here for now. His cousins were here, held by Pépé and this valley at their heart, and not scattered to the four winds as they might be one day soon, when Matt became the heart and that heart just couldn't hold them.

All that loss was for later. Today was a good day. It could be. Matt had a hangover, and he had made an utter fool of himself the night before, but this could still be a good day. The rose harvest. The valley spreading around him.

J'y suis. J'y reste.

I am here and here I'll stay.

He stretched, easing his body into the good of this day, and even though it wasn't that hot yet, went ahead and reached for the hem of his shirt, so he could feel the scent of roses all over his skin.

"Show-off," Allegra's voice said, teasingly, and he grinned into the shirt as it passed his head, flexing his muscles a little more, because it would be pretty damn fun if Allegra was ogling him enough to piss Raoul off.

He turned so he could see the expression on Raoul's face as he bundled the T-shirt, half-tempted to toss it to Allegra and see what Raoul did—

And looked straight into the leaf-green eyes of Bouclettes.

Oh, shit. He jerked the T-shirt back over his head, tangling himself in the bundle of it as the holes proved impossible to find, and then he stuck his arm through the neck hole and his head didn't fit and he wrenched it around and tried to get himself straight and dressed somehow and—oh, *fuck.*

He stared at her, all the blood cells in his body rushing to his cheeks.

Damn you, stop, stop, stop, he tried to tell the blood cells, but as usual they ignored him. Thank God for dark Mediterranean skin. It had to help hide some of the color, right? Right? As he remembered carrying her around the party the night before, heat beat in his cheeks until he felt sunburned from the inside out.

Bouclettes was staring at him, mouth open as if he had punched her. Or as if he needed to kiss her again and—*behave!* She was probably thinking what a total jerk he was, first slobbering all over her drunk and now so full of himself he was stripping for her. And getting stuck in his own damn T-shirt.

Somewhere beyond her, between the rows of pink, Raoul had a fist stuffed into his mouth and was trying so hard not to laugh out loud that his body was bending into it, going into convulsions. Tristan was grinning, all right with his world. And Damien had his eyebrows up, making him look all controlled and princely, like someone who would *never* make a fool of himself in front of a woman.

Damn T-shirt. Matt yanked it off his head and threw it. But, of course, the air friction stopped it, so that instead of sailing gloriously across the field, it fell across the rose bush not too far from Bouclettes, a humiliated flag of surrender.

Could his introduction to this woman conceivably get any worse?

He glared at her, about ready to hit one of his damn cousins.

She stared back, her eyes enormous.

"Well, *what?*" he growled. "What do you want now? Why are you still here?" *I was drunk. I'm sorry. Just shoot me now, all right?*

She blinked and took a step back, frowning.

"Matt," Allegra said reproachfully, but with a ripple disturbing his name, as if she was trying not to laugh. "She was curious about the rose harvest. And she needs directions."

Directions. Hey, really? He was *good* with directions. He could get an ant across this valley and tell it the best route, too. He could crouch down with bunnies and have conversations about the best way to get their *petits* through the hills for a little day at the beach.

Of course, all his cousins could, too. He got ready to leap in first before his cousins grabbed the moment from him, like they were always trying to do. "Where do you need to go?" His voice came out rougher than the damn burlap. He struggled to smooth it without audibly clearing his throat. God, he felt naked. Would it look too stupid if he sidled up to that T-shirt and tried getting it over his head again?

"It's this house I inherited here," Bouclettes said. She had the cutest little accent. It made him want to squoosh all her curls in his big fists again and kiss that accent straight on her mouth, as if it was his, when he had so ruined that chance. "113, rue des Rosiers."

The valley did one great beat, a giant heart that had just faltered in its rhythm, and every Rosier in earshot focused on her. His grandfather barely moved, but then he'd probably barely moved back in the war when he'd spotted a swastika up in the *maquis* either. Just gently squeezed the trigger.

That finger-on-the-trigger alertness ran through every one of his cousins now.

Matt was the one who felt clumsy.

"Rue des Rosiers?" he said dumbly. Another beat, harder this time, adrenaline surging. "113, *rue des Rosiers?*" He looked up at a stone house, on the fourth terrace rising into the hills, where it got too steep to be practical to grow roses for harvest at their current market value. "Wait, *inherited?*"

Bouclettes looked at him warily.

"How could you *inherit* it?"

"I don't know exactly," she said slowly. "I had a letter from Antoine Vallier."

Tante Colette's lawyer. Oh, hell. An ominous feeling grew in the pit of Matt's stomach.

"On behalf of a Colette Delatour. He said he was tracking down the descendants of Élise Dubois."

What? Matt twisted toward his grandfather. Pépé stood very still, with this strange, tense blazing look of a fighter who'd just been struck on the face and couldn't strike back without drawing retaliation down on his entire village.

Matt turned back to the curly-haired enemy invader who had sprung up out of the blue. Looking so damn cute and innocent like that, too. He'd *kissed* her. "You can't—Tante Colette gave that house to *you?*"

Bouclettes took a step back.

Had he roared that last word? His voice echoed back at him, as if the valley held it, would squeeze it in a tight fist and never let it free. The air constricted, merciless bands around his sick head and stomach.

"After all that?" He'd just spent the last five months working on that house. Five months. *Oh, could you fix the plumbing, Matthieu? Matthieu, that garden wall needs mending. Matthieu, I think the septic tank might need to be replaced.* Because she was ninety-six and putting her life in order, and she was planning to pass it on to him, right? Because she understood that it was part of his valley and meant to leave this valley whole. Wasn't that the tacit promise there, when she asked him to take care of it? "*You*? Colette gave it to *you*?"

Bouclettes stared at him, a flash of hurt across her face, and then her arms tightened, and her chin went up. "Look, I don't know much more than you. My grandfather didn't stick around for my father's childhood, apparently. All we knew was that he came from France. We never knew we had any heritage here."

Could Tante Colette have had a child they didn't even know about? He twisted to look at his grandfather again, the one man still alive today who would surely have noticed a burgeoning belly on his stepsister. Pépé was frowning, not saying a word.

So—"To *you*?" Tante Colette knew it was his valley. You didn't just rip a chunk out of a man's heart and give it to, to...to whom exactly?

"To *you*?" Definitely he had roared that, he could hear his own voice booming back at him, see the way she braced herself. But—who the hell was she? And what the *hell* was he supposed to do about this? Fight a girl half his size? Strangle his ninety-six-year-old aunt? How did he crush his enemies and defend this valley? His enemy was...she was so *cute*. He didn't want her for an enemy, he wanted to figure out how to overcome last night's handicap and get her to think he was cute, too. Damn it, he hadn't even found out yet what those curls felt like against his palms.

And it was *his valley.*

Bouclettes' chin angled high, her arms tight. "You seemed to like me last night."

Oh, God. Embarrassment, a hangover, and being knifed in the back by his own aunt made for a perfectly horrible combination. "I was *drunk*."

Her mouth set, this stubborn, defiant rosebud. "I never thought I'd say this to a man, but I think I actually liked you better drunk." Turning on her heel, she stalked back to her car.

Matt stared after her, trying desperately not to be sick in the nearest rose bush. Family patriarchs didn't get to do that in front of the members of their family.

"I told my father he should never let my stepsister have some of this valley," his grandfather said tightly. "I told him she couldn't be trusted with it. It takes proper family to understand how important it is to keep it intact. Colette *never* respected that."

His cousins glanced at his grandfather and away, out over the valley, their faces gone neutral. They all knew this about the valley: It couldn't be broken up. It was their *patrimoine*, a world heritage really, in their hearts they knew it even if the world didn't, and so, no matter how much they, too, loved it, they could never really have any of it. It had to be kept intact. It had to go to Matt.

The others could have the company. They could have one hell of a lot more money, when it came down to liquid assets, they could have the right to run off to Africa and have adventures. But the valley was his.

He knew the way their jaws set. He knew the way his cousins looked without comment over the valley, full of roses they had come to help harvest because all their lives they had harvested these roses, grown up playing among them and working for them, in the service of them. He knew the way they didn't look at him again.

So he didn't look at them again, either. It *was* his valley, damn it. He'd tried last year to spend some time at their Paris office, to change who he was, to test out just one of all those many other dreams he had had as a kid, dreams his role as heir had never allowed him to pursue. His glamorous Paris girlfriend hadn't been able to stand the way the valley still held him, even in Paris. How fast he would catch a train back if something happened that he had to take care of. And in the end, he hadn't been able to stand how appalled she would get at the state of his hands when he came back, dramatically calling her manicurist and shoving him in that direction. Because he'd always liked his hands before then—they were strong and they were capable, and wasn't that a good thing for hands to be? A little dirt ground in sometimes—didn't that just prove their worth?

In the end, that one effort to be someone else had made his identity the clearest: The valley was who he was.

He stared after Bouclettes, as she slammed her car door and then pressed her forehead into her steering wheel.

"Who the hell is Élise Dubois?" Damien asked finally, a slice of a question. Damien did not like to be taken by surprise. "Why should Tante Colette be seeking out her heirs *over her own?*"

Matt looked again at Pépé, but Pépé's mouth was a thin line, and he wasn't talking.

Matt's head throbbed in great hard pulses. How could Tante Colette do this?

Without even warning him. Without giving him one single chance to argue her out of it or at least go strangle Antoine Vallier before that idiot even thought about sending that letter. Matt should have known something was up when she'd hired such an inexperienced, fresh-out-of-school lawyer. She wanted someone stupid enough to piss off the Rosiers.

Except—unlike his grandfather—he'd always trusted Tante Colette. She was the one who stitched up his wounds, fed him tea and soups, let him come take refuge in her gardens when all the pressures of his family got to be too much.

She'd loved him, he thought. Enough not to give a chunk of his valley to a stranger.

"It's that house," Raoul told Allegra, pointing to it, there a little up the hillside, only a couple of hundred yards from Matt's own house. If Matt knew Raoul, his cousin was probably already seeing a window—a way he could end up owning a part of this valley. If Raoul could negotiate with rebel warlords with a bullet hole in him, he could probably negotiate a curly-haired stranger into selling an unexpected inheritance.

Especially with Allegra on his side to make friends with her. While Matt alienated her irreparably.

Allegra ran after Bouclettes and knocked on her window, then bent down to speak to her when Bouclettes rolled it down. They were too far away for Matt to hear what they said. "Pépé." Matt struggled to speak. The valley thumped in his chest in one giant, echoing beat. It hurt his head, it was so big. It banged against the inside of his skull.

Possibly the presence of the valley inside him was being exacerbated by a hangover. Damn it. He pressed the heels of his palms into his pounding skull. What the hell had just happened?

Pépé just stood there, lips still pressed tight, a bleak, intense look on his face.

Allegra straightened from the car, and Bouclettes pulled away, heading up the dirt road that cut through the field of roses toward the house that Tante Colette had just torn out of Matt's valley and handed to a stranger.

Allegra came back and planted herself in front of him, fists on her hips. "Way to charm the girls, Matt," she said very dryly.

"F—" He caught himself, horrified. He could not possibly tell a woman to fuck off, no matter how bad his hangover and the shock of the moment. Plus, the last thing his skull needed right now was a jolt from Raoul's fist. So he just made a low, growling sound.

"She thinks you're hot, you know," Allegra said, in that friendly conversational tone torturers used in movies as they did something horrible to the hero.

"I...she...what?" The valley packed inside him fled in confusion before the *man* who wanted to take its place, surging up. Matt flushed dark again, even as his entire will scrambled after that flush, trying to get the color to die down.

"She said so." Allegra's sweet torturer's tone. "One of the first things she asked me after she got up this morning: 'Who's the hot one?'"

Damn blood cells, stay away from my cheeks. The boss did not flush. Pépé never flushed. You held your own in this crowd by being the roughest and the toughest. A man who blushed might as well paint a target on his chest and hand his cousins bows and arrows to practice their aim. "No, she did not."

"Probably talking about me." Amusement curled under Tristan's voice as he made himself the conversation's red herring. Was his youngest cousin taking pity on him? How had Tristan turned out so nice like that? After they made him use the purple paint when they used to pretend to be aliens, too.

"*And* she said you had a great body." Allegra drove another needle in, watching Matt squirm. He couldn't even stand himself now. His body felt too big for him. As if all his muscles were trying to get his attention, figure out if they were actually *great*.

"And she was definitely talking about Matt, Tristan," Allegra added. "You guys are impossible."

"I'm sorry, but I can hardly assume the phrase 'the hot one' means Matt," Tristan said cheerfully. "Be my last choice, really. I mean, there's me. Then there's— well, me, again, I really don't see how she would look at any of the other choices." He widened his teasing to Damien and Raoul, spreading the joking and provocation around to dissipate the focus on Matt.

"I was there, Tristan. She was talking about Matt," said Allegra, who either didn't get it, about letting the focus shift off Matt, or wasn't nearly as sweet as Raoul thought she was. "She thinks you're hot," she repeated to Matt, while his flush climbed back up into his cheeks and *beat* there.

Not in front of my cousins, Allegra! Oh, wow, really? Does she really?

Because his valley invader had hair like a wild bramble brush, and an absurdly princess-like face, all piquant chin and rosebud mouth and wary green eyes, and it made him want to surge through all those brambles and wake up the princess. And he so could not admit that he had thoughts like those in front of his cousins and his grandfather.

He was thirty years old, for God's sake. He worked in dirt and rose petals, in burlap and machinery and rough men he had to control. He wasn't supposed to fantasize about being a prince, as if he were still twelve.

Hadn't he made the determination, when he came back from Paris, to stay *grounded* from now on, real? Not to get lost in some ridiculous fantasy about a woman, a fantasy that had no relationship to reality?

"Or she *did*," Allegra said, ripping the last fingernail off. "Before you yelled at her because of something that is hardly her fault."

See, that was why a man needed to keep his feet on the ground. You'd think, as close a relationship as he had with the earth, he would know by now how much it hurt when he crashed into it. Yeah, did. Past tense.

But she'd stolen his land from him. How was he supposed to have taken that calmly? He stared up at the house, at the small figure in the distance climbing out of her car.

Pépé came to stand beside him, eyeing the little house up on the terraces as if it was a German supply depot he was about to take out. "I want that land back in the family," he said, in that crisp, firm way that meant, *explosives it is and tough luck for anyone who might be caught in them.* "This land is yours to defend for this family, Matthieu. What are you going to do about this threat?"

Chapter 4

Jerk. Layla parked her car in front of the stone house and yanked the key out of the ignition. Asshole.

And here she'd been thinking he was so darn cute.

A vision flashed through her mind again of him standing rigid, his cheeks reddened by sunburn, the T-shirt caught around his neck, and his eyes as desperate as some bird trapped in a soda can ring.

So easy, it would have been to walk forward and rest one hand on that incredible chest and say, *Hey, there. Easy now. Let me help you with that T-shirt.* The little stroke her fingers might have made before she could stop them. *We'll just pull it right off, how about that? I'm not quite ready to cover up this view.*

Not that she would have *done* that, obviously, with a complete stranger. But still.

They'd been pretty nice, generous thoughts to be having about someone who turned out to be a *complete jerk.*

Yelling at her like that. Turning that beautiful, mysterious gift of a house amid roses into some kind of personal crime on her part. Like it was her fault someone had traced some long-broken line of descent down to her?

That was all she needed. She came all the way here to clear up some bizarre inheritance issue and stop that Antoine Vallier guy from badgering her, when she needed to be focusing on her *career* and producing some kind of album that wouldn't make everyone shrug and say she was clearly a one-hit wonder.

And what did she get? Some grumpy bear of a neighbor who gave her a hard time for even being there.

She scowled at the house.

And then her scowl slowly softened. Set up several levels of roses from the rest of the fields, the house was nestled back into the slope where the land had climbed out of the valley and was heading up into the steep wooded hills. Terraces of roses draped below its stone, like the slow folds of a mountain's fancy dress.

It, too, was old stone, like the big house in which she had spent the night and the smaller house she could see a couple of hundred yards away from here, on the same terrace level. Red tiles roofed the gold stone. A huge, ancient rose climbed up the side of the door and covered part of that roof, not the flustered, open pink of the roses below, but something with full, deep fuchsia blooms. Herbs grew in walled beds against the house, and she brushed her hand over them, releasing lavender, rosemary, and thyme to twine their scents with that of the stone and roses. The beds looked surprisingly weed-free and neat for a house she had assumed long unattended. A thick mass of jasmine grew up another wall, incredibly sweet.

It was so...*quiet* here. If she stood still long enough, she might hear time sifting over stones.

Somebody had given this to her?

Somewhere back in her history, this had been part of her family?

Her ears prickled for noise and finally, through this great absence of clamor, started to pick up bees buzzing from roses toward their hives somewhere, a stir of a breeze in the pines rising up the hill, some deep male call across the fields below. Probably Grumpy Jerk's deep male call, so she shouldn't appreciate it, but that bass note to the quiet made the fingers of her left hand itch and stroke across the fabric of her jeans.

There wasn't even the sound of a text here, dinging her for all the things she was supposed to be giving of herself to everyone else. The hills circled around and shut her off from that hungry world.

Just herself.

Her.

She ran her left hand over rose petals as she walked toward the door, and all the muscles in that hand seemed to release their tension, the relaxation washing up her arm and on through her body. She stared at her hand a second, almost not recognizing it with its muscles relaxed.

The key that had come with the letter five months ago was old and heavy iron, like something out of a fairy tale. A musty scent released from the house when she got the door open, the odor mixing with the herbs and stone and roses.

She picked her way into the shadows inside. More quiet, so intense and so old that it begged her to let her voice ring out through it. To remind the old stone of what it had felt like when children clattered through here laughing.

Heavy, dark brown beams bore the weight of much stone above her head, some cobwebs gathering in their corners. Narrow, twisting stone stairs led upward from the main room, looking as if they had once been covered with a soft ochre wash to complement the colors of the tiles, but that had been worn off by years of feet, so that it remained on the bare stone like traces of make-up after a grande dame of the theater wiped her face clean at the end of a long performance.

It was lovely with age, this place that had anchored itself here before the Internet ever existed, when even a performer might have been able to go hours sometimes, probably days, without ever knowing what someone else thought of her or needed of her.

Hadn't Edith Piaf lived around here part of the time? Maybe this was why she had come.

Layla pulled a window open, then forced the shutter wide, white paint coming off in her hands. Light fell in on this quiet, aged place. She leaned out a moment, staring at the roses below. Hills climbed all around the valley, keeping it safe. In contrast to the crowded coast, which in theory should be nearby—not that she knew how to find it again—this valley seemed only gently populated. On the hills opposite her, climbing past the road, she could spot a sparse scattering of houses here and there, high up against a dark green tree line. On a high slope there, someone had planted a vineyard. Those silvery trees must be olives. Another square patch must be lavender, not yet in bloom. But all of those things were on the hills.

The sea of roses held sway over the bottom of the valley, making it seem like a fairy tale in which a woman could curl up and go to sleep, dreaming her dreams.

She leaned against the window frame, watching the harvesters leave strips of green in their wake, the pink retreating as if the green was an inexorable tide. Out of so many dark heads below, it was probably her imagination that she recognized one moving among them, taking charge.

Jerk. She went out to her little van to bring in her suitcase.

Tante Colette never had any descendants.

She gave that house to you?

What did that mean?

But Layla had had her own lawyer check out the letter and accompanying documents, of course. The house had been well and truly deeded over to her. And her grandfather *had* been born in France, way back before the war. It made some kind of sense, didn't it, that some heritage might one day find its way to her?

She went back to her little van and stood gazing a moment at her favored guitar, sitting there staring at her accusingly, the most obvious and reachable thing in the van, blaming her for not reaching for it.

It's a guitar, Layla. It does not have eyes, and it can only speak if you make it.

Preferably in a non-repetitive way that does not make that damn critic at Entertainment Weekly *say ironic things about sensitive female chord progressions and repetitive ideation, but which also pleases your fans, who*

clearly like "senstive female" chord progressions and the
things you've had to say so far.

A bee buzzed past, and in the quiet, she could taste its vibrations on her tongue, feel them tingle faintly in her fingertips, like the strings of a guitar that she had barely touched but which she had not yet allowed to make sound. That deep voice called again below.

It was going to be very dark and lonely here tonight, without even a guitar to keep the shadows at bay.

She reached for it, and for the first time in months, it felt oddly reassuring to her hand.

Chapter 5

The thick wood door thudded behind Matt as he stepped into the room. Antoine Vallier glanced up, looking far too tan and satisfied with himself for a lawyer. Pale, geeky, and cringing before his doom, that was what Matt was looking for right about now. Because Tante Colette might be protected from his rage by all the teas and soups she'd fed him all his life, and Bouclettes might be...well, she thought he was hot...but *someone* had to pay.

Antoine didn't exactly cringe, but he stood quickly as Matt strode toward his desk. "Antoine Vallier," Matt said grimly, grabbing onto the edge of the desk to lean in. Fortunately, the heavy, old desk could support a little aggression. "You're not looking for a long career around here, are you?"

The blond, younger man braced himself, lit by the late afternoon sunlight slanting through the narrow streets of Grasse into his office. "Damien has already been by."

Matt did a quick search of Antoine's body, but he didn't see any precise, lethal cuts starting to bleed out. "You must have talked fast. Go ahead. Just tell me every single thing you told him, and we'll compare notes."

Antoine attempted to lift an eyebrow in a sardonic way. "Nothing, in other words."

Unfortunately for Antoine, Damien's lifted eyebrow made the younger man's look like a kid's attempt to play at being a grown-up. Since Matt had been enduring the way Damien raised an eyebrow ever since his younger cousin turned thirteen, he could just see how the previous encounter between Antoine and Damien had gone—the great eyebrow-raising face-off, as Damien's oh-so-sardonically decimated the younger Antoine's.

Merde. Now he was feeling sorry for the lawyer. How did you strangle a man you felt sorry for?

"And I didn't tell Raoul anything either," Antoine Vallier said. "He was here an hour ago."

Damn it, everyone got first chance at strangling Vallier while Matt was tied up with the harvest. His cousins *always* got to have all the fun while he handled the responsibilities. Raoul got fourteen years in Africa, for God's sake, while Matt was harvesting flowers and plowing dirt, fixing machines that went wrong, and only getting to break up a knife fight between harvesters once every year or so for adventure. Okay, fine, Raoul had gotten shot in Africa, but clearly if he hadn't been enjoying himself, he would have come back sooner, right?

"You're still alive. So why don't you quit pretending you didn't talk?"

Antoine added a second lifted eyebrow, in his efforts to keep acting superior. Amateur. "Despite your family's pretense at being some kind of perfume Mafia, we both know none of you want to go to jail."

"Exactly," Matt said. "That's why we offer so many scholarships to bright, shining young people on paths to become local judges around here. We've been doing that for quite a few decades, in fact." He let Antoine see the edge of his teeth and pretended it was a smile. "Lots of good will. All perfectly legal."

Antoine Vallier gave him a sharp smile right back. "I paid for my own education."

Damn it. If France would only make its universities more expensive, the Rosiers would have a lot more leverage in some of these cases. Matt pressed his hands on the edge of the desk and leaned in. "Vallier, explain to me in small words so that I can understand. What exactly did you have in mind for your long-term career here when you decided to align with a ninety-six-year-old woman against, well...me?"

Antoine very delicately snorted. "Colette Delatour is going to live to be one hundred twenty-three, just to beat the Provençal record. I wouldn't count her out yet."

That anxious squeeze around Matt's heart whenever he had to think about his great aunt's age eased a little, at Antoine's conviction. Naturally he didn't tell the idiot that.

"I think your own life expectancy needs to be what you're worrying about right now, Vallier." He flexed his hands in a show of size and power. "You've dug yourself a very deep hole, and this would be a good time to start digging yourself out of it. Talk. Who is this woman, and why did Tante Colette give her that land? And are there any more surprises waiting for us? Any other descendants of someone I've never heard of that you're tracking down on her behalf?"

Antoine gave him a thin smile that was mostly designed to show off how tightly his lips were sealed.

"Vallier. I know you're fresh out of your internship and you probably have a lot of ideals. Do yourself a favor. Break them."

"I can't do that," the lawyer said regretfully. "You know I'd love to, but...I have to think about my long-term career prospects."

Matt leaned his weight a little more against the desk, letting big shoulders cross well into the other man's space. "That's what I'm trying to tell you, Vallier."

Antoine Vallier pulled out a pack of cigarettes and lit one.

Merde. Matt straightened. He had a very sensitive nose. The Rosiers were, in fact, quite famous for that sensitivity, even if Tristan was the only one of their generation to become a top perfumer himself. Everyone in Grasse knew not to light cigarettes immediately next to the Rosiers.

Even, surely, idiot lawyers fresh out of school?

Antoine Vallier very politely blew his cigarette smoke toward the open window, but the breeze coming up from the sea blew it straight back in, against Matt's face. Matt tried to make his nostrils pinch together as he held his ground.

"The thing is, Matthieu. May I call you Matt?"

"No," Matt said incredulously.

"Monsieur Rosier, then," Antoine Vallier said. "Although that gets a little confusing, considering how many of you answer to that name. Your grandfather, your uncles, the four of you cousins…"

"Five." Matt didn't count Lucien out, no matter how long the second eldest of them had been gone.

"Fuck, I have two more of you to deal with before the day is done?"

"Right now, just worry about surviving me."

"*Enfin.*" Antoine Vallier waved his cigarette. The stink of it washed over Matt as if he was back in Paris, stirring up the last lingering hint of nausea and headache from that morning's hangover. "The thing is…now imagine that I break client confidentiality and tell one of you thugs all you need to know."

"'Thugs'?" Matt figured he and Raoul could almost take that as a compliment, but he was kind of offended on Damien's behalf. Damien didn't do thug. He did lethal, elegant assassin.

"What do you think will happen to my long-term career here if I do?"

"You'll live to see it?"

"I'll never have another Rosier client, or a Delange client, or anyone you Rosiers know as long as I live. And you know a lot of people." Antoine Vallier gave that thin smile again and tapped his cigarette into the ash tray *right* under Matt's nose.

Matt brought a hand briefly over his mouth to try to wave the air away, then caught himself revealing the weakness and turned his hand back into a fist on Antoine's desk.

"But imagine that I stand up to you and keep my client's confidentiality, no matter how much you threaten to destroy me," Antoine said. "What do you think will happen then?"

"I'll destroy you?"

"Maybe," Antoine Vallier said. "But I bet the next time *you* want something done that needs to remain absolutely confidential no matter how much pressure is brought to bear...you'll come to me."

And he oh-so-politely blew his stream of cigarette smoke out the window—right into the breeze that blew it straight back into Matt's face—and smiled. Without showing a single tooth.

Damn.

Matt drew back, impressed. This guy and Damien might actually deserve each other as enemies. Be fun to watch them in the same room together, that was for damn sure. "Look, I don't mean to play good cop," he began.

Antoine Vallier gave that elegant snort again. "Don't worry, you're entirely failing to come across as one."

"But you'd really be much better off telling me everything you know and making this easy on yourself," Matt added. "All I'm going to do is strangle you if you don't. Some of my family members, on the other hand..."

Antoine stubbed his cigarette out. Then put it in the ashtray, instead of tossing it through his window to pollute the cobblestone streets of Grasse below. Matt gave him one tiny point for that. He liked Grasse's streets. "I'll take my chances," Antoine Vallier said. "Because there's no way in hell I'm crossing your aunt Colette. You must agree, or you'd be talking to her and not me."

Merde. Matt should have known a ninety-six-year-old Resistance hero who had ferried thirty-six children across the Alps must know how to pick a team that didn't crack.

***

So then he didn't really have any choice. Unless he wanted to get arrested for choking the information out of that damn idiot lawyer, he *had* to face his Tante Colette.

Every step up that medieval stair-street, lined with an ancient grape vine thicker than his wrist, brought Matt one step closer to the woman who had always been his refuge. Who had always let him sit in her kitchen or her garden, who had fed him soup or tea until his soul got addicted to the stuff and needed it to re-center.

He didn't knock, because she didn't like it when they bothered her with their knocking instead of coming in. She was in the old, walled garden, tucked up against the great medieval wall of the hilltop town of Sainte-Mère, this garden that had always seemed so magical that he and his cousins had invaded it once at night to steal *raiponce*, rapunzel, and Lucien had ended up with a broken arm.

The garden stole the last of his ability to growl and snap, as did the sight of his aunt, white hair pinned up neatly, sitting on the stool he had made for her when he was seven so that she didn't have to kneel anymore when she gardened. "Tante Colette," he said, and that lined, old face turned his way.

Twenty years ago, she would have spotted him long before this. How must that feel, to have once survived a war by not letting anyone ever sneak up on you, and then slowly lose your peripheral vision? Find your hearing dulling?

"Matthieu." Cool, assessing dark eyes searched his face.

They made him feel sixteen years old again. The sixteen-year-old who had sat here and sat here until suddenly, into the quiet, he was talking about what it felt like to have Raoul, his top rival but also the person he hero-worshiped the most in the world, ditch the whole valley because Matt was heir to it. The way it felt to lose a cousin because of his existence, and the way it felt to have that same cousin say, with that one gesture, *Your existence is worthless anyway. I've got a much better life waiting for me out in the world.* The way it felt to have that same gesture that indicated his worthlessness be the very act that put even more pressure on him to be *worth the valley.* Able to carry it on his shoulders all by himself.

And yet never be by himself. The pressures from his family were relentless.

How could he roar or growl or argue with Tante Colette? The things he did to win or dominate or at least not let anyone mess with him—how could he do them with her?

"A—a woman came today." He had to take a breath past that tightness in his chest. "She said you gave your house in the valley to her?"

Tante Colette's head lifted, this little *ah* of a movement, as if she'd spotted some rare eagle flying in the sky. "*Did* she?" she said softly. "She finally came?"

After that morning's already brutal blow, Matt wouldn't have thought that one more mattered, but it turned out it did. "Finally?" How long had Tante Colette been planning this without warning him? *Merde,* five months at least. All the time he had been fixing up that house, she must have meant those repairs for someone else.

"What is she like?" Tante Colette asked hungrily. "Is she anything like her great-grandmother? She doesn't look much like her in the photos."

"I don't even know who her great-grandmother is," Matt said between his teeth.

Tante Colette stroked the lemon balm in front of her, a hint of its scent reaching Matt. "Bring her to see me, and I'll show you both her great-grandmother's photo. I'll tell you her story."

Matt shoved his hand through his hair. His chest hurt so bad. Worse than all the times he had sought refuge here as a boy, when some pressure of his grandfather's, some battle with his cousins got too much for him, when his heart felt tender and he couldn't show that to all the men around him who must only ever see tough, bossy strength. But he could tell his tough, quiet, no-nonsense, war hero aunt. "I don't understand. Tante Colette, that land is supposed to stay in the family."

I don't understand. I thought I could trust you. Pépé always worried about you having that land, but I never did. I thought you liked me.

Thought that he might have to fight constantly to keep his position among his competitive cousins, but here, he could lower his guard.

Colette's face had so many wrinkles these days. When he'd been born, she was sixty-six. He'd never known her without wrinkles. But how had she gotten so *old?* "I've told you before that the way your grandfather defines family is unnecessarily limited."

That didn't even make sense. And the actions of a ninety-six-year-old woman that didn't make sense and disinherited her true family could almost certainly be fought in court. The problem was, he was damned if he'd attack his aunt in court as not being of sound mind while she was alive to be hurt by that. And he still nurtured this hope that Antoine was right and that she would beat the old Provençal record and live to be one hundred twenty-three.

Which would mean they couldn't start a court battle over that property for nearly thirty years, and no court was going to support them kicking out Bouclettes after they had let her keep that house for decades.

He searched his aunt's face, his throat tightening hard. "And—and you cared about this unknown descendant of someone you used to know more than...more than"—me?—"your real family?"

Her expression grew cool and haughty. Tante Colette's pride and strength had weathered time well. "I believe your grandfather doesn't consider me part of the real family."

That old, stupid fight. Seventy years, the two of them had been dwelling on that damn thing. "*I* do."

Her expression softened a little, a rare thing for Tante Colette. "You know, Matthieu, a valley is a very big thing to be. But you're human. So you're much more than that."

He tightened his arms over his chest defensively. He used to dream of as many adventures as his cousins had. He'd just done so much better at shouldering responsibility than at adventuring. You had to get your chores done first, before you ran off and played with the world. And in the end, it turned out he was better at chores than at playing. He must be the only man in the world who could date a supermodel and turn *that* into a chore.

"One little piece of your land to someone else, Matthieu. Maybe it's not the beginning of the end. Maybe, since you're human and humans, even more than valleys, are famously good at adapting, you need to learn to be a little bit more flexible."

Flexible. About his valley. As if *she* was in the right.

And he couldn't even roar or growl or do *anything* in protest, because it was Tante Colette.

She frowned a tiny bit, shaking her head as she studied him. "When you tighten that fist of yours, it takes something pretty drastic to force it open."

Well, he should hope so. He looked at his hand—currently fisted. That was one of its purposes, wasn't it? A hard grip that didn't let go? Didn't open up just at the wrong moment when someone else was trying to wrench something away from him?

"It's a metaphor, Matthieu."

Fuck, now she was being enigmatic. And for once in his life, he did not feel like sitting by her in the garden, working his brain through her riddles, until his heart had calmed and those riddles—and therefore he himself—made sense to him again.

But he couldn't growl at her, and he couldn't yell at her, and he couldn't grab chunks of this old medieval wall and try to tear it down to relieve some of these emotions. In fact—hell, was that another crack in the wall he needed to come fix soon?

The worst thing he could do was turn abruptly on his heel and stomp out. And even then, he felt guilty for not saying good-bye.

All in all, was it any wonder that by the time he was done trying to deal with his aunt, he had to hike up through the hills above his valley, growling and gripping trees and shaking them? Pine was so much safer to strangle than bare throats. Damn it, how did his family always do this kind of thing to him?

He finally subsided onto his rock, tucked under a cypress tree, weary and wounded, like some bear wanting to suck on a thorn in his paw. Glumly, he gazed down over his valley, including those beautiful, freshly-stolen acres of roses that looked exactly like all the other acres—they didn't stand out like a raw wound in any way at all.

But they now belonged to some curly-haired interloper who thought he was a jerk and who was now playing *music* as if all was right with her world. The notes filtered to him softly, a song he almost recognized, too far away to fully catch. Then they broke off in the middle and started again, and he realized she must be playing the guitar herself, not a recording.

He quieted slowly as he tried to hear it, everything in him gradually going still as he listened for the elusive tune. Was that "La Vie en Rose"? But then it drifted away into some other melody he'd never heard before.

Did she play so softly because she felt alone and friendless and exposed and didn't want to draw too much attention from a hostile world? Or more specifically from a next-door neighbor who had slobbered on her when drunk and then shouted at her the next morning when all she was doing was asking for help?

He buried his head at last in his arms and growled in despair. At having his valley wounded. At having an impossible family. At having a curly-haired, kissable enemy. And *merde*, at what an asshole she must think him.

Chapter 6

Layla woke with a song in her head. It was elusive, like a bee buzzing past her, like the silk slide of roses. She had to chase it, its sweetness escaping her, luring her on, as she tried to find the golden richness of it. A bear lifted its head from that golden richness, a madness of bees buzzing around him furiously, and growled at her to protect his honey.

Damn. She needed to get out her bass guitar.

She went out on her patio with both guitars, and stopped still. The fields were full of roses again. Literally covered, like yesterday. Just as if they'd never been stripped clean, as if they could bloom and bloom forever because *that was who they were.*

She sat down on an old lichen-covered bench, watching the light brighten over those fields as she switched back and forth between guitars, testing chords. Watching the trucks come into the field, people climb out.

As the harvesters poured into the fields below and a certain dark head emerged from a truck, she got up from the lichen-covered bench on the little patio that overlooked the roses, flexing her left hand to ease the muscles from the strings, realizing she was starving. Wow. It had been a *long* time since music pushed its way out of her so eagerly she forgot to eat. There was a giddy, uncertain joy to it, as if all the doctors had told her she would never walk again and she'd managed at last to wiggle her toe.

She was slightly impatient with her stomach for getting so growling and insistent, but that was biology for you. It insisted on reminding a musician that she had to eat.

There proved to be only one Petit Écolier left in the package on the passenger seat, too.

Rats.

She went back inside and for the first time that morning tried to turn a light on. Nothing happened.

All right now. What had happened to the electricity? She shot a fierce, suspicious scowl in the direction of the Growly Bear below and took her shower in freezing cold water—hardly the first time in all those festivals and shoestring road tours that she'd had to do that, but she'd really never developed a love for it. If she found out he'd done something to her electricity, she'd...she'd...well, she'd do something. It would be devilishly punitive, too.

The last thing—the very last thing—she wanted to do, hair dripping and skin covered in goose bumps but fingers tingling pleasurably and not from a hand grip exerciser, was ask Big Grumpy Jerk for help. But she thought she spotted some other faintly familiar heads below. Maybe one of the nicer cousins could help her? Wasn't that Allegra's boyfriend, Raoul? Given Allegra's overt, ready friendliness, how bad could he himself be?

And as that box of rice was resolutely refusing to restore life to her phone, it was either ask them or make her way toward the church steeple in the distance and start asking for help in whatever café Layla found there. She needed groceries and an electrician, or to find out how to contact the local electric company. Maybe she could find a phone and set up a meeting with that lawyer, Antoine Vallier, so she could closet him in his office and find out more about this inheritance.

She drove down to the harvest crew, stopping on the edge of the dirt track by the two cousins the farthest from the Big Grump. Allegra's boyfriend Raoul stood with a leaner man with black hair and a kind of elegant mercilessness to his movements that made her think of James Bond playing cards with some terrorist spy— Damien? Was that his name? Unfortunately Layla didn't spot Allegra herself anywhere. Maybe she was one of those rare graduate students who actually treated her dissertation like a full-time job and was busy writing it.

Raoul and the other cousin were at the end of a row, laughing as they dumped pouches of roses into a burlap sack, having apparently been in some kind of competition as to who could clear their row the fastest, but when Layla stepped out of her car, they turned toward her, their faces growing neutral.

The scent of roses swirled all around the twin punch of masculinity from the two.

Over at some distance, Growly Jerk's head turned. He still hadn't figured out how to put his shirt back on, she noticed right away.

Noticed it kind of deep in her body, where the noticing clenched.

Layla did her best to ignore it, and him. "Excuse me," she said carefully to Raoul, her best bet. At least he had a nice girlfriend. "I wondered if you could help me with directions."

Raoul bent that unusual russet and charcoal head of his to look at her map. Hesitating, he glanced toward his grumpy cousin in the distance and then cleared his throat, a rumbling sound. "I'm sorry. I've, ah, only recently moved back here. I'm afraid I wouldn't be much help. But you know who's good at directions?" He nodded toward Matt.

Oh, no way in hell did she want to talk to Growly Bear. Hear *"to you?"* roared over and over again as if "you" was a lowly worm.

"Couldn't you at least tell me where I *am?*" she demanded, holding the map toward Raoul again.

His amber eyes flicked over it with obvious recognition. But then he squinted across the rose fields as if the thing had been written in ancient Egyptian. "I, ah, tend to rely on my phone," he said apologetically. "Matt's your man."

Maybe these guys were *all* jerks. Layla looked at the other cousin, the controlled, elegant James Bond one, whose hair was as dark as Matt's but much more contained, without that upward lilt of half curls at the end of every lock. "Could you—?"

Gray-green eyes flicked over the map. Damien looked at Raoul, then past her toward Matt, then back at her again before he finally took a deep breath. "You'll have to ask Matt. I...can't help you." His eyes flinched closed in pain.

The one who looked the youngest—Tristan?—drifted up, an ease in his skin that made him seem so much more relaxed than his cousins. Even his dark hair had a relaxed wave to it, as if it did what he told it to without much effort. "You came back!" he said cheerfully. "We'll try to get Matt to behave this time." He glanced behind him and stage-whispered, "We're still working on his dating skills. He managed not to hit you over the head and drag you off to a cave by your hair, so I think that part where he picked you up and hauled you around the room was progress, really."

"He has the manners of a bear," Layla said stiffly. "All I want is directions."

Tristan's eyes flicked over her map, that quick look that held complete comprehension of maps in it. He glanced at his cousins. "I, ah...I'm terrible with directions," he told her. His brown eyes danced. "I got lost on the way to Grasse once."

"This is true," Raoul said. "*Merde*, did I get in trouble for that one."

"He was only five," Damien, the elegant one, explained to her. "Raoul was supposed to be keeping an eye on us."

"But my point," Tristan continued cheerfully, "is that you'll have to ask Matt."

Raoul squinted amber eyes at the sky. "He's so much better with directions than the rest of us," he managed, his voice coming out of him as if it had been dragged painfully through gravel. Damien patted him on the shoulder and confined himself to nodding in agreement about Matt's superiority with directions, his eyes wincing in pain even at that. Raoul reached out and gripped Damien's shoulder. She had the brief impression of two men bearing each other up at the side of a grave.

Tristan grinned. "This is truly a beautiful moment," he told her. "I think my heart grew a size, just witnessing it." He turned his head to yell, "Matt! Put your shirt on! Your girlfriend needs you!"

A dozen rows over, Matt tried to pull his T-shirt over his head. There was a brief blur of arms jerking, a T-shirt getting stuck haphazardly on broad shoulders, and then finally he threw it in a ball at his feet and kicked the thing. It tangled on his shoe, and he stomped on it twice to get it free, and then strode over, his face sunburned so red it was all Layla could do not to pull out sunscreen right there.

And she didn't even care about that jerk.

"You should put on sunscreen," she heard herself say. And curled her toes tightly in lieu of kicking herself.

Big Matt stopped still and looked from her to his cousins and back to her again. If anything, his sunburn darkened. He folded his arms over his bare chest, which was just...*God*. That should be criminally liable, to look so good half-naked and be such a jerk at the same time. Dark curls of hair scattered across a broad chest, biceps bulged under tension, and broad shoulders narrowed down to taut abs. All of it just faintly, barely gleaming from the work in the morning sun.

"Or instead of sunscreen, you could put on a shirt," Tristan supplied helpfully. "Oh, wait—" He grinned. "You're still learning how to dress yourself."

Matt glared at him.

Tristan put a hand up to his mouth and turned partly away, coughing. Damien patted him hard on the back, pressing his lips resolutely together as the corners kept twitching.

I could help you put that T-shirt on, you know, Layla thought. *You're just not patient enough. It needs to be slowly...slowly...stroked down over that—*

59

Hey! What are you doing? she shouted at her imagination.

"What do you want now?" Matt growled at her, tightening his arms around himself.

"I only need directions!" Layla snapped back at him. "I can't believe how unhelpful you people are being!"

Matt blinked. He slid the oddest glance toward the other men, almost—vulnerable? "They couldn't give you directions?"

Tristan shook his head woefully. "Even Damien," he said sadly, "proved unequal to the task."

Matt stared at them for a moment. And then his sunburn seemed to get worse than ever, and he rubbed his chest, as if it felt strange to him. Clearing his throat, a rough growl of sound, he took her map from her. "Where do you need to go?"

"I've been lost enough around here, thank you," Layla said. "I don't need you to get me lost some more, just to punish me for inheriting a house."

Matt scowled at the map. "Where do you need to go?" he growled again.

Tristan coughed a little into his hand. "Ahem, Matt. People skills!" he stage-whispered.

Matt glared at him.

"He's really a nice guy," Tristan told her out loud, cheerfully, as if Matt wasn't even listening. "No, I swear."

Matt transferred his glare back to the map.

Again, Layla fought the urge to just lay her hand against his chest. It was a really hot chest, that probably explained it. She kept imagining all that growly tension relaxing away from him in surprise. And then what would he be like? That cute, enthusiastic, uncontained man he had been drunk?

"Where?" Matt insisted. He cleared his throat again. And then managed to get words out that were still rough, but considerably quieter. "Where do you need to go?" he repeated, carefully.

"I don't even know where I *am*."

"You're in the Rosier valley," Matt said blankly and put a callused finger to her map. "Here."

Layla peered around his big hand and tried to figure out where Nice and Grasse were in relationship. What direction were they facing? She cast a quick look at the sun. Okay, she was pretty sure it rose in the east, even in France, so now she had to re-adjust her whole compass. Last night she had thought that was west.

Matt started to speak and paused long enough to clear his throat again. "Where do you need to go?" Again, the growl was kept low, more an underlying roughness than an open rumble. It felt gentler this way, like being rubbed with something textured. The map left almost no distance between them. Was that his skin that smelled of roses, or the roses all around him? Mixed in with the rose scent was something warm and male that made her want to press her face close against hard muscles and take a deep breath.

"I'm not sure," she admitted. "I need to get my electricity fixed. Since it went out last night." She narrowed her eyes at him suspiciously.

"Why are you looking at me?" he asked as indignantly as if he'd been acting like a perfectly sane person since she met him. "I'm the reason the electricity in that house works in the first place."

"I knew it! I knew you would know how to cut it off. Trying to scare me away?"

He gave her a look of deep aggravation. "It's probably a *fusible*."

Her face scrunched as she tried to figure out the word. When most of your French came from your mother and an occasional random encounter with your father, you were really dependent on their vocabulary, and her parents' certainly hadn't included words that involved home repair. *Fusible*. Must be fuse.

"The—" He held up one of those tanned hands and moved his thumb back and forth as if over a switch. The scent of roses on his hands was so strong she had a sudden, flashing vision—more a *sensation* than a vision—of two paths of scent, the size of big hands, being drawn all down her body.

Ooh. Oh. *Stop that right now*, she told herself.

"I'll fix it," he said finally, giving up on the thumb gesture. Which was just as well. That small waggling back and forth had made her start thinking about at least three different places on her body which would like that motion, and not a single one of those places was supposed to be uttering an opinion right now.

"You'll fix it?" She stared. "I thought you didn't want me here."

He shrugged big, grumpy shoulders. "I'll fix the kitchen sink, too."

There was something wrong with the kitchen sink? She frowned up at him. Why did she keep wanting to lay a hand on those grumpy shoulders and soothe them?

Probably because shoulders that broad and muscled operated like a magnet to the female hand. Any excuse to pet all that grumpiness off him and see what he was like when he was just one sexy, happy man. She cleared her own throat. "Don't you think you should put your T-shirt back on? So your shoulders don't get as sunburned as your face?"

He touched a hand to his cheeks and cursed.

Tristan started coughing again, and Damien's twitching lips split into an open grin before he turned completely around to gaze at one of the great hills that framed the valley. Raoul watched the whole thing with a relaxed, wolfish smile on his face, while he idly scooped up a handful of the roses he'd been harvesting and let them fall back into the sack. Layla wanted to plunge her hand into one of those sacks nearly as badly as she wanted to touch Matt's bare shoulders.

I mean, I could help, Layla thought again. *With the T-shirt*. Just stroke it soothingly down...

Will you stop it? she snapped at herself.

Well, I could, herself said sulkily back.

"I'm fine," Matt growled, back to grumpy.

She deepened her frown at him. *Don't start with that grumpy stuff again.* "And what about groceries? I need to find a store nearby." *I can't exactly rely on you for food, water, electricity, all contact with the outside world...*

Although actually being cut off from all contact with the outside world sounded *heavenly.*

"There's an *épicerie* in the village." He gestured with his hand toward the church steeple at one end of the valley. "Pont-le-Loup. If you need more than they have, head south from there until you get to a roundabout, then go east there, and head south again when you get to the next roundabout after that—"

Layla put a hand to her head.

Matt broke off. "Here," he said after a moment, and ran that big thumb along a tiny part of the map. "To here."

Layla squinted at it, and then surreptitiously angled her body so that the sun was to her left. Okay. So, that meant she was facing north, which meant *that* way was south, so on the map—

Matt sighed and held out his hand, big palm up. "Give me your phone. I'll put the address in."

Layla hesitated, glancing around at all the not-exactly-friendly strangers who would know she had no way to call for help. It was really unfortunate that cutting oneself off from all contact with the world was so inconvenient in practice. It had sounded way, way better when she had, ah, accidentally left her phone in her pocket in a fountain. "Umm...it's having a little trouble charging."

"Do you have paper? I'll pretend I'm a phone."

Layla had a sudden vision—again, more of a *sensation,* really—of her texting things all over his body.

Boy, your social media addiction is really bad, she told herself severely. At least, that was what she was going to blame it on.

He followed her to her car, while his relatives went back to work with some reluctance but kept them in view, several grins in evidence. She flipped quickly past the few pages in her journal with their sad two lines of lame lyrics that went nowhere, as if all the music had been wrung out of her and the tired old rag of herself hung up to dry. No one needed to see that stuff. She found an empty page and handed the journal to him.

He began to write in square, firm handwriting:

1. Turn RIGHT onto road.

2. 2.94k to village.

3. At roundabout, FIRST EXIT.

His gruff voice elaborated as he wrote: "A three-story house with blue shutters will be on your left. It has lace curtains. If not, if it's a house with blue shutters and roses climbing up the walls but no curtains, you've taken the wrong exit. There's a little bar two buildings farther down, with a faded red awning. Be careful, there's a pale orange tabby cat that likes to lie right in the middle of the road there, and he will not move. You have to stop the car and pick him up and carry him to the garden of the little house with the jasmine climbing up the green gate. That's where he belongs. Then you—"

Layla watched his square hand around the pen, his big body bent over the hood of her car as he wrote. His bare back curved and she stalwartly fought the need to reach out and see if it was as smooth as it looked. As warm. To see if his voice would grow more or less gruff when he was being petted.

He knew a particular cat might be sleeping in the middle of the road on her route. And he stopped and picked it up. He made sure *she* stopped and picked it up.

From this angle, his face was in shade and the sunburn didn't look as bad, his skin less ruddy under the matte tones. Her head tilted.

It wasn't sunburn, was it? Sunburn didn't subside like that.

This big, growling man had been blushing.

"You're way better than a smartphone," she said wonderingly. Actually he was more like a...guitar. Someone she wanted to run her fingers over to see what sounds she could pull out.

He made a sound of acknowledgement that was pretty darn close to a grunt.

She grinned. Definitely a bass guitar. "And you have a much better voice. Do you think I could record you giving the directions instead?" Except, of course, she didn't have a phone to record with. If she wanted to hear that rough bass talking to her again while he blushed, she'd just have to figure out a way to keep getting him to do it.

A musician had to, you know, coax her instruments into making the sounds she wanted sometimes.

She bit back a grin.

He stopped writing and turned his head just enough to look at her. The color started to mount back into his cheeks again.

Her smile started to escape her efforts to restrain it. "Do you need help with your sunscreen?"

That stern upper lip relaxed its pressure on the full lower one. He stared at her, frozen.

Her smile deepened. Whether it was the pure fun of flirting in French—a language that had, after all, been refined for centuries to that purpose—or the vulnerable blush on someone that big and rough and growling, this whole moment was developing a delicious zing. "You're pretty cute, you know that?" she tested softly.

The streak over those strong cheekbones turned ruddy bronze. He looked back at her journal, and the pencil lead broke. He stared at it, apparently not having a clue what to do with himself.

Which was so empowering. It gave her *all kinds* of ideas about what to do to him.

She curled her fingers into her palm and dug the nails in, reminding herself this was the real world and not some fairy tale just because it was in France in a valley of roses. She had an album to write. The last thing she needed to do was get distracted.

In fact, was she so willing to be distracted because it was easier than facing the dark void of that album again?

"His name is Hendrix," Matt said roughly, to the broken end of the pencil.

Her eyebrows went up.

"The cat. Madame Grenier, his owner, was a fan. Of Jimi Hendrix. She went to see him at Isle of Wight when she was in her twenties."

"Isle of Wight?"

"It's a music festival in England," Matt explained.

Yeah, no kidding. "She was at Isle of Wight when Jimi Hendrix played? Wow." Pure fan awe filled her. "And The Doors and everything? Oh, man." Just for a second, longing ran through her to be a fan in the crowd again, never to have tried to make it as a musician herself. To be a fan back *then*, at Isle of Wight, or at Woodstock. Just a fan. Nobody looking at her or judging her or demanding things of her, simply a girl on the grass, hanging out with friends and wrapped up in music.

Madame Grenier must be about seventy, she realized. And this man knew her stories of forty-four years before? When he picked the cat up off the road and carried it to her, and she wanted to talk to someone about her life, did he stop and listen to her?

I wonder what it would be like to touch one of those muscled arms? Just curl my hand over his biceps. She scrubbed her itching fingers hard against her jeans.

You are such an idiot, she thought to herself. *Aren't you ever going to learn to quit throwing your heart at the latest bad boy like some stupid...musician?*

"She used to have a gray tabby named Jimi, but he died," Matt told her journal.

You're rambling.

It was *insane* how badly she wanted to stroke all his confidence back into him.

Or maybe, even better, make the last of his confidence break down into something flustered and hungry. He was such a big guy. His voice could boom so loud. The whole thought of him helpless to her was delicious.

"So, uh, and then you go left," Matt said, scraping words onto paper with what was left of the broken pencil lead.

The low, rough texture of his voice made all the hairs on her arms prickle. She wasn't processing a word he said. Still, his voice was so deep and gorgeous, maybe it was imprinting on her brain and she could replay the words once she was in the car and didn't have the proximity of that naked torso and that blush distracting her. She had *really* good retention for great voices. If she could get him to add a little melody to it, she might be able to remember every word out of his mouth.

He extended her journal, but when she tried to accept it, his fingers tightened. "I, ah...I was really drunk that first night. I know that's not—I'm sorry."

That rough voice cracked her. "Hey." Her hand slid far enough over the journal to graze the inside of his wrist. Just a hint of his texture, soft and hot and vulnerable there at the inside of that strong wrist. His skin felt like his voice. "Look, there's no point agonizing over it. I get that you didn't mean it. I didn't make anything of it."

He frowned in visible confusion. "Make anything of it?"

"I know you didn't really fall in love with me at first sight or anything. Don't be silly."

All that color flooded back up under his bronze skin. "Of *course* I didn't...I...that is...I—*fuck*," he said between his teeth, turning his head away.

She pulled back a step, tugging hard on her journal to get him to release it. "I'm not going to start asking you to marry me and have my babies," she said dryly.

His jaw dropped. He stared at her in pure horror.

Man, he was easy to mess with. Full of herself, she stole an opportunity and patted his biceps. "You're okay," she told him. "Don't worry about me."

Wow, that was a nice tingle to carry away in her palm.

Chapter 7

"Did you like how we sent her your way for the directions?" Tristan asked cheerfully. "That was beautiful, wasn't it?"

Matt grunted from under the conveyor belt, trying to ignore his cousin. Damn belt. What a time to break down, the first day of the harvest. Could anything else go wrong with his awesome thirty-first year?

Yes, probably. It could start to rain.

"Just *think* of what you could have done with that," Tristan said, putting a thrilling ring into his voice. It echoed in the high-roofed space of their extraction plant, that building on the edge of the fields to which all the fresh roses were carried. "Sent her to Timbuktu, even. Where did you send her, by the way? I haven't seen her car come back."

Yeah, Matt was getting pretty worried about that. She'd left before lunch, and it was four in the afternoon. Sure, she'd probably stopped for lunch or something herself, but still...between the state of that damn car and her visible confusion about what was north and what was south, anything could have happened. He'd called Madame Grenier earlier—after making sure none of his cousins were in earshot, of course—but Mme Grenier couldn't even remember how long it had been since Bouclettes had come by. Apparently Bouclettes was a "young woman who knew her music", though, "not like some kids her age". Also, Madame Grenier approved of her manners, particularly toward cats that lay in the middle of the road.

"I sent her to the damn store," Matt snapped at Tristan.

A huff of breath as Tristan threw one of the sacks of roses up to Raoul on the upper platform. They had to get those roses processed tonight, and Cédric, their extraction plant manager, had had to leave for some play his daughter was doing. Until Matt could get this damned conveyor belt fixed, they were going to be transferring that last truckload of roses up to the vats above the hard way. It would have been a pure, slogging pain to have to transfer the last load bag by bag alone, but his cousins had, of course, joined in and turned it into a game.

Nice to have people who were happy to hit you in the face but always had your back. Even if they were a damn pain in the ass.

"I *knew* I should have been the one to give her directions." Tristan sighed. "Poor girl."

Matt banged his wrench unnecessarily against the nearest solid metal. Better than Tristan's ankle. "My directions were perfect."

"Now, see, Matt, what's wrong with you? Why were your directions perfect? Aren't you supposed to be getting that land back somehow? Pépé said so."

Matt pressed his teeth together hard to contain a frustrated growl. He didn't like to let his cousins visibly get to him, but damn it, how the hell *was* he supposed to get that land back? How was he supposed to fight a woman that small? She spent too long getting back from the grocery store, and he was about to beat something in worry over what might have happened to her. If anything did, it would be his fault.

Anything that went wrong in this valley was his fault.

"I mean, *I* thought sending the enemy invader over the Alps or something would have been the perfect way to discourage her," Tristan said. "Look what it did to Hannibal."

Yeah, right. Matt rolled his eyes and banged some more things. As if any of his cousins would have actually done that.

Still, maybe it explained why his cousins had pretended they couldn't give directions earlier. At first it had been so weird, like they were...matchmaking or something. Crushing their own competitive instincts to let him look good.

Instead maybe they'd been dumping the responsibility of helping her or hindering her onto his shoulders. Nobody wanted to play the bad guy.

Matt always got to have that role.

"Fine." Tristan gave a much put-upon sigh. "We'll just have to figure out some other way."

Oh, *bordel.*

"I know!" Tristan said, in dramatic delight. "We'll sabotage her house! Cut wires, break a pipe...make her miserable, you know."

"I just spent five months getting that house into shape!" Matt roared, shoving himself out from under the conveyor belt. "Tristan, if you touch one damn thing—"

He stopped. Tristan was grinning. Damien was doing that controlled, elegant smirk thing of his. Raoul, up on the platform above, was laughing so hard that Damien took advantage of the moment of weakness to throw a sack of roses up there extra hard, aiming for Raoul's head.

Raoul managed to save himself at the last second, caught the sack as he ducked away, and then turned and poured its roses into the vat behind him.

"Although it sounds as if you already started on the sabotage," Tristan said. "Didn't she say her electricity went out? What were *you* up to last night, Matt?"

"Sleeping," Matt snapped. Well, tossing and turning and beating his head against his pillow. Getting up to pace his terrace and stare out at his valley or at the house where Bouclettes slept. "It was probably a damn fuse. The wiring in most of that house is decades old. I'm going to fix it as soon as I get this damn conveyor belt working again."

Tristan grinned. "That will help scare her off, all right. You fixing her house up for her. You've got to think of the market value, Matt. It's already going to cost us a fortune to buy it back from her, even in the state it's in."

Well, what was he supposed to do? Leave the place in a mess? Leaking sink, poor wiring...damn it, his aunt could have warned him that he was fixing the house up for *someone else* and that he had a deadline to get everything done. Also, it wouldn't have hurt to mention that the someone else was really cute.

Just give a man a little forewarning so he didn't make a complete idiot of himself in front of her, for example.

And if Tristan looked any more amused, Matt might throw this wrench at him. "Fuck off, Tristan." He went back under the conveyor belt.

"Or *I* know!" Tristan exclaimed. "I've got a much better plan. Instead of scaring her off, one of us could *seduce* her into our clutches. Convince her to sell the land back to us through pure sex appeal. I'll have to take care of that one, Matt, sorry. No woman is going to be seduced by one of you guys."

Matt shoved himself back out from under the conveyor belt, sitting up so fast he nearly bonked his head. He glared at his youngest cousin dangerously.

"What?" Tristan asked innocently. "Flirting is my forte."

Yeah, and it really was. If Tristan started flirting with Bouclettes, she...he...damn it. Matt tightened his hold on his wrench against the wave of images. "Stay the hell away from her, Tristan."

Tristan looked exaggeratedly crestfallen. "But she's just my type."

Every woman was Tristan's type. And he was every woman's type, too. Matt thrust to his feet and took a step toward him, menacingly.

Tristan couldn't contain himself anymore and started laughing.

Damn it. Matt's cousins were so annoying.

"You forget," Damien drawled. "She thinks *Matt* is the hot one."

Matt's face flamed.

"Allegra swears she wasn't making that up," Raoul said from above. "As hard as it is to believe."

Tristan shook his head in wonder. "You'd better grab this one, Matt. It's not every woman who finds it hot to be hauled around by a drunk caveman and then yelled at when she's lost and asking for help. It must be your way with a T-shirt."

If Matt's face burned much more, it would catch fire. "I'll tell you what," he growled. "*Either* you guys can let me fix this conveyor belt in peace, *or* I can hit you with something. Which is it going to be?"

A flood of roses engulfed his head, drowning him temporarily in pink petals and scent. He shook himself out of it, looking up.

Raoul grinned and dropped the empty burlap sack so that it floated down over Matt's face. "Oops," Raoul said. "I must have confused the vat with the vast empty space that passes for your brain."

"Seriously?" Tristan said. "Rose fight? Damn, but I've missed those." And he grabbed a sack of roses off the truck and swung it at Matt.

Matt dropped his wrench and dove for him to try to protect his head—sacks of roses were cushy but a lot heavier than pillows—and the two men toppled to the ground on top of the roses Raoul had spilled. "Damn it!" Matt roared, loud enough to fill the building, which was the minimum volume to have any impact on his cousins when they started this kind of shit. "You're wasting the harvest! That's four hundred euros, Raoul."

A sack of roses swung through the air and hit Tristan on the butt. Laughing, Damien used the rebound off Tristan to help swing the bag toward Matt and catch him in *his* butt. Even in rose fighting, Damien killed two birds with one stone. Matt grabbed Tristan's sack from him and went for Damien with it, and then Raoul was on

73

the concrete floor joining in, and then...it all got a little bit out of hand. Roses flew everywhere.

It was some time later before Matt finally sat up, shaking petals out of his hair and clothes, having been tackled, in the final act, by all three of his cousins at once so they could bring him down. Just like the old days, actually, when there were five of them and the only way to keep one of them down was if all the others piled on him in a heap. Even Tristan, five years younger than Raoul and Lucien and two years younger than Matt and Damien, had been a wriggly little brat, impossible to contain.

They hadn't wrestled like that in a long time. After Raoul and Lucien left, all their games and wrestling matches had lost their savor.

Matt did his best to act grumpy and not just relaxed and happy as he gazed out over the disaster of roses spilled across the concrete floor. The place looked like the old *ateliers* used to, back before they had their own processing facility, when they used to spread the roses to protect them from rot and wilt, tossing them every once in a while before they bagged them up again to haul them off to Grasse.

"Now we're going to have to clean this mess up and get these roses into that vat." He made his voice extra growly to make sure his cousins didn't start thinking he was getting soft or anything. "We are not wasting this much of the harvest."

His cousins, roses still falling out of their hair, grinned, already reaching for rakes on the wall of the plant. "Go fix the conveyor belt, you big grump," Tristan said. And winked. "I'll take care of handling your curly-haired female problems."

So Matt had to dive for him all over again.

Well, what? It was very relaxing.

***

Damn country. Layla puffed as she hauled the too-heavy groceries through the door, tired and pissed off.

74

She needed a new phone. Did they make ones anymore that didn't allow producers to text or email?

Getting to the grocery store had worked just fine, Matt's directions clear and easy to follow—and she'd had a nice little chat with Madame Grenier, too, after she'd handed the older woman her cat. It turned out Madame Grenier had one of the old pink and yellow Isle of Wight posters signed by half the performers—Jimi Hendrix, Pete Townshend, Roger Daltrey, Joan Baez. She'd let Layla *touch* it. Layla's fingertips still tingled.

Between touching Matt the Grumpy Bear and touching that poster, her fingertips were having quite a day. They'd actually danced on the steering wheel on the drive to the store, testing out chord progressions that were lively and rhythmic, not ones so whiny and tired she had to rip the notes in half and throw them in the trash.

But then, post grocery shopping, she had had the brilliant idea of trying to find Antoine Vallier's office in Grasse without Google Maps and also maybe a store where she could buy a new phone, and she had gotten so hopelessly lost that dusk was falling now, and the cheese she had bought had stunk up the whole car.

And it was official—she hated spaghetti-thin, twisty cliff roads. Especially the fourth time she crept down the same one, in a cycle of lostness.

Her chocolate had probably all melted, too. After she'd bought half the aisle. (Well, what? A well-traveled woman knew when to take advantage of her host culture. A whole aisle of chocolate bars was not something one found in a supermarket in the U.S.)

God, she was glad to be back home. That was...back in the quiet and roses of the valley. Obviously not her *home* home.

Stepping into the old farmhouse kitchen, she started to set the ten-pound bag of chocolate bars on the worn old table.

And then saw the body sprawled across her kitchen floor.

She screamed, jerking backward, sack in hand. The sack dragged at her arm, and she hefted it, ready to do battle with chocolate if she had to, as the body came to life.

There was a thump, a curse, another curse, and then a huge form lunged upright in the kitchen, giant wrench raised high to—

She screamed bloody murder.

"What?" a deep voice boomed over her. "What? What? *Merde, what's wrong?*" He lunged for her.

She swung the bag with all her might, and ten pounds of chocolate collided with a broad shoulder and unfortunately only glanced against the head. The bag split, and Matt staggered against the counter under the rain of chocolate bars, dropping the wrench.

It hit the floor and maybe something else because he cursed again, jerking one foot up. "*Bordel de merde.*"

"What the hell are you doing in my kitchen?" she yelled, grabbing for the next grocery sack. Cheeses. She should have chosen stinkier ones.

"I—the kitchen sink was leaking!" Matt yelled, rubbing his head. "*Aïe!* Damn it."

"*How did you know that?*"

"It's my valley!" he roared so loudly she fell back against the counter.

She took a deep breath and stared at him—and then abruptly dropped the cheese and pressed her hands to her face. "Oh, holy *crap*, you scared me to death."

"I told you I was going to fix it! And I fixed your *putain de fusible!*" His arms folded across his chest.

Yes, a light was on in the kitchen. The refrigerator was humming again. Little things she should have noticed before she even came into the kitchen, except she was so tired. And he *had* mentioned the kitchen sink that morning, hadn't he? She'd been too busy thinking about his shoulders and what they would do if she touched them to pay much attention.

She took another deep breath, her skin still jittery from the shock of it. "*Shit*," she said, heartfelt.

Matt glowered, his arms tightening. "Where the hell have you been anyway? The store is only twenty minutes away!"

"I got lost!" she snapped, the whole day of frustration piling up on her.

"You did not get lost with my directions!" he said, affronted.

"I decided to risk going farther afield." She glared back at him. Tears stung ridiculously, trying to turn the glare into something else. She'd had a hard day. She'd actually been having a hard few months, full of this endless cycle of pressures and expectations she couldn't meet, like twisting forever on those damn cliff roads and never getting anywhere she could rest.

And her whole body wanted to collapse now in relief, nestling itself against a big, strong man in gratitude for him saving her from an axe murderer. A wrench murderer. Whatever. Saving her, in this case, just by not being the axe murderer in question, nor a dead body, nor all the things that had flashed through her mind as she'd reacted instinctively.

"You went somewhere else? Why the hell did you do something like that without checking with me?" Matt demanded.

She gaped at him. "Excuse me," she said dangerously. "I've traveled by myself all over Europe and the United States, and you, some random stranger with a temper problem, want me to *check with you* before I go anywhere?"

"That's not what I meant!" He looked ready to pound his head against something. "Check with me for directions! And how the hell did you manage to travel all over Europe if you can't even get from here to Grasse? What happened on your last trip, you got lost trying to get from London to Paris and ended up wandering through Istanbul and Prague before you could figure out where you were?"

"Okay, you know what..." She folded her arms and glared at him. "You can go now." She'd used train passes back then, for God's sake. Only on this trip had she had the brilliant idea to buy the little blue van off a friend in Berlin and use it to get around. Much easier to carry her instruments that way, right? Plus, it reminded her of the old days, when she'd driven that old beat-up van her mother had helped her buy all over the U.S., chasing festival opportunities in the summers between school terms. Music had just flowed out of her, back in those days. That had been who she *was*.

"Not if you want to be able to use your kitchen sink, I can't." He dropped back down to the floor and stretched out, scowling at her one last time before his head disappeared into the cabinet. From under the sink came a muttering stream of curses, like a bear grumbling in his cave.

She stared down at him. Now that she knew it was alive and didn't belong to an axe murderer, that was one really nice body to have stretched out there on those worn tiles. Big, half-filling the kitchen. A very reassuring strength to have around, to fight the lingering ghosts of axe murderers. He couldn't even see her ogling it either. As long as he kept working on that sink, she could ogle it a long time.

One knee drawn up, jeans hugging lean hips, a T-shirt clinging softly to stomach muscles drawn in extra tight with the work he was doing. Wide shoulders, the undersides of muscled arms visible as he used the wrench. "I see you got your T-shirt on," she said regretfully.

Then clapped her hand to her mouth. Oops. That regretful tone must be due to the shock of the moment.

He made a low, growling noise, clearly still grumpy.

Damn, she loved the growling noise. It just hummed through the air and through her bones. Her hands actually curved, fingers shifting to press down strings and strum, as if she could capture the sound, caress it, play it.

Be one hell of an instrument that could capture *that* sound. Her fingers flexed into the air, in frustration over all the moments that her music could never capture. And her gaze scanned the real instrument of that sound, that broad chest and that stretch of tan throat, and her fingers—all by themselves, she *swore* her brain knew better—thought about ways they could play more growls out of him. The tickling way they could run up his ribs right this second, get him to growl in protest, then maybe test the resilience of those chest muscles and see what other sounds he made when he was...

She curled her fingertips tightly into her palms and tucked them behind her, locking them between her butt and the counter to make them behave.

It was *hard* to make them behave. Her gaze drifted to where his drawn-up knee pulled the jeans against his crotch, and her impish, idiot fingers all the sudden thought about what sound he might make if she touched him *there*, and—

She smashed her butt harder against her hands, pinching them against the counter.

Probably be one hell of a sound, though, her brain thought wistfully.

Oh, fine, now her brain was going to turn idiot, too.

Yeah, but...admit you want to hear that sound.

"I'll just, ah...clean up," she said, and crouched to start collecting the chocolate bars that were scattered all around his body. A couple of them were even tucked half under his butt. She smiled a little, and then gave her fingertips a little rap against the hard tiles to try to knock some sense into them.

The hard stomach drew in even tighter. She followed that tightness up his torso—and started when she found that, in the shadow of the cabinet, he'd curled his head up enough to gaze at her.

"Nice T-shirt," she said dreamily. It was, too. This lovely golden-brown, fine cotton that kindly clung to all the definition of the muscles stretched out before her. The scent of roses came off him, mixed erotically with dirt and grease and sweat. "Although not as good as being naked."

The breath whooshed from him. A small thump as he hit his head on the pipe.

She clapped her hand to her mouth. Oh, good God. She had not just said that, had she? *If this is your newest way of procrastinating on that album, Layla Dubois, you have lost your mind.*

"Uh—don't get any ideas!" She held up a hand hastily, as if that could really ward off someone his size.

"Hard not to, now," he growled, low and deep. *Oh, yeah. Already a promising sound there.* One that vibrated through her whole body. He pushed himself out from under the cabinet enough to half sit up, one arm looping around his knee and the other hand rubbing his forehead.

She stared, still crouched on the floor close to him, really not wanting him to get any ideas and...really wanting him to. To just reach out and grab her and...show her some of his ideas.

Good lord. This must be where those repairman-housewife stories got started. And she'd always judged those poor women. Hot stranger, in one's house, fixing things...she could suddenly, utterly see the temptation to turn that into intense, stolen sex.

She slid back a bit, the movement shifting her out of her crouch to her knees. "I don't know why I said that."

Dark brown eyes tracked over her body. His voice went so deep the rub of it in her nipples *hurt.* "Want me to see if I can find out?"

"Oh, I—" She pushed herself back more. But in the process, her knees spread just a little. "No."

His gaze tracked back down over her body and lingered a second at the seam of her jeans, then trailed back up her torso, stopping like a hot stamp on her breasts before it reached her eyes again. As his gaze locked with hers, she flushed suddenly, all through her. "Sure?" His voice burred so deep she wanted to beg for it.

To just *wallow* in that sound, all over her body.

"No," she said. "I mean—yes! Yes, I'm sure."

Wait, had she said yes or no now? Those brown eyes caught on hers, clearly not sure either and intently hoping for the best.

She held up both hands. "No."

He took a long, slow breath, holding onto that upraised knee as if it was his own lifeline, and just watched her. Waiting.

Waiting for her to maybe change her mind, she realized. Or make it up.

Oh, *hell*, the crazy, stupid, intense arousal that pressed through her at his waiting.

"Please don't," she said. Because if he did reach for her, if he tested her response at all, she might just...go with it. Be swept away. And then where would she be?

Besides satisfied? protested her rebellious body.

Matt frowned just a little. "Bouclettes, you already said no. You don't have to add a 'please' to that for me."

She drew a breath and forced herself to break his gaze, blurrily eyeing instead the scattered chocolate bars.

"You don't have to add a 'please' to a 'yes' either." That deep voice rubbed over her.

She wet her lips.

"Yeah." A rumble like thunder. "You could just say it like that."

She pressed her lips together and shook her head, not daring to look at him. She desperately wanted to do something stupid.

He reached for a rag and very carefully, very thoroughly, wiped his hands clean.

Oh, lord.

"I said no."

"I'm not touching you, Bouclettes."

Damn. Why was that so *hot?* To not be touched? Why did it make her want to be touched so badly?

"That's good," she managed.

The deep vibrations of his voice just wrapped her up and caressed her, easing into a tone so gentle it was all she could do not to curl up in it. "Why is that good, *chérie?*"

She scrubbed her hands over her face, trying to rub some sense into herself. "Because I don't know what I'd do if you did," she confessed.

He drew one hard breath in, his fist clenching on the rag. Their gazes locked and *sizzled.* "That is a hell of a thing to tell a man while you keep asking him to do nothing."

"I know."

He shook his head slow and hard. "No. I bet you think you know. You think you can imagine it. But I bet you have no idea how hard it is to not just...*do.*"

She drew another breath and scooted herself to the other side of a table leg. A flimsy, silly barrier for all it was a sturdy old table. But she could hold onto it and stare at him from its pseudo-refuge.

She felt more like a lion caging herself so she wouldn't attack her prey rather than, say, prey hiding from the lion.

But maybe he misinterpreted, because he frowned and looked down, releasing all that delicious pressure. He took his own deep breath in and let it out now, heavily. "So...you like chocolate," he said randomly, picking up a few of the bars. And then a few more. A smile started to curl the corners of his lips. "A lot."

"They had all these flavors!"

Just that hint of amusement did the most amazing things to his mouth—easing the pressure that firm upper lip kept on the full, sensual lower one. Letting a hint escape of how much sensuality was there waiting to be freed. That lower lip, when the upper one relaxed, looked—vulnerable. Erotic. Looked like something a woman could lick and nibble and...

Stop it already.

His smile deepened, and he rose, setting the bars on top of the table. "I think you pierced my eardrums. *Merde*, but you've got a voice on you."

Ah...yes. That had been commented on before.

He reached out a hand for her, and she hesitated one second to gaze at the size and strength of it before she put her hand in his. It closed with just the right firmness, entirely engulfing hers as he pulled her easily to her feet.

She sighed, gazing up at him. He didn't look the least bit grumpy now. Intrigued, alert, ready. But...there was a gentleness to that alertness, a patience. He didn't move in on her with that big body. She could tell he wanted to. But he let her keep the corner of the table between them.

"I think you'd better give me your key to this house," she said regretfully.

Oops. She had meant to say that *firmly.*

That smile warmed the brown of his eyes to the most amazing color, rich with gold. "I'll leave the door unlocked on mine."

Hey. She started to blush. "That will *not* be necessary."

He laughed out loud, and pleasure leaped through her, to have made the grumpy bear laugh. "No, it will be something a lot more fun than necessary."

She put her hands on her hips. "Seriously. Don't leave your door open. I'm not coming."

"All right, Bouclettes. I got it. You didn't mean to go that far." He moved away to turn on the faucet and let it run a moment, checking under the sink. Then he nodded and started packing up his tools. A little color showed on his strong cheekbones and a little smile still curved his mouth while he cleaned up, just this sexy, happy curl.

She liked it.

Of course, she liked the scowl, too. It made her want to poke him and pet him and see how easy it would be to make that scowl disappear.

Men with hot bodies had it *so* easy where women were concerned, she thought with a sigh of despair at herself. They could get away with just about anything as long as they flexed their muscles from time to time. She'd burned herself on a couple of hook-ups like that before, post performance at a festival, when everyone who had been on stage was feeling kind of high with the glory of it, all wide open from having poured their hearts out to the crowd. But then you woke up in the morning wondering what the hell you had done, and why you had been so careless with your own heart. The music circuit was a small world, and you ran into those guys again, and saw them hooking up with some other high-on-performance woman, and...yeah, it felt crappy.

In other words, if starting something with him was her subconscious way of avoiding working on that album, it was a really bad idea. Oddly, though, she didn't feel as if she was avoiding the album. She actually kind of wanted to sit down and play with bass notes all evening. Drift some silken sweet sounds over them like a fall of petals. Let the breeze from the pines blow through. See what happened to them when night fell...

Matt glanced down at her as he headed out of the kitchen with his toolkit, his step slowing as if he might just stop and not leave. But he kept going. Outside the house, he set the toolkit down and turned to face her in the doorway.

"You still have the key," she said.

He braced his hands on the doorjamb, on either side of her above her head. *That* moved him into her space— caging her in with his size, and all his body wide open to her. But of course, she could always take one step back and shut the door. "It's in my back pocket," he said. That little smile as he held her eyes, and that deep, deep voice. God, a smile was a gorgeous look on him. She wanted to play with it, run her fingers over it, nurture it. "And I think my hands are dirty."

His jeans looked as if they'd been through a lot more than dirty hands. And, anyway, he'd just wiped his hands off so carefully she'd been *sure* he was about to touch her with them. But now they gripped the doorjamb above her, not touching her at all.

Meaning she would have to touch him, if she wanted any touching to occur.

His *back* pocket. Her palm itched to slide over the curve of that taut butt. "If I—if I got it out, what would you do?"

The biceps to either side of her face grew more pronounced. He gazed down at her, eyes not grumpy at all, oddly quiet. Intent. "What would you want me to do?" His voice didn't boom. It slid over her, textured, strong and rich, entirely reassuring.

"N—nothing," she admitted. Well, that was kind of what she wanted. With, like, the only two neurons that seemed to be functioning in her brain right now, that was what she wanted. The other two hundred billion seemed to want something entirely different.

Evidently a big, hot body that smelled of roses short-circuited all synapses.

His low, deep voice rubbed over her. "Well, I guess I'm going to do nothing, then."

Oh, really? Would you really do that for me? Hold all that big, aggressive need to do still for me?

He tightened his hands on the doorjamb. "I told you, it's not that easy to do."

But he waited, quite still except for the flexing of his arm muscles.

She slid her hand into his back pocket slow, slow, slow, afraid of what she was doing but tantalized by it,

85

too, by that firm curve, by the warmth and snugness of the pocket, by the arms framing her that hardened and didn't move. By his eyes watching her. Intent and pushing his will on her, as if he knew exactly what he wanted to do to her, but with maybe this hint of caution, too, as if he wasn't quite sure what she might do to *him*.

She came out with the key, iron and warm, but she didn't step back into the house with it and shut the door. She stared up at him, liking her little space inside the cage of his body so much she could have stayed there for an hour, with that warmth so carefully not touching her.

He took a deep breath and sighed it out. "I promised to do nothing, didn't I?"

She nodded mutely.

Another huff of a breath, and he shoved himself away from the doorjamb and her. "Well, that was a lot harder than I expected."

He picked up his toolkit and studied her another long moment, as if she was really hard to figure out. "I don't believe we've been properly introduced yet," he said slowly and held out his hand. "I'm Matthieu Rosier."

Her hand disappeared into his, slim and strong but engulfed by his strength and size. "Layla Dubois."

He didn't release her hand. "You stole my land," he said, still studying her as if something here was a complete mystery to him.

"It was a gift."

"I want it back."

Anxiety swamped her immediately, the clamor of the world coming back, just outside this valley, drowning out her music. Drowning out that buzz of bees she had been chasing on her guitar that morning, those soft silk petals. The bear in that song might be loud enough to be heard over the clamor, but all the rest would be lost. She had to catch it first. "I can't...I can't do that."

His lips pressed together, emphasizing all that tough, stubborn strength in his face. "How much do you want?"

She had no idea. "A few weeks?" Who was she kidding? She hadn't managed to write anything worthwhile in the last six months. There was no way she was going to pull fifteen or so solid songs out of her a— hat in a few weeks.

He blinked, visibly confused. "What?"

"What are we talking about?" she asked, confused, too.

"How much do you want for it?" His voice had tightened, like his face. "This house and land. What's your price?"

Oh, God, she was really, really bad with money. It was a family curse. Her mother was an art professor, she herself was a musician. And her mother had *supported* her in that career. She hadn't even told her daughter to become an accountant or anything instead. Layla had even turned down major recording contracts in favor of the indie route because she preferred the artistic control. She wasn't sure she had the genes for practical decisions. "I don't want to sell it," she protested. "I don't even know why it came to me yet. And I like it here."

I was writing a song this morning! Do you realize what that means? That I'm not some zombie up there on the stage playing a guitar anymore. That I can still create.

She expected another flare of grouchiness on his part at her refusal, but her last sentence seemed to distract him. A little light came into his eyes, even, as if she had paid him a compliment. "Do you?"

She gestured out over the roses with her free hand. "It's beautiful." *It's quiet. It teases the music right out of me, lures it into the open. It's like the old days, when I wasn't trying to* think *the music out, I could just* feel *it.*

The light in his eyes grew brighter. "You really think so?"

She nodded.

His hand didn't seem to know how to let go of hers. But then, she didn't try to wiggle free either. It was such a nice, strong, warm hold.

"I'll try to take good care of it," she offered. "I won't sell it to the highest bidder or anything."

A hint of brooding snuck back into his expression. "The highest bidder is likely to be one of my cousins. They have more liquid assets."

Not having ever had an extended family, she had no idea how to address that. Well, she had one. "How about if I promise to sell it to you if I ever do sell it?" What was her little chunk of this valley even worth? It was right off the Côte d'Azur, but clearly agricultural.

His face tightened again. "Layla. This valley is supposed to stay in the family. It's *mine.*"

"I'm pretty sure this part never was yours, or it wouldn't have come to me," she pointed out.

He scowled, temper flaring in his eyes.

Since she shouldn't let herself stroke his chest and smooth his T-shirt down, she offered him something else: "You can keep picking my roses."

That made his head rear back. "Of course I can keep picking those roses! We just planted those bushes three years ago, they—" He broke off as she put her free hand over his lips.

"Or you *could* say, 'Thank you very much for being so cooperative,'" she suggested sternly.

He studied her, one eyebrow going up. Then he leaned a tad into her, pressing his will onto her as if seeing how she held up to it. "I could say that. But they are *my* roses."

Ha, as if he was the first man who'd ever tried to get her to bend to his sheer force of male will. Busking around Europe and then dealing with the music industry had brought her into contact with plenty of men who wanted the little female to cooperate. Little females who couldn't afford a personal bodyguard had to learn how to look out for themselves in the world. So she only raised her eyebrows, amused. "Every single last petal?"

"Every single one."

"You're very possessive, aren't you?"

He nodded unhesitatingly, as if she had just affirmed one of his more admirable qualities.

She locked eyes with him. "I'm not good with possessive people." The words were so inherently true to who she was, that it was odd they seemed to rub her throat wrong coming out, as if she was telling a lie. A little frisson of loneliness ran inexplicably across her skin.

He met her locked gaze easily, as if he liked that meeting of wills. "Anyone ever try to possess you?"

"Oh, all the time," she said wryly. They bought her on a CD or downloaded her onto their phones and thought they owned her forever after. Sometimes she felt they owned her, too.

His thumb rubbed over the back of her hand, this sweetest stroke of a callus. "How'd that work out for them?"

She lifted her chin. "I'm pretty hard to hold." *I'm still me. Free. And I can write this damn album without worrying about what all those people who bought me last time are going to think when they buy me again.*

He looked down at his hand, currently holding hers so easily and surely, and made the slightest moue of disagreement.

For some reason, that made a tingle run through her. "I don't like to be owned," she said firmly.

Matt's hand squeezed once, strong and gentle both, around hers. "'Holding' and 'owning' aren't the same thing." He released her hand. "*Bonne nuit,* Layla."

"*Bonne nuit.*"

He got maybe ten paces before he glanced back over his shoulder. "I meant it, by the way. This valley is mine." A faint smile. "And my door's unlocked."

Chapter 8

Layla woke full of music. Her lips actually buzzed with it, as if it had been trying to hum out of her all night. She climbed out of bed and padded to the window, gazing at the way the soft gray dawn lay over the wealth of pink petals. Fresh buds had bloomed during the night, as if the roses' song was one that could be renewed over and over, no matter how many hands grabbed at those roses during the day. A thousand hands could strip those flowers off for themselves, but the rose bushes remained *roses*.

She whistled softly, but her whistle couldn't catch it, and she picked up her guitar, trying to sift the sound of that dawn softly from it. Just this quiet, simple thing, this peace that teased at the guitar, that invited it to lilt more and more joyously, to expand the picking of a melody from its strings into fuller and braver chords that wanted to run out into the valley and play. A song that somehow grew from a shy, quiet thing to a child bursting out of bed in the morning, thrilled at a brand new day and a whole valley to explore.

Like Grumpy Bear might have woken up when he was a kid, maybe, with his black hair all tousled around his head. Maybe not so grumpy back then, just excited, running to his cousins' houses, all of them tumbling out to play...

It made her happy, that song. It made her happy with how easily it *came*, as if she was that girl wandering the world again. Weird that it wasn't so much about the freedom to roam and the wanderlust of life—like her first album—and more about a place, but she kept singing bits of it to herself in the shower, searching for words.

The words didn't want to come, though. She tossed the marker she always kept on hand across the bathroom and wiped her few attempts off the shower wall with her forearm, scowling at the blue ink running slowly down her skin.

She had just gotten out of the shower when she heard the knock. She finished pulling on her shorts and squeezed some frizz-control product into her palm as she headed for the door.

Grumpy Bear—Matthieu—stood half-turned away, gazing out over the rose fields while he waited. His hair was damp, too, one or two little black locks already curling up as they dried. He turned toward her as soon as the door opened, one hand going behind his back, his gaze flicking over her once.

"I was just thinking of you," Layla said, burying her hands in her curls to scrunch in the product. Normally she would hang her head toward the floor for this part, but she had a sudden thought of that dark brown gaze moving over the stretch of her back toward her butt and she kept upright. "In the shower."

He blinked. A little surge of energy seemed to run through his body, a man getting ready for action.

"Because the water was warm!" Layla tried to explain hastily. "You know, it *felt* good."

His lips parted. He stared at her.

"Because you fixed the electricity!" she shouted. "I was thinking of you because I was so glad to have warm water again!"

He stared at her another long moment and then grinned suddenly. God, a grin looked good on him—all that grumpiness laughed away. All that energy and happiness surging in its place. It made energy and happiness surge through her, too. "I was thinking of you in the shower, too, Bouclettes."

Her entire body went red. She put up hands to ward him off. Or possibly to hold herself back.

That made his grin fade a bit, as if it wasn't entirely sure it was welcome. He thrust a plastic container into one of her hands. "For you." His voice had gone suddenly gruff.

She studied him as her fingers closed around the container, intrigued by that gruffness. Maybe under that aggressive growling of his, under that cocky, close-her-in-a-doorway confidence, he too had a...tenderness, a soft vulnerable spot that he preferred not to reveal to anyone who could abuse it.

Smart guy. She'd gotten up on a thousand stages and shown all her vulnerable spots to the world, and the world had said, *Ooh, yummy. Give us some more. But not the* same *more and not a* different *more and have you noticed you use a lot of sensitive female chord progressions? Not that there's anything wrong with being* female *of course, you must be misinterpreting our tone.*

Yeah. Matt was probably the smart one—not showing his heart at all. Keeping it here tucked up in a valley.

"It's just something my cousin Gabe made for my birthday. Not those idiots—" Matt jerked his thumb toward the field in a way that was presumably indicative of the cousins she had seen the day before. "A more distant cousin. Gabriel Delange. The chef." He eyed her as if he expected her to know the name, but, as often happened at the worst moment possible on the music circuit, she didn't. It was hard to get so famous that *everyone* recognized you.

Especially if you're nothing more than a one-hit wonder, a little voice reminded her.

Damn it, shut up, she told it.

Who wanted to be famous, anyway? Even having a reputation was unnerving. People *expected* things of you. And those expectations seemed to reach right into the heart of who you were and take it over, try to keep it for themselves.

"Three-star chef?" Matt tried. "Famous pâtissier?"

Contrary to popular opinion, it took quite a while for a musician to make enough money to indulge regularly in three-star restaurants. A long time after you first got picked up by Pandora, that was for sure. Bar food was more her style. She opened her free hand to show ignorance.

"Anyway, I thought you might like it." He cleared his throat and nudged the container in her hand again, making her realize she was still staring at his face.

"Thank you," she said, confused, looking down. And then she saw what was in the clear plastic container—a delicate chocolate rose, perfectly formed to look not like a classic tea rose but like the ruffled ones that grew in these fields. "Oh. *Thank* you. This is beautiful."

"To eat his famous rose, you have to go to his restaurant. It melts. This is just something he made as a joke for me." Matt shrugged big shoulders as if they didn't quite fit on his body just then. "Since you said you liked chocolate…"

She smiled. Her heart had just turned to mush. "That is—really, really sweet."

Color tinged his cheekbones. "No, it isn't."

Her eyebrows went up a little.

A bit of growl entered his voice. "I'm not sweet. I didn't even make that."

Damn, that was such a hot growl. "I was talking about the chocolate," she reassured him. "Obviously not *you*." She smiled.

He gazed at her suspiciously a moment. And then he pulled his other hand from behind his back and offered her a real pink rose. Definite color streaked his cheekbones as he handed it to her. "I made this one."

She couldn't help it. That just lit her heart up. She snatched the rose out of his hand and took a step back, before that crazy heart could shine right out of her chest so brightly that he spotted it in all its vulnerability and then did something careless with it. Like break it.

"*Aïe.*" He lifted a finger to his mouth to suck where a thorn had raked his skin when she grabbed the rose.

"Sorry."

He shook his head and shrugged, watching her.

"Excuse me. I think I need to—" *Go cradle a rose and act all mushy and ridiculous over it for a while. It's probably best if I do that in private.*

Write a song, maybe. Something soft and sweet and silky as roses. No, but with this gruff, rough undertone. How to do that?

"Do you want to come help?" Matt asked abruptly.

She blinked her way out of the beginnings of a song, confused.

"With the harvest. Just for a little while," he added quickly. "Just as long as it's fun. You don't have to stay."

She took a step back toward him, angling her head to study his eyes. "Do a lot of people only stick around you as long as it's fun?" she asked quietly. "And leave you to handle the job when it gets boring, and hot, and dirty?"

"They come when they know I need help," he corrected firmly. "Yesterday, they were there all day and they're coming out this morning, too. And yes, when it's fun. They like the harvest. But on a day-to-day basis...this valley is my job. Not theirs. They don't have to spend their whole lives here."

He was only defending his cousins, casually, but at heart she was a songwriter even more than a performer, someone who craved the right words for the right tune, and his words caught at her. "And you do?" *Is your whole life trapped here?*

He frowned a little, looking around at the roses that spilled below them, at the hills that framed them. "It's my valley."

She stepped back into the doorway, lured toward him just when she had thought to hide herself and her silly, extravagant feelings somewhere private and safe. Fascinated by this blend of responsibility, big, strong grumpiness, and the sweetness that was almost like a secret he was afraid to share. The man who roared...and then saved a cat. Or made a rose.

"If I show you what it's like," he said, rough and strong, his hands flexing by his sides in big fists that had no idea what to do with themselves, "maybe you'll understand. Why it has to stay in the family."

"And by 'family', you mean you?" she asked curiously.

"It's my valley."

"You're the entire family?"

He scowled, folding his arms across his chest. "Do you want to come or not?"

"I do, actually," she said quietly, and his face relaxed.

"Really?"

"Really." It sounded like spending the day in the middle of a song.

***

In the fields, Matthieu helped her put on one of the apron-like things the harvesters wore as they moved down the rows—essentially a giant pocket that tied around the waist, into which the flowers were dropped. "When it gets filled up, dump it in the nearest burlap bag," he said.

She reached for the first rose cautiously, afraid to do something wrong.

"Just press your thumb right in the center," Matt said behind her, and his big hand curled gently around a rose near her hand, thumb pressing down on the little nub of yellow at the center of the loose, ruffly pink petals as his fingers cupped it. The rose looked absurdly small and delicate in that work-hardened palm.

Layla looked back at her own rose. Her fingertips were callused and strong, too, especially the left ones—a guitarist's hands—and her hands, too, were bronze, for she had been born with skin that loved to soak up all that sun on festival stages. But her hands were much slimmer, and she would have assumed the pink rose would look more natural in her feminine hold.

She looked back at the big masculine palm cupping its delicate pink so surely, that thumb pressed so easily and firmly onto the nub at its center.

Oh...her mind just went somewhere...it really didn't want to come back from.

It gave a whole new concept to what looked "natural".

She stroked the petals of her own rose, only a few inches from his hand. Such exquisite texture. The rose bushes on either side of her came up to her shoulders, and the scent caressed everywhere.

"Be firm," that deep voice said from just behind her, completely confident now, with no hint of the vulnerability he had almost revealed that morning. "Take control of it."

She ducked her head to hide a smirk. One day she was going to quote those words right back at him when he was—*whoa. Slow down.*

You're just passing through here. You've got an album to produce.

If you stay here a little while and concentrate*, you might even be able to write some songs for it.*

With a tiny, competent twist, the rose came off in his hand, and he dropped it into her apron pocket. His arm circled her body, brushing her own arm when he did it. Was that the heat of the sun or the heat of his body that she felt so keenly against her back? His chest wasn't touching her. It must be the sun. But super-imposed over the roses before her was a vision of his naked torso from the day before, those broad shoulders and those hard abs and that fine V of dark hair aiming down a flat belly. It made her feel so small and vulnerable and oddly sheltered. Dangerously safe.

If she turned around, how much would it take for her to get that growl and blush to come back?

She turned. His gaze snapped up from somewhere lower on her body to her face. She smiled, feeling saucy. Feeling a really outrageous urge to flex her butt muscles a little bit in case that was where his gaze had been. "Let me know if you need help getting your T-shirt off," she said. Be nice to make that vision of his naked torso come true.

Brown eyes locked on hers.

She grinned, pretty full of herself. Sometimes it was really fun to be outrageous. Besides, in comparison with all the other visions she'd been having of him—and them—that one was practically G-rated.

His voice lowered into that deep, deep register that just vibrated into her bones. "Any time."

Ooh. *Any* time, hmm? Her gaze drifted down over those hard, cotton-veiled abs, quite a cruel temptation. In fact, those abs might very well be the most fantastic excuse for not working on her album that a songwriter could ever come up with.

He took a hasty step back. "Any time we're in *private*. Not when all my family's watching!"

She grinned. "You know, I have an advantage over you."

He made an incredulous sound. "Only one?"

Wait, how many advantages did he think she had over him? And what were they? "I'm used to having people watching."

He blinked and shook his head. "You're *what?*"

"So I don't get too intimidated by having eyes on me. I actually, I think, feel a little cockier and more outrageous."

He took another, much longer step back. And it was *hilarious*. She loved having the power to make a big, strong, go-for-what-he-wanted man back up. "You behave." His voice was a grumble of warning. Or a plea for mercy?

She grinned. "It's okay. I understand. I have a shy side, too."

"I'm not *shy*," he said, outraged.

"Of course not." She actually reached out to pat him soothingly on the arm. If he'd been a little closer, she would have managed it, too. As it was, her hand moved in the air and then had to drop, disappointed, to her side.

"I'm not." A stomp of his voice into the earth.

No, of course not. That's why you blush so easily.

"I just don't believe in letting my family or my workers see a weak spot, which is *not* the same thing."

"No," she said soothingly. And maybe it wasn't the same thing. Maybe it wasn't that he was insecure—it was just that he refused to show the chink in his armor to the world around him.

It must take a *lot* of growling to hide a heart tender enough to make roses.

She wished she knew how to growl. Maybe she should have gone into heavy metal. "What advantages do you think I have over you?"

An incredulous rake of his gaze over her, head-to-toe, that left her tingling everywhere. "All advantages."

Oh, come on, be more specific. "You're this much bigger than I am." She stretched her hands apart to encompass the notion of twice her size.

"Yeah, well, while that would come in very handy if you were a guy I was trying to beat up, it's not real useful in this situation, is it?"

She considered, and a smile softened her mouth. "*I* kind of like it," she murmured.

"I can't *do* anything with it," he said, frustrated. His hands flexed in the air in this way that charged excitement all through her body, as if he had a whole host of visions of things his size would make it possible for him to do with her that he wouldn't let himself do.

So much energy sparkled over her skin that she didn't quite know what to do with herself. "That's part of the fun," she admitted. Testing and teasing all that strength of his and knowing he would hold it in check for her. That he wouldn't, for all his grumbling, wannabe aggressiveness, use it to do anything she didn't want.

"I'm glad to know I'm entertaining," he growled and turned abruptly to the rose bush to start clearing it of roses. He had half of it done before she could even pull her gaze away from the long, blunt fingers deftly cupping rose after rose, the thumb pressing firmly, the way the soft pink petals disappeared for a moment completely in that big, callused hand as he collected five or six at once and dropped them in the pouch.

He slid a glance sideways at her. "You didn't explain how you're used to people watching you pull off a man's T-shirt."

"Well, I used to do this number in a sex shop where I—"

He jerked away from her.

"I'm kidding! I'm a musician. I perform on stage. I only meant I was used to being in front of a crowd of people and not letting them intimidate me. An audience probably exacerbates my tendencies to over-express myself."

He cleared a few more roses, deft, firm fingers moving amidst soft pink. "But you are expressing your *self*," he said finally.

"What?"

"Right now. You're not acting or pretending. You're letting too much of yourself out into the open. Of what you really think and feel."

Well, well...she started to flush, unexpectedly, and even though he was ostensibly gazing at the roses he was picking and not at her, a little smile started to curve his mouth, releasing that sensual lower lip.

"I'm just being me," she said hastily. "Don't worry about it. I already promised not to ask you to marry me and have my babies." *I'm a free spirit. A rolling stone.*

I just need to get back to those days of freedom and wandering, when it was just me and my music. Then maybe I'll be fine. I'll have music again.

One eyebrow went up a little. He still didn't turn his head, but she was beginning to suspect he had very good peripheral vision. "If it's any reassurance to you, I promise not to have your babies."

Okay, and what did that mean, exactly, that he left off the other half of her promise? Her whole body did this weird, panicked gulp, like in her dreams sometimes when she thought she was playing her guitar softly to herself and looked up to find ten thousand eyes on her. Most of them, these days, staring out over picket signs that said, "Is this all you got? One hit and you're done?"

She shook herself, focused on her own bush, and carefully picked her very first rose.

The petals fell apart in her hands, and when she tried to drop the rose into her pouch, pink fluttered around her fingers, half the petals drifting to the ground. And she wanted to just flutter after them. Lose herself to this and be caught in big, callused palms.

"Not like that," he said. Now, when she was actually getting something wrong, not an iota of impatience showed in that deep voice, any more than it had when he was giving her detailed directions or talking about the cat he had to move out of the way of his car every time he drove through the nearest village. Or letting her hide behind a table leg as she teased him and hit on him and he let her, without pressuring her for more. That grouchiness of his wasn't impatience. It was just his armor, wasn't it?

"Look." He shifted back to her, body carefully held so as not to brush hers, but so very, very close as he reached for another rose right in front of her and showed her again. "Put your thumb down firmly on this little nub here."

She stared at that firm thumb on that little nub. This was turning out to be the most confusingly erotic day.

"Don't be afraid of it. You have to take the whole flower or the bush wastes its energy making rose hips later." As he spoke, he absently snapped off an older

100

stripped stem left on the bush. "See, you're not the only one. The workers get careless."

"Show me one more time?" she asked innocently. And felt a little guilty when he did show her with that surprising patience and sincerity, no idea where her dirty mind was taking his hand. She ducked her head, feeling her cheeks heat again.

"You need a hat," he said. "And sunscreen. You're already starting to show color."

He disappeared while she focused on the rose bush, slowly getting the hang of how much pressure and twist was the most effective. It was an easy gesture, nothing complicated about it, really...as long as you were firm with that little nub. Her lips twitched, and she bit hard on the lower one, beginning to suspect she really was drunk on something. Quite possibly that heady combination of roses and male. The roses slid softness and scent through her fingers, such a sensuous sensation that she could have picked roses all day.

Or at least half a day. The more her fingers slid over them, the more they longed also for the more demanding textures of the strings of her guitar. They wanted to alternate—a little silk, a little tension. To capture this silk in that tension.

She saw why so many of his cousins came and helped as much as they could, taking time away from whatever other responsibilities they had. A day in the sun and roses, with all that camaraderie? Over at a truck half-filled with rose-stuffed burlap bags, his cousin Tristan was shrugging another burlap bag off one shoulder and grinning as he said something to Matt that had Matt giving him a warning, grumpy glance, his color high.

Meaning the comment had to be about her, right? The guy was so darn adorable. He made her feel like some frivolous butterfly dancing around the head of a great bear that had just crawled, grouchy and hungry, out of its cave in the spring. She knew she only had a metaphorical butterfly's day here. She had a career waiting for her, crouched right outside this valley like a stalker waiting for her to come out the back stage door. But how was she supposed to resist playing with that grumpy bear, when he was such irresistible *fun*?

He came back over to her, walking as if he had to make sure the earth felt the imprint of every step. "Here." He pulled a broad-brimmed straw hat over her head. Then he held up a bottle of sunscreen and squeezed it into *her* palm. Darn. "Get your arms and your face," he said.

So she tried.

Well, she kind of tried.

It wasn't her fault she was so bad at getting sunscreen on her face, was it? No mirror, after all.

"Good?" She looked up at him brightly. Hey, this straw brim was fun. Made her feel all Scarlett O'Hara flirtatious, peeking from under it.

Alas, she suspected it didn't have quite Scarlett's effect with her wildly curly hair—more like putting a hat on an electrocuted porcupine—but *she* didn't have to see herself.

"You...just..." His fingers stretched out, got restrained back into a fist, flexed out again. "Right there, it..." His hand worked in frustration, just shy of her face.

She rubbed ineptly. "Better?" she asked cheerily.

He looked down at her a moment. Brown eyes narrowed a fraction. A little shot of adrenaline charged through her, like maybe she was about to pay the consequences of her teasing. *Ooh, yeah.*

"Hold still," he said finally, and big palms framed her face. Two callused thumbs rubbed gently but firmly over the bridge of her nose, then down across her cheekbones, smearing in cream. The scent of rose oils on his hands dominated even the sunscreen smell. It was all she could do not to turn her head enough to bury her face in that big tough palm and see what it was like to smell only him, no sunscreen as distraction.

Her lips parted, and all that merry, teasing happiness in her went very, very still. Her face framed in his palms, he let his gaze drift down to her mouth and linger there a moment. Long black lashes, curled at the tips, didn't quite veil those rich brown eyes. That stern pressure of his upper lip slowly relaxed, releasing the sensual, full lower one as his lips softened apart.

She touched her tongue to her own lips in reaction, involuntarily, and his gaze swept back up suddenly to her eyes.

"You're...gentle," she said wonderingly.

He frowned a little, even as a touch of color snuck across his cheeks. "What did you think I would be?"

A little smile ran through her. "Bossier. I thought you'd take that sunscreen and *make* it do what you wanted."

His own smile snuck out, that sensual lower lip escaping further from the bossy control of the upper one. His thumb snuck another caress of her cheek that made her feel so happy. Alive. Touchable. As if she was a rose petal. "It's only sunscreen," he said. "Pretty pliant."

She laughed. His gaze caught on that laugh.

"And it's just a little face," he said softly, still framing her cheeks with both hands. The calluses rubbed carefully against her skin, his hands covering pretty much the whole of each side of her head. "I wouldn't want to be too rough with it." His fingertips caressed very gently into the edge of her hair.

A woman could nestle her head into that caress, kiss the base of his wrist, forget anything and everything.

His family. He didn't want you to make him look vulnerable in front of his family.

And maybe she didn't want to be that exposed, that fragile, either. She'd only been fooling around, right? Gentleness, and her reaction to it, put them in completely new territory.

You know, just because a guy is hot, surrounded by roses, and speaks French is no reason to believe you're immersed in a fairy tale. This is real life to him.

And it's not real life to me. No matter how real and magical it feels.

Maybe if they could stop speaking French. It had always been her heart language, her secret language, the one she spoke with her mother and grandparents there in that emotional safe space of her home growing up and rarely out with the rest of the world. It was probably leading her astray to use it so much with him. Misleading her heart into thinking he was her safe space, too.

She drew a breath. "Do you speak English?"

"A little bit," he said carefully in that language, and every erogenous zone in her body just abandoned all resistance. Okay, then, switching to English was *not* going to help in this case. Apparently she was more vulnerable to accents than she had previously realized in all her travels around Europe.

She held up a hand, struggling for an even, sane breath. "Stop. Don't do it anymore."

"Why not?" he asked, still in careful English.

She lifted her fist to her mouth and bit into the side finger. *Because I can't handle that much hotness right now. It's hotness overload. I think I need a break before I do something* really *crazy.* "Umm...I need to practice my French."

"Probably," he agreed, back in that language. She gave a little gasp of relief. "Because I'm not sure you entirely realize the things you say to me sometimes. That is, I think you know what they mean, but I'm not sure you realize how hard they hit."

"I should stop, shouldn't I?" she asked wistfully.

He considered that a long moment, big and brawny, all strong cheekbones and stubborn jaw and half-curled hair and those brown eyes, when they focused on a woman like that, just utterly lovely. The whole of him was so big and testosterone-charged, and yet...there was something about those eyes. And that blush that sometimes betrayed his soft heart. "Why?" he asked finally.

Why was she acting like this? "I have no idea," she said frankly. Because he made her feel happy? Because he made her feel free and alive, like she used to back in the days when she wandered Europe playing at markets and tiny festivals and picnicking on the edge of streams and the music flowed freely? "But you started it. That first night."

"Yes, but you're not drunk, are you?"

Fine. Go ahead and rub it in that you *were, when you came on to me,* she thought, a little sulkily. "Maybe I'm drunk on being here?" She opened her arms to indicate the valley of roses, or Provence, or France. This place that made her feel as if she was twenty again, backpacking through Europe after her study abroad program ended, with her guitar and a dream. This place that made her feel alive *even when she wasn't playing a new song.*

He frowned, a hint of that grouchiness back, as if maybe he really preferred her not to have an excuse, and folded his arms. God, that did such great things to his biceps. But it left her cheeks feeling utterly bereft of the warmth and texture of his hands. "I actually meant, why do you think you should stop saying things to me?"¬

"Otherwise you might get ideas," she admitted. He had a lot more feelings than a guitar, and playing with him might lead to someone getting hurt. Both of them, maybe. When she started playing with an instrument, she always, always ended up pouring all her heart into it.

His frown deepened into a scowl. He shoved the toe of his shoe into the soft earth. "Men have been known to do that, after being told they look good naked."

"Exactly," she said uncomfortably.

He pulled back a step, the grumpy bear entirely awake again. "What, are you afraid I'm going to turn out to be an axe murderer or something? That I'm going to strangle you and leave your body buried in the rose fields?"

She blinked.

He scowled.

He looked so darn adorable when he scowled like that.

Her lips quirked. "Are there a lot of dead bodies buried in these rose fields? Because you thought of a location for mine awfully quick."

"You'd have to ask my grandfather where the dead bodies are." He glowered at his shoe. "I'm pretty sure not in the rose fields, because we have to dig these bushes up every seven years or so, and we were *always* on the lookout for bones when we were kids."

She gaped at him.

He hesitated, gaze sweeping her face, and then rushed on, honest to God as if he was trying to reassure her. "If they ever did use the rose fields, I'm sure it was only a stopgap because there was loose dirt, and they moved the bodies again as soon as they could. But honestly, I would be surprised. Anything done close to the rose fields would have been so easily tied to him and his family, when there was all this *maquis* around he could have done it in." Matt gestured to the hills.

Layla stole a quick glance at the old patriarch over by the truck. Those light blue eyes of his were trained on her right at that moment, not menacing exactly, just matter-of-fact, as if it wouldn't be the first time he'd made the decision to pull a trigger with a human skull in his sights, and it wouldn't necessarily be the last.

"You're trying to scare me away," she decided. "I'm not that stupid. If you want that property back, you had a better chance at it when you were walking around half naked. Actually, maybe if you wanted to try fixing the sink half naked, that would—"

"*La Résistance!* He's Jean-Jacques Rosier. You haven't heard of him? He was a Resistance hero in the war. Like his stepsister, Colette Delatour. The woman who gave you that house."

That caught her. "You knew her well, then? Can you tell me more about her?"

He stared at her. "You can *meet* her. She's still alive, you know."

Alive? Antoine Vallier's letter had completely failed to communicate that the woman who gave her this mysterious gift was still alive. Layla brought her hands to her lips, both excited and unnerved.

"She'd like to meet you," Matt mentioned. "She told me so yesterday."

It gave her goose bumps suddenly. She had wanted to know more about this heritage, but to meet a real, live person...to really find out what it meant...it was like that build-up of nerves before she went on stage. She stared at him, wishing she could bury herself in his big, strong embrace until her nerves calmed down.

"If she tries to pass on any Renaissance treasure to you, be aware that it's stolen, too," a voice said behind her, and she turned to find the old patriarch had snuck up on her.

Damn. How did the man move like that at his age? He had to be at least ninety, didn't he, if he'd fought in the Resistance during World War II?

"Renaissance treasure?" She might have sidled closer to Matt. Well, what? He probably wouldn't let his grandfather shoot her, would he?

"Just remember that the ethical thing to do would be to return that treasure to its proper family."

"Pépé, will you let me handle this?" Matt grumbled.

"Of course, that would be the ethical thing to do with that property she gave you, too." Blue eyes fixed on her.

"Look," Layla began, not at all sure how to handle the entanglement of family heritage issues when she had no idea what they were. Plus, family heritage had never been an issue for her. Her grandparents on her mother's side had pretty much lost everything to bombardments in Beirut—it was how they'd ended up immigrating to the U.S.—and her grandfather on her father's side had come to the U.S. as a teenage refugee, so up until the letter from Antoine Vallier, family heritage hadn't been on the table. "I—"

And just then a scream split the air.

"Oh, fuck," Matt said and shoved past her.

Layla stumbled out of his way and then spun, trying to figure out what was going on, while around the field, four male cousins and one grandfather changed from relaxed males to lunging, lethal action.

One of the male harvesters had a knife drawn—a woman was screaming at him, but Layla couldn't make out even what language she spoke. French? Arabic? Another man was backing away warily, fists ready but no weapon to defend himself.

Oh, *shit*. Layla had seen a few fights break out at festivals, and this couldn't possibly end well. Her hands flew to her mouth—and then Matt's big body burst straight through a row of rose bushes and rammed into the knife-wielder from the side.

The man went down, crashing through more roses, and Layla ran forward, straight through bushes herself, unable to see. Thorns ripped at her, and she reached the scene to find Matt on the ground grappling for the other man's wrist, slamming the knife hand into the ground as he drove his other fist into the man's face.

Blood spurted everywhere, on Matt and on the man he was fighting to hold down. The woman was screaming, Matt was shouting, something like, "You fucking idiot!" and some other men were shouting, and then—

All the sudden the man on the ground went limp, all the fight leaving him.

Knocked unconscious?

No. It was more as if the sense had been knocked into him. Blood streaming from his nose, he gave his head a slight shake and stared at the woman, who had stopped screaming and had her hands to her mouth, staring back at him. Suddenly, the female harvester started to sob. The man closed his eyes a second, obviously realizing what he had just done.

Then Raoul and Damien were on them, Raoul kicking the knife away and each locking up one of the man's arms as they dragged him to his feet. Matt stood up and back, blood running down his arm.

Oh, God.

"Matt, you're bleeding," Raoul said.

"Yeah, the roses. I went straight through them." Matt wiped absently at his arm without looking down. "You have to move fast or else Pépé still tries to handle these things all by himself." He sent a dark look at his grandfather, who was moving in on the scene with what was still a remarkable pace for his age, and turned toward the man who had drawn the knife.

"That's a pretty big thorn scratch," Raoul said dryly.

Matt glanced down. His eyebrows went up at the blood running over his arm, and then he swore and turned to the man he had hit. "Couldn't you have started a fistfight? Did you have to pull a knife? What the fuck? What's going to happen to your kids if you go to jail?"

Tristan grabbed Matt's wrist to lift his arm up and heaved a dramatic sigh. "Damn it. I hope we're not in the waiting room as long as last time."

"Are you kidding me? It's the *rose harvest.* I don't have time to go to the doctor."

"Sorry," Tristan said, his voice careless even while he managed to sound completely firm. "It's not deep, but he got you up half your forearm, Matt. You need stitches."

Layla crept closer, horrified by the violence and deeply anxious over the blood on his arm. How deep was that slice running up the outside of his forearm? Matt caught sight of her and winced, trying to turn his body so that she couldn't see it.

"Can't one of the women do it?" his grandfather asked. "What's the matter with this generation, didn't you learn any proper skills?" He shot Layla a sharp, impatient glance.

Layla gaped at him.

"You didn't learn how to embroider?" Pépé asked, exasperated.

"I—I think I cross-stitched something when I was eight or so," Layla said. "*Not* on human bodies."

"Well, Colette would come in handy for once," Jean-Jacques Rosier said reluctantly. "I suppose one of you boys could call her."

Matt perked up. "Yeah, Tante Colette could do it. She sews better."

"We're taking him to the doctor," Tristan said firmly.

"Can I have somebody's T-shirt or something to wrap it up?" Layla asked, her voice coming out high and tense. How could they all act so *casual* about all this?

"Yeah, we don't want to get it all over the seats in my car," Tristan agreed. "Damien, your shirt is ugly. Let's use it."

Matt grinned at that, making Layla stare. He'd just been in a knife fight, and he was laughing at some stupid joke?

He looked down at her, caught her shocked gaze, and clamped his lips together quickly, grin disappearing.

"I'm holding a violent criminal," Damien retorted to Tristan. "So I'm afraid it's going to have to be yours."

Tristan sighed again, very heavily. "I don't suppose you—?" He glanced at Layla invitingly.

"Don't make me hit you," Matt said.

"Oh, fine, fine, fine. But you're going to regret it, you know." Tristan pulled his T-shirt over his head.

Revealing a long, lean, ripped torso, broad, supple, muscled shoulders narrowing down to washboard abs and a flat stomach. All of which he stretched leisurely as it was revealed.

"Show-off," Matt said. "Give me that." He grabbed the T-shirt and started trying to wrap it around his own arm.

"Matt, you know you're no good at T-shirts," Tristan argued, grinning, flexing his muscles a little and winking at Layla. "You'd better let me do it, or you're going to end up with it stuck around your neck or something. And as charming as that look is on you..." He tried to take over the wrapping. Matt growled at him, jerking his arm farther away.

"I'll do it," Layla said. She had to do something before she hyperventilated. And, and...his arm. The blood on it was making her sick to her stomach.

Matt went still. And then just yielded his arm to her, his head bent to hers.

She frowned as she wrapped the T-shirt tightly. "Isn't there a first-aid kit in the truck?"

"Yes, but the doctor's only a few kilometers away," Tristan said. "No point making Matt go through all that antiseptic twice."

"I don't mind," Matt said.

She looked up at him. He...oh, for crying out loud. He was blushing. Just that hint of deeper bronze in his cheeks as he tried to keep his lips firm and stubborn, as if they could fight that color down if they only compressed themselves hard enough.

"Not that you have to do anything," he said quickly. "It's nothing. Honestly. This kind of thing happens all the time." He stopped, and his eyes widened a tiny bit. "I mean...it never happens. Of course. This is—that is—I never—"

Tristan pushed his shoulder, laughing. "Let's come back when you're bravely bandaged. *Allez*, wounded fighter coming through." He dragged Matt to his silver Audi, parked along the edge of the field.

***

111

When Matt glanced back as the car pulled away, he found that Layla had trailed half the way after them and was standing still, her eyebrows flexed together. Beyond her, Pépé was facing the two men and the woman, the knife-wielder still held by Raoul and Damien. Matt winced a little in sympathy for the man now on the receiving end of that level, whiplash voice. *Been there.*

But whether the man realized it yet or not, Pépé would handle him fairly. Of all of them, Pépé knew the most intimately what it was like to be in a country where the police force was a foreign enemy—even if, in his case, that country had been his own—and what it was like to have kids whose lives hung in the balance if he slipped up. And he knew one hell of a lot about violence and how to judge what a man was or wasn't capable of. Like, were the kids and wife better off if the man *was* in prison?

It was good to have Pépé still there. Good to have time to acquire a little more wisdom before he had to become the patriarch himself—maybe the *last* family patriarch—and know everything about human nature without the benefit of thirty more years to learn it.

Okay, fine, Pépé himself hadn't had the benefit of that much time. He'd led a Resistance cell before he was twenty, living proof to all his grandsons that a man had no right to excuses. No right to shirk his duty, no right to weakness. A man did what he had to do.

And he didn't get distracted by a scratch on his arm. Although, given that Pépé had met their grandmother when she was the next leg on their ferrying of children through the Alps, he suspected even Pépé could get distracted by a cute girl.

Matt sighed and sank back in Tristan's leather passenger seat, closing his eyes. Layla's face swam before him, the way her hands pressed over her mouth in horrified rejection of what she had seen. Damn it. How many other ways could he find to make a crappy impression on her?

What an idiot he'd been to bring her those roses. A woman could draw all the wrong conclusions from something like that—think, for example, that a man actually cared about the crappy impression he was making. That he wanted to make a different one and just kept screwing up.

That he was an utter fucking idiot, in other words.

"How bad did it look?" he growled, and tried to fold his arms over his chest. Ow. He loosened the left one.

Tristan looked completely confused. "Your arm? Well, you'll need stitches, obviously, but you've had worse. At least it didn't bleed as bad as that time Damien fell out of a tree and busted his chin open and—"

"Not—*no*. The—" How to even explain? "If you were, I don't know, like…a *female*, and you saw me hitting that idiot, how would it look to you?"

Tristan blinked at the road a minute. "Uh…like you have a nice, strong right and good reflexes? Not afraid of much? Think all problems are yours to solve first?"

Matt frowned at him. "Are you sure that's what a girl would think?"

"Are we still allowed to call them girls if we're trying to imagine their perspective? I think Allegra said something about using the word *women*."

Hunh. Matt flexed his hands and then held them about ten centimeters apart. "But they're about this big."

"Look, if you want to argue with Allegra about it, go ahead. For someone who acts so friendly to everyone, she's pretty damn stubborn. On the plus side, if you argue with her too long, Raoul gets pissed, so you and he can have that fight you've been longing to have."

Matt gave that some wistful consideration. He'd been wanting to get in a fight with Raoul for about fourteen years—ever since Raoul had walked out on them just when Matt was getting big enough to maybe, for once, actually win—but at the rate things were going, if the two of them did get in a fight, Bouclettes would somehow manage to see it and probably think Matt was…violent or something. It would be terrible to keep giving her such an accurate impression. "So if you were a *woman*, and you saw some guy break up a knife fight, and then he bled all over the place...would you be horrified?"

Tristan again stared at the road blankly. "Well, I don't *think* so, but women are weird sometimes. I mean, you'd put that kind of brute edge in a perfume, but I generally avoid showing it openly in real life. I hear dinners in nice restaurants are a much safer technique."

Damn it. He'd been trying to lead up to that, that morning, with Gabe's chocolate rose and all his hints about the desserts she could have in the actual restaurant. And then she'd gotten so...cute or something, standing there with those wet curls slowly dampening her white tank top and holding onto his idiot rose like it was something precious, and he'd chickened out. If you asked a woman on an obvious date, well...she could rather obviously say no. And then where were you?

Wishing you hadn't given her such a fragile part of you as that rose, that was where.

See, when he picked up a woman in a bar, he didn't have this problem. First of all, he wasn't stupid enough to give them roses. And second of all, a bar setting left no room for hesitations. He just went for it and usually got it. And then for some reason, everything started degenerating in the morning. That *always* happened to him. It was almost as if a bar wasn't a good place to meet someone for a long-term relationship or something.

Still, better a local bar than a perfume launch party, that was for damn sure. When you went after a woman with no hesitation at a perfume launch party, you suddenly found yourself dating a supermodel, and just when you were thinking that must mean you were hot shit, you found the soul being sucked right out of you. Famous women...God. Never again.

Better the cute girl next door any day. Even if she had stolen that house next door from him.

He sighed. It really, really complicated his life that the house hadn't been stolen by a man, or at least someone who didn't have quite so many curls and that kissable a mouth. On the other hand, if he tried to

114

imagine the last two days with a man in her place, well, the problem got solved a lot faster, but a bleakness almost like grief invaded him, as if someone had reached into his life and stolen all the color out of it.

Which, given that he spent all of May immersed in pink and green, was really ridiculous.

"I wish Tante Colette had warned me I was fixing that house up for her," he said suddenly, restlessly.

"Yes, I noticed that was a bit of a shock to you," Tristan said dryly.

"I mean—there are all kinds of unfinished projects still. I didn't know someone was going to be living in it so soon." He gave a huff of frustration and glowered at the gorge falling away as they climbed up out of the valley. "I would have prioritized."

Out of the corner of his eye, he could see Tristan gazing at the road with a bizarre blend of amusement and affection, perfectly comfortable half-naked against his leather seat. "Never too late to get them done."

"Yeah, but Bouclettes—I mean, Layla—nearly split my eardrums yesterday when she found me in the kitchen," Matt said, despairing and grouchy.

Tristan's eyebrow went up. "Umm, Matt...was she *expecting* to find you in her kitchen?"

"It's my valley," Matt said indignantly. How many times did he have to remind people? "Besides, I told her I was going to fix it." He glowered through the window. His arm was starting to realize it hurt. "And I think I still have a concussion." From hitting his own head on the underside of the counter. Thinking he was alone, peacefully working in a house to get it all right, and then suddenly hearing an ear-splitting female scream from a few feet away had scared the hell out of him. It had taken about an hour for his heart rate to calm down.

Actually, his stupid heart *still* didn't seem to have calmed down.

But that might be more to do with all the things she had said after she stopped screaming. Like about him looking so much better naked.

His glower started to ease away, despite the throbbing in his arm, as his butt tightened into the memory of her hand sliding into his pocket to get the key.

"Bouclettes, hmm?" Tristan grinned a little at the road. "Like Goldilocks?" *Boucles d'Or.* "I like it. Are you the three bears?"

His cousins were so annoying. Matt grunted.

Tristan's grin widened. "Excellent grunt. *Great* role-playing there. I bet you get the part of the biggest bear." His expression went innocently wicked. "Wasn't he the one whose bed fit just right?"

Oh, *yeah*, Matt would like to see how she fit in his big, white bed, when he...he caught himself and glared at his cousin. "Don't make me hit you while you're driving."

"No," Tristan agreed solemnly. "After all, look at how close we are to a cliff's edge here. You wouldn't want to find yourself suddenly falling too hard would you?"

No. He wouldn't. Because Tristan was wrong about his fairy tales. The biggest bear was the one the curly-haired interloper never chose. Everything about him was too hard and too big.

Chapter 9

"It's people like you who make my taxes so high. Going to the doctor for a scratch like that." Pépé beckoned Matt over and peeled back the gauze enough to eye the arm Matt held out in resignation.

Matt double-checked Bouclettes. She sat near the head of the table where his grandfather was, with Damien and Raoul and Allegra, who must have come out of her dissertation-writing hole to join them.

He hadn't expected to find Layla still there when he got back, under the great old plane tree near the original family home from which Pépé still reigned over the family, that table full of memories, where they often lunched together during peak season when his cousins pitched in. He'd kind of thought she would have fled by then, having found out that all those silken, sweet roses came with a lot of grit. Hot sun, thorns, bee stings, long, repetitive hours, and people who acted like idiots.

Run off and sold her land to a hotel chain or something because it wasn't worth her time—too boring or annoying or difficult.

But here she was, taking on his grandfather. He'd arrived to hear Pépé blandly referring to times when a man had to shoot a threat to his valley and Layla defiantly complimenting him on his routine for scaring tourists. From the way Damien and Raoul had been choking with their efforts not to laugh, he'd missed some of the good parts. Unfortunately, his grandfather had immediately gotten distracted by Matt himself and the excessive gauze the doctor had insisted on putting around his arm.

"You would have had much neater stitching from Colette." Pépé dropped the edge of the gauze in disgust. Steri-Strips covered most of the stitches, but that didn't stop Pépé from making a judgment of them.

"If you were lucky, Tante Colette might have even stitched you one of those pretty lavender sprigs she likes to put on pillowcases," Tristan said helpfully, exactly as if he hadn't been the one to insist on the doctor in the first place.

"Or maybe a bird," Raoul agreed. "She does really pretty birds."

Matt bit back a grin. It felt like the old days—Raoul helping his younger cousins ride him. It felt...good.

Layla was watching him from across the table, eyes rather solemn now as she looked from his face to his arm. He tried to school his expression into an appropriate one for a man who was having, to be honest, a fairly ordinary day. Should he look solemn himself? Casual? Smile? Pretend he was in agony and needed someone to cuddle him? When he was a kid, his grandfather and cousins told him to tough it up when he tried that one, but maybe there might be some potential with Layla...?

"Could you tell me how to get to your aunt Colette's house?" Layla asked Matt.

Oh. She wasn't even thinking about him.

"I should go see her." She sounded unnerved by the idea.

"Sure," Matt began. Damn it, why did his voice always sound so rough? Forced too often to carry across fields and rise above all his cousins. He tried subtly to clear his throat. "I—"

"Getting to Sainte-Mère is very complicated," Tristan spoke over him. See? That was what Matt got for trying to soften his voice. "One of us should go with you."

Matt whipped his head around. Oh, no, one of his cousins sure as hell should not. Tristan? Damien? Raoul possibly, as long as Allegra went with them, but—

"Matt probably," Tristan said casually. "He can't possibly work the rest of the afternoon with that." He gestured to Matt's arm, as if that would in any way affect his ability to do anything whatsoever, except possibly wash his hair.

"What are you talking about?" Matt demanded. "Someone's got to be here to handle the harvest."

Raoul turned over his fork in a big hand, pressed the tines down into the tablecloth, and lifted his amber gaze suddenly to hold Matt's. "I'm here."

Matt stared back at him. And now neither of them could look away, gazes locked, neither willing to be the first to yield, until—

Fingers touched Matt's arm and Raoul shattered from his brain as Layla eased up the edge of the gauze to peek under for herself. She had surprisingly callused fingertips, the toughened spots rough and delicate against his skin.

The delicacy, that was what was so strange. As if his wounds deserved caution and care. And they didn't, obviously, because he was far too tough for that, so his brain got trapped in the cognitive dissonance. He had no idea what to think about it, but it felt good—strong hands that were tender. With him.

It felt *weird.*

Merde but it felt sweet.

Layla dropped the gauze as soon as she realized he was watching her. Then smoothed it down, that little rough delicacy shimmering from that one spot all through his body. He took a slow, deep breath and then another, and then brought up one finger to graze the back of her hand, near a red spot on her knuckle. "Did a bee get you?"

She nodded. His thumb stroked around the red bump without touching it. The one tiny circle of his thumb, like magic, seemed to draw a circle around both their bodies, making everyone else fall away outside it. "Did someone get you some spray?"

She lifted her gaze from their hands to his face, staring at him, her eyes so damn green. No, but they weren't a bright green, were they? It was more like early morning in the rose fields, when the soft gray light sifted over the leaves and they were touched with dew...

"You have a *knife wound* in your arm," she said, with this kind of über-insistent tone, as if she was using small words to penetrate his brain. "And you're worried about my bee sting?"

Well...yeah. He kind of felt as if he should have been around to suck on it for her. Just draw her knuckle into his mouth and...

He realized every single person at the table was staring at them, some of them with pretty open glee on their faces, and that little magic circle shattered as he braced himself.

Layla, however, was the one who deflected all teasing by starting her own. "Well, it's a much neater job than *I* could have done," she told Pépé, indicating his stitches.

Pépé sighed. "Kids these days. Am I the only one who bothered to teach anyone in your generation any proper skills?"

Layla rested her chin on her hand and narrowed her eyes at the old man. "You taught your grandsons how to embroider?" she challenged sweetly.

He did that tiny curl of his lips. "No, I taught them how to shoot an olive off a tree at two hundred meters. And skin bodies."

Layla blinked. And recovered her narrowed eyes. "Of olives?"

Damien bit back a grin. "They've been at it like this since we broke for lunch," he told Matt.

"Of a rabbit," Matt intervened. "Pépé, you are not helping."

"What? I can't make conversation with our guest?" Pépé asked innocently.

You know, the nice thing about four cousins close to his age, Matt thought, was at least he could hit one of them if they drove him crazy.

"Well, it's too bad about the embroidery," Layla told Pépé, her chin up, and gestured at Matt's arm again. "At least that would have come in handy."

"Who said the shooting never comes in handy?" Pépé asked.

Matt thumped his forehead into his hand and groaned.

Tristan grinned and grabbed Matt by his good arm, pulling him toward the extraction plant. *Merde,* what had gone wrong in the plant now? Damn it, if that conveyor belt was acting up again...

"You know what skill I missed the most while I was gone?" Raoul asked behind them, breathing deep as if pursuing scents from his past. "Truffle hunting. Are we going to do that again next winter?"

Matt had a sudden memory of the five of them roaming the woods in the cold, gray early mornings of November and December, following the old truffle dog, Rudi, their grandfather pacing with his long strides while the boys tumbled and played Robin Hood, or Roland and the Saracens, or *Star Wars,* and occasionally paid attention to the actual truffle aspect. When the dog found one, the kids would all throng to the spot, pushing at each other in excitement as they fought to dig it up, breathing in that rich, unique scent and dreaming of the omelets their grandfather would make them that night. Damn, but he still missed that dog.

And those days. He glanced back.

"Snails first," Pépé said, bright-eyed. "That season's only six weeks away."

"You have a season for hunting snails?" Layla asked incredulously.

Pépé gave her an indignant look. "You can't just gather them whenever you're hungry, you know. You'll decimate the population, and then no snails for the future."

"What a terrible loss," Layla said dryly.

Everyone at the table stared at her as if she had lost her mind. "Exactly," his grandfather said firmly.

Layla opened her mouth and then apparently thought better about whatever comment she was going to make concerning the value of snails to future generations. Americans were weird about food sometimes, there was no getting around it.

Of course, the main problem with snails was that you had to prepare them, and pulling dead snails out of their shells was a nasty way to spend an hour or two. Except that you soon quit paying attention to the snail itself in the slow rhythm of the work and the things you could talk about with your grandfather while you did it.

An intense, wistful hunger flashed across Raoul's face. He'd chosen to stay away from them for years, off adventuring in Africa while Matt handled the valley that bound him. Had Raoul truly missed things while he was gone? Things Matt had? Allegra closed her hand over Raoul's, as if she saw something Matt didn't. Raoul's big thumb shifted enough to tuck her hand in a little more securely over his.

Matt turned away. Not jealous of Raoul having a hand to hold exactly, just...wistful. Vulnerable. And he hated to be vulnerable in front of his cousins. Instead, he tried to focus on whatever problem Tristan needed to show him in the damn extraction plant.

Tristan stopped inside the doors, where the stink of solvent washed over them. Cédric, the extraction plant manager, was up on the platform above and lifted a hand to them.

"You got your priorities straight, Matt?" Tristan asked quietly.

Matt glanced at his youngest cousin, confused by the tone. They teased each other roughly. Quiet sincerity was a dangerous power, used sparingly, because it left all of them feeling a little too naked to each other.

"Your whole life you've been here every single day of the rose harvest. You can't possibly think you'll lose your spot here because you take an afternoon off to court a cute girl."

Matt's cheeks heated immediately, damn them. He tightened his muscles, trying to make himself look even bigger and tougher to make up for it. "I don't *court* people."

Not since his supermodel dating disaster last year, that was for sure. Even before then, he'd never been that good at it. If you met someone, you just went after her and got her on the spot, right? Where did the courtship part fit in?

"A little chocolate and some flowers never hurts, Matt."

Matt folded his arms over his chest, struggling to get his cheeks to cool down. "That sounds like something you would do, Tristan. Talk about a damn cliché."

Unless that gift of a flower was a test. Unless deep down, what a man was really trying to do, was see what a woman who messed with him so easily did when given a tiny piece of his actual heart.

She'd acted...wow. As if he'd given her something miraculously precious. And he hadn't been able to think straight since.

Sometimes the corners of Tristan's lips curled up in this contained way that reminded Matt remarkably of Pépé biting back his inappropriate sense of humor. It wasn't in the least promising for what Tristan was going to be like in old age. "Because you take the afternoon off to reluctantly drag your feet around after a girl you have no interest in just so she doesn't get lost, then. How about that?"

That did sound better, actually. "But somebody has to make sure the harvest goes right."

"It's the harvest, Matt, not rocket science. I think we could probably handle it."

Yes, he knew it wasn't rocket science. He knew Tristan and Damien and Raoul had all gone on to far more glamorous jobs while he was a farmer and a mechanic, tied to earth and growing seasons and the grease of the machines he had to fix to keep things running. He knew that his own attempt to become the glamorous adventurer himself had proven how badly that role fit him. But farmer's job or not, it was still his to handle.

Because the rose fields weren't his cousins'. They were his. It made everything about him become untrue, if they weren't his. Matt took a tight breath, that breath that felt as if he was wearing plate armor two sizes too small. He had never, in his whole life, figured out exactly how to deal with this issue—the fact that his very existence was the wedge that split his cousins from this valley and the fact that if they could have his life, they wouldn't actually want it.

Tristan laughed, releasing the tension. "Why don't I put it this way? You can either let one of us help the girl while you handle the harvest, or you can help the girl while we handle the harvest. Which one is it going to be?"

Matt stared at his younger cousin a moment. "Have I hit you recently?"

"Not since we were kids, but the weirder thing is, it's been at least that long since I've hit you." Tristan grinned, grabbed his shoulder, and shoved him back toward the table. "Too bad I can't start now, what with you being gravely wounded and all."

Matt felt Layla's green eyes watching him the whole walk back across the gravel. It made him feel as if his feet crunched too loudly, so big and solid compared to that butterfly playfulness of hers.

When a man spent a lifetime struggling to assert for himself a large, dominant space amid four big cousins, his uncles, and his grandfather, he just grew up as big as he could. Matt hadn't realized how much too big that was for the average person until he'd spent those months in Paris, and felt as if he was trying to cram himself into a box that was too small. God, Nathalie, the model he had dated, had wanted him so small she could take him out to wear as jewelry from time to time, when she was in the mood for him as an accessory. She'd wanted him so small that he'd ditch his own valley, his entire family heritage, just to date her. And he hadn't been able to shrink.

I can't try to fit in that box again. He looked at Layla helplessly. *I think this is just the size I am.*

She looked back at him solemnly, making him miss that sparkle in her eyes when she messed with him.

Damn, but he liked it when she messed with him. As if she was a kid and he was this glittery something she couldn't resist reaching for. It made him feel so befuddled, and it didn't help with his size problem at all...because it made him feel three meters tall. No boxes big enough.

And when she didn't mess with him—when he handed her one of his roses, this symbol of his whole life and heart, the symbol of the very thing her presence in this valley threatened, and she clutched it to her chest and her eyes got damp with how much it meant to her— he didn't even know quite what to feel. So many unidentifiable emotions kept pressing up through the wariness and fascination, fighting for room.

Her eyes were serious now and a little anxious. When he sat down beside her, her hand slipped to curl over the side of his palm.

He looked down at that small hand against his big one, this great stillness invading him again, as if he was poised on that precipice Tristan had mentioned. "Would you mind going with me to meet your aunt Colette?" she asked, low. "So I don't get lost?"

He'd grabbed her up drunk and kissed her, he'd scared the hell out of her by trying to fix her kitchen sink, he'd probably terrified her into imagining her body buried in the rose fields, and he'd gotten in a damn fight in front of her. He was, in theory, her enemy, even if he had no clue how to fight her invasion into his valley. He was twice her size.

And yet...she seemed to be turning to him for reassurance.

And just for that second, with her hand on his, he wanted to offer her one of his roses every day for the rest of his life to see if she would react, every single time, as if he had given her something precious.

He turned his hand over and covered hers. His hand didn't fit hers at all. It was too big. And yet inside his hold, he could feel the tension relax out of her hand, feel the way it nestled into his as if he'd made it feel safe. A quiet eased through him, and he forgot his cousins. Forgot even his grandfather.

For the weirdest moment, he forgot about his *valley*. He was just...him. *You'll never get lost with me here, sweetheart. I can make sure you never get lost again.*

"No, of course not, Bouclettes." He squeezed her hand. A smile softened her face as if he had done exactly the perfect thing. And for a moment, he felt as if he fit in her world just right. "I wouldn't mind at all."

Chapter 10

"We've got a problem," Damien said as soon as Matt and Layla were gone and Pépé had left the lunch table to go take that nap he wouldn't admit he needed. Damien thrust back in his chair, lounging like a panther stuck too long in a cage.

"And you haven't solved it yet?" Tristan raised his eyebrows. "What is it, a comet headed toward the earth?"

"A comet headed toward *Matt*," Damien said, and Tristan and Raoul both sat up straight and then leaned forward, a surge of energy running through them.

"What's going on?" Tristan asked. "Is it Abbaye? Did those damn accountants of theirs finally convince them they had to buy their roses from Bulgaria and fuck quality and a hundred-year reputation?"

Damien made a little slashing motion with his hand. In a James Bond film, that motion would have hit some evil super villain in the neck and knocked him out. Although Tristan personally kind of preferred to imagine Damien as Bagheera taking out his prey. "Not yet."

Tristan drew a breath. There were very few people he hated more than accountants. They were like alien octopus invaders, getting their ugly tentacles into everything good and saying it cost too much, and their invasion fleet always loomed on the edge of the valley, menacing, held back only by that thin wisp of extravagant arrogance that said, *No. We don't care whether the ordinary person can smell the difference or how much it cuts into our bottom line. We, the Top Perfume Houses in the World, get our roses* here. *Not from much, much cheaper non-France places. Or synthetics.*

Sometimes Tristan actually considered abandoning Rosier SA and opening his own niche perfume house so he wouldn't have one more beautiful idea ripped to shreds by those damn accountants.

But Damien...Tristan sighed a little. Yeah, he couldn't abandon Damien like that. It might break that secret heart of his.

The same way they couldn't abandon Matt, no matter how damn grumpy he was.

"So what is it?" Raoul demanded. He had that hunting-wolf look in his eyes that would make a rabbit cower in the snow, and it eased Tristan's own heart a little. He liked having their oldest cousin back and still, apparently, quite willing to beat the crap out of anyone who messed with his younger cousins. Four against the world was better than three. And—a wistful twinge—five would be best of all. If Lucien ever came back.

Damien thrust his phone at him. Raoul looked at the screen a moment and raised his eyebrows, then passed it to Tristan. It showed a photo of Matt's curly-haired girl, only she wasn't wearing shorts and a tank top and picking roses with a borrowed hat on her head and looking up at Matt with sparkling, fascinated teasing every time he got anywhere close. She was sleeked out in some evening gown, a little, elegant purse clutched nervously in front of her, her eyes very big and her smile carefully posed. *Belle Woods arrives for the Grammys,* the caption said.

Tristan's stomach sank.

"Well, shit." He looked up to meet his cousins' eyes.

Raoul looked thoughtful but not much alarmed. But Damien definitely got it, his expression grim, like James Bond when he realized the first woman he'd slept with in that movie had once again turned out to be using him in her plans for world annihilation.

"Damn it, I liked her," Tristan said. "*Hell.* She's already got him wrapped around her little finger. You know, you could have slipped me your phone before I encouraged Matt to take off with her for the afternoon so he could fall even harder for her."

Damien opened one hand. "You all have time to threaten Antoine Vallier for information, but none of you can pursue a Google search of her name to see where it leads you?"

"You tried to threaten Antoine?" Tristan asked, startled. "How'd that work out for you?" He'd gone to school with Antoine. Nerves of steel, that guy.

Both Damien and Raoul frowned.

Tristan grinned. Maybe he should buy Antoine a drink. He always liked it when a younger guy managed to best the older ones.

"It had its moments," Raoul said. "What did you do, Damien, run a background check on her?"

"She's on Wikipedia," Damien said dryly. "You type 'Layla Dubois' and the first search result is the 'Belle Woods' Wikipedia entry. If I ever abandoned Rosier SA and ran off and left it all to you, the company would fail in months, wouldn't it?"

Raoul bared his teeth at his cousin menacingly.

"*Merde*, don't do that!" Tristan said, horrified. "It's all I can do to sit through those damn board meetings every quarter. Hell, Damien. That's why we pay you so damn much."

"So what's the problem, exactly?" Raoul asked, pulling the conversation back to its point. "So she's famous. She very obviously doesn't go around rubbing people's noses in it, and it's not as if Matt hasn't dated women far more famous than she is."

Even Damien's look at Raoul was openly appalled.

"Exactly," Tristan said, horrified. "Raoul, you weren't here. *Merde*, what a nightmare Nathalie Leclair was."

"Nobody told him to date a supermodel," Raoul said dryly. "Of all people, you guys should know better than to date someone in that world."

"Matt's not around the fashion industry side of things much." Tristan waved a hand. "He got sucked in before he knew better. And, hell, but did she work him over. You know how he is about trying to fix problems. She had an *infinite* number of problems for him to fix.

And then the scenes, the jealousy. Fortunately, he wised up and broke up with her, but then she'd go after him in public places, pretending like she really, really wanted to make up, and engineer arguments around cameras, so they could catch him scowling and her looking like a vulnerable victim, until she'd made him the media's pet monster. *Matt.*"

"Well, he clearly learned from it," Raoul said. "Layla seems like a much better choice."

Damien and Tristan frowned at him.

"Are you being deliberately dense, or what?" Tristan asked finally.

"Are *you?*" Raoul asked. "Do I need to explain the facts of life to you two again?"

Tristan folded his arms across his chest. "Oh, please," he said very dryly. "Do tell me all the secrets to success with women."

"Finding the right one," Raoul said promptly. "Not, for example, attracting all of them as if you were some damned lamp and they were moths." He gave Tristan a sardonic glance. "That gets sticky."

Tristan gave him a sweet smile even though he felt like baring his teeth. That was his cardinal rule: never let his older cousins get to him. As kids, they'd torment him mercilessly if he did. But given how many women there were out there, and how many of them liked to flirt with him, where *was* the one who could walk on the beach with him, the one whose scent would blend with those of the sea to make them richer and more beautiful, rather than clash? Why couldn't he find her?

"So Matt found the wrong one, learned something from it, and now seems to be focusing on a much better choice," Raoul told them.

"She's famous, likely to wake up that whole Nathalie scandal again the second some picture of the two of them gets out and the media decides to rub Nathalie's face in it as 'dumped for Belle', and there's no way someone who's just starting to hit real success in her music career is going to abandon it all to stay here in this valley," Damien said between his teeth. "She just won a Grammy for her first album! Hell, she'll probably sell the place to some actor pal who needs a summer home, and before we know it, he'll have sold it on to some hotel chain. How do you figure that as a 'better choice'?"

"The way she looks at him," Raoul answered quietly. The little smile that softened his lips made it instantly clear that he was thinking about Allegra. Nobody but Allegra made Raoul's lips soften like that. "Fascinated and teasing and in over her head."

Tristan and Damien both gazed at him. Tristan didn't know about Damien but he, personally, hated that sense of being outside some secret club of true love looking in—as if Raoul knew all kinds of things about happiness that they didn't.

"How, exactly, does that solve all these other problems?" Damien asked acerbically.

Raoul shrugged one big shoulder. "You'd be surprised."

Tristan frowned, feeling like he had as a kid before his birthday, when his cousins kept teasing him about this really cool present they had hidden for him.

"I think you're worrying about the wrong person here, anyway," Raoul said. "Matt's tough."

Well, that just shot Raoul's credibility all to hell. "He's a damn marshmallow," Tristan said. "That's why he growls so damn much—to hide it."

"Who do you think we should be worrying about, Raoul?" Damien asked. "Pépé? Tante Colette?"

Tristan made a tiny snort. "They're way the hell tougher than Matt." As tough and spare as nylon rope, those two.

"Her." Raoul gestured to the phone with its photo of a woman smiling confidently for the camera while her fingers clutched nervously at her purse. "She's obviously trying to be incognito here, and we just sent her out in public with Nathalie Leclair's ex. That's worth a few

131

photos on celebrity sites, if anyone spots them and realizes who she is."

Damien frowned. "Fortunately all the paparazzi are down in Cannes right now, focusing on the festival."

"Unless a photographer decides to follow some stars up to Aux Anges," Raoul said. Gabe and Raphaël's Michelin three-star restaurant was packed with movie stars for the two weeks while every celebrity in the world descended on nearby Cannes.

"She's not that recognizable," Tristan pointed out. "*We* didn't recognize her. It's not as if she's a household name."

"Yes, but paparazzi are a different breed," Damien said. "That's their livelihood—being able to recognize celebrities, even small celebrities. Anyone whose name might be enough to get their photos sold to some site or magazine."

Damn it. Tristan frowned, deeply unhappy now. "Are we going to have to talk to Matt about all this?" And ruin the way he and Layla were currently pulling toward each other like bees to roses? That was crappy.

Raoul stretched out long, blunt-tipped fingers and studied them. "I think he should talk to her, and she should talk to him, and we should stay the hell out of it," he said.

***

Wow, Matt drove well, Layla thought. These roads weren't scary at all with Matthieu Rosier at the wheel. He focused on the roads as if he liked them and expected them to do what he told them.

He drove fast, much, much faster than anything Layla would have dared. But he never drove too fast for the road. His car held the curves of those narrow, twisty cliff-drop roads easily at the speed he demanded of it. When he came behind tourists creeping along carefully, he slowed down and left several courteous car lengths between them, not honking or even growling under his breath, waiting calmly until the tourist turned off or the road opened up and he could speed up again.

The hand of his injured arm curved around the wheel of his rebuilt car—some kind of sixties sports car, she was pretty sure—with a kind of competent affection. Big hands. Both focused on the job, one on the wheel and one shifting. If his wounded left arm bothered him, he gave no sign. The subtle scent of roses filled the car.

There were moments when the growls slid off him, when everything about him seemed to ease. The afternoon before in her doorway, as he looked down at her. This morning in his fields, as his hands framed her face. And here now, in the car. Was it because the car did what he told it to without resistance? Or could it conceivably have something to do with her? Could she possibly have the effect on him she kept fantasizing about, the ability to lay her hand on his chest and ease him all the way through?

"You could drive these roads in the dark without headlights, couldn't you?" she murmured. "Have you always lived here?"

"Except for a few months up in Paris last year. Do you want the top down? Or would it mess up your hair?"

"Whatever you want." The scents of herbs and pine outside were nice, but so were the roses and the quiet inside. She could go with either. She smiled at him.

He took a long, slow breath and put all that focus of his back on the road. His hand left the gearstick long enough to pull out his phone and start music streaming through the car speakers—nothing vintage about his BlueTooth. The song made her smile a little, since she'd opened for the band several times. Good people. Hearing their song reminded her of all the friendships she had formed in her years trying to make it as a musician, of the crazy post-performance nights, hanging out and talking about the trials and joys of pursuing their music dreams, over mojitos or beers or a couple of bottles of wine, depending on where they were in the world.

"What do you do that puts you out there in front of crowds and new people all the time on your own?" he asked suddenly. "Your music? Is it that intense?"

"Oh, I—" On cue, the custom station he was streaming segued into its next song. She supposed it made sense, given that the previous one was by a band she used to open for, that this one be one of hers. "You, ah—you like Belle?"

She double-checked his phone. Hey, sometime in the past, he'd given the song a thumb's up.

He looked a little surprised by the change of subject. "Belle?"

"That's who's playing."

"Yeah, sure." He smiled a little. "*That's* the music you were playing the other night. You know, you do a great cover of her songs."

Layla laughed before she could catch herself. "Umm...thanks."

"I suppose you hate to hear that you sound like another artist. You want to be your own person."

Well, that was true. She did. And it felt insanely hard to do these days, after her sudden burst to semi-fame. Her nostalgia for the old days was so acute it hurt—those days scraping by, playing with friends in bars, trying to get any festival to take her. Back then, no one knew much more about her than the sound coming out of her guitar right then. Sometimes she wanted to wish it all away, the success, the awards, the demands, in exchange for the girl who busked her way through Europe on what people tossed in a hat and from whom music poured freely.

But that, of course, would mean she'd failed in her dream. That she'd never made it big enough to find herself staring into this great, gaping void of other people's expectations, thinking, *I got nothing.*

She took a deep breath, and that sense of *nothing* shimmered like a mirage before all the *things* that filled her lungs. An air rich with scents and with the vitality of the man beside her. Cliff-hills rose and narrowed around them as they headed into the pass that led out of the valley. All the rest of the world seemed so far away here. Songs lurked in the scents of rosemary and thyme and pine and roses in this car, teasing at her to hit the right note and distill their essence into words and melody. That would be *fun*, to capture a scent in song, and nobody else but her might ever even realize what perfume teased through the notes. It would be like—

"How do you make a living from music?" Matt asked curiously. "I never thought that was possible."

"Well, it *is* the perennial question," she said wryly. "I've done a lot of bartending in between gigs."

A faint smile. "That's why you don't get easily unnerved by a big party and a drunk man."

That and her instincts had done the quintessentially stupid thing and just decided to focus on how hot he was that night. And really, ever since.

"You know, selling that house back to me might make up for a lot of bar gigs," he pointed out. "I suspect I could come up with a bit more than some drunks might throw into a hat."

"And just imagine if I got you four cousins bidding against each other!" Layla exclaimed enthusiastically. "I'd never have to sing for my supper again!"

Matt's eyebrows slashed down, his hand tightening on the gearstick, this sudden blackening of all the air in the car.

"Hey." Layla touched his arm quickly, horrified to have ruined the mood. "Joke. I wouldn't do that. Are you really afraid that could happen?"

He shrugged, this hard, almost sullen shrug, his face dark and brooding.

"I was only teasing," she said, very sorry now. "I really wouldn't do that."

"I'm sure they'd oblige you." He scowled.

Layla called up a vision of the three other big men who twitted him and helped haul a violent man away from him and showed up to help with the harvest, despite how obviously below their pay grade picking roses was. She didn't have any cousins, so maybe she had no clue, but... "Do you really think so?"

Matt just scowled, all his grumpiness back in force. It was probably just as well he was driving, or he'd have his arms folded across his chest again.

"I won't sell it to your cousins. Who haven't, by the way, offered."

"Really?" His grumpiness softened in this wary way, like a man slowly lowering his weapons and not quite sure it wasn't a mistake. "Even Damien and Raoul didn't, when I was at the doctor's?"

"Never mentioned it. Your grandfather did offer to take me out hunting in the *maquis*, though."

Matt grinned, his grumpiness disappearing.

"Oh, that's fine? Because, frankly, *I* would prefer a bidding war over having my body buried in the *maquis*."

"He's just testing your mettle. I think he likes you."

Layla felt absurdly pleased that the old pseudo-pyschopathic war hero might like her.

"Not enough to let you have a part of this valley or anything, but it's my job to handle that problem."

"And here we are, driving through some *maquis* right now." One of those terrifying cliffs rose inches away from one side of the car and fell to the other, a dramatic drop into scraggly oaks and juniper and wild herbs that clung to the steep slopes. She opened her eyes wide, clutching the window and seat to either side of her like the heroine in a silent film when the villain was about to tie her to the train tracks.

Matt laughed and reached out to touch her arm this time, gently. "I wouldn't do that either, Bouclettes."

"Because you like me?" Layla teased.

That little smile curled his mouth, his eyes on the road as he took a sharp turn. "Maybe just a bit."

She hugged herself in happiness, and his gaze slid sideways at the movement, running over her and lingering on her expression, his own so wondering and questioning and...yes, happy, too.

But then, as he focused on the road again, his lips turned down, more serious, more brooding. "Don't sell to my cousins," he said abruptly. "I'll come up with the money."

Her arms tightened on herself at the way he kept trying to buy that happiness away from her. As if he wanted to press his thumb down on that fresh-blossoming song in her and rip it right off. Nip it in the bud. "Would that be hard? To come up with the money?"

His lips firmed, that bossy upper one back to trying to press that sensual lower one into line. "Most of my assets are in land. But...I can do it. Get a loan or sell some of my shares in Rosier SA. It's my valley."

She frowned a little, searching his face. So his aunt, this unknown benefactor of hers, had ripped a chunk right out of him. To do either of those things—sell shares or get a loan—would make him weaker when he had to face any other financial challenges life might throw at him. She'd done a festival for Farm Aid. She had at least a vague idea of the challenges anyone in agriculture faced.

"How much money are we talking about?" she asked warily.

His upper lip pressed down harder on the lower one. "It depends on whether you start a bidding war. A million or so."

Holy crap. Layla pressed her head back against the window, blinking. "Isn't it agricultural land?" A *million*? Somebody had given her land worth a million dollars? No, crap, euros. That was even *more*.

His lips twisted. "That's one of the challenges of maintaining this valley whole. Land around here is worth more to a developer than you can make off of it, growing roses. It's got a protected status, in terms of taxes, because of the cultural value of what we do, but if ever one of us cracks and starts selling chunks of it to a hotel chain, then it's all over."

Good God. His aunt must be out of her mind. How the hell could she have done that to Matt? Turn something that mattered to him over to a stranger? "*I* won't sell it to a hotel chain," she said. "I promise." Crap, could she even afford the taxes on the place? She bet no one was going to give a Grammy-award-winning rock star American tourist a tax break, no matter how many times she told them that all those streaming sites had killed a musician's actual income and she made, at best, a middle class salary—which was totally dependent on her producing another album for the money to keep coming in.

Matt's upper lip was so bitter, so hard. "You'd be better off letting Damien and Raoul buy it before that. They'd try to beat the hotel's offer."

And he, himself, probably couldn't. Layla reached out and squeezed his arm again. "I don't know if you may have picked up on this when I told you about busking around Europe and bartending between gigs, but I'm really not that practical about money. I tend to go with what matters."

Her own words rang through her, like something had brushed this little bell of truth somewhere deep inside her. She didn't think about what the world wanted, what would make a second album *successful,* how she should sing and what she should sing about to have another hit. That was her producers' job. She gave them twenty songs that came out of her heart, and they chose from there, selected and crafted and arranged to hit the widest demographic. That was why she was paying those guys such a fortune—to produce her work in a way that would reach her audience, without asking her for artistic compromise.

So that she could concentrate on what mattered.

Like the way Matt's upper lip eased a little when she'd made that statement. That was how bad she was. A million dollars—she couldn't even quite understand what that was, when it came to her and to her life. Probably something convenient to have. But the way his mouth eased, as if somewhere inside him his heart had eased a bit, too...that was priceless.

It made her own heart ease. It made her dreamy and hungry, as if she could run her fingers over that curve of his lips, and that would be even better than writing a song.

"I don't mean to be rude, but it sounds as if you're not that practical about money either," she said, with another gentle squeeze of his arm in lieu of that caress of his lips.

He stiffened instantly, but his indignant frown was his grumpy one, not that dark, bitter wound of a moment before. "What are you talking about? I'm as hard-headed and practical as they come."

"Of course you are," she said. "I picked that right up when you were telling me how much more money you'd make without ever having to work again, if you sold this valley to developers and let them uproot all your roses."

"It's my *valley*," he said, as if she was incredibly dense. "I can't *sell it*. It's who I *am*."

"Yeah, I'm starting to gather that," she said softly. She dropped her left hand back to her knee, rubbing her calluses against her skin. She had to meet this Tante Colette and discover what was going on with this crazy heritage of hers, but one thing was clear—Layla couldn't keep it.

You couldn't keep part of who a man was for your very own.

Not as a game. Not as a little break from career pressures.

Not even if, for the first time in what seemed like forever, being in that valley eased all the panicked sense of emptiness in her, that sense of nothing left to be or give. Not even if it seemed to fill her up, so full again that songs bloomed out of her the way they once had—not as if she was scrabbling desperately on hard gravel to get anything to grow, but as if they were growing in rich earth, as if she couldn't stop them, no matter how many she produced, more would come.

They were part of who she was.

An odd realization hit her. She couldn't expect Matt to give up a part of who he was on behalf of her music. But with her music, she constantly ripped out chunks of who she was and gave them to the rest of the world.

"Do you fertilize your roses?" she asked suddenly.

"What?" Matt looked totally confused by this non sequitur. "Of course we fertilize them. And trim them, and treat them for disease, and...trust me, once the harvest season is over, there's still plenty left to do for those roses. To get them to bloom that well, you have to nourish them and take care of them the rest of the year."

Her head relaxed slowly back against her seat. Hunh. She couldn't actually remember the last time she had nourished herself or taken care of herself. She'd been so focused on blooming, blooming, blooming, and desperate when no more blooms came.

"How long do they bloom?" she asked.

"About five weeks or so. It depends on the weather each year."

Five weeks. And nearly eleven more months of nurturing, for those five weeks of bloom.

Maybe she was really out of balance.

"And once every seven to ten years, we have to uproot them and replace them because they've run out of blooms. We cycle different parts of the fields."

Damn it. Or maybe it was just time to uproot her, because she'd run out of blooms?

No way. Not after only one hit album.

She wasn't going to count that album she put out in high school, because that one was a permanent embarrassment to her these days.

They came around another curve, revealing an old, walled town on one of the heights, and she pressed her lips together in determination.

She couldn't keep her place in that valley, but she could borrow it. Right? Just long enough to...get some fertilizer in her. To prove to herself that it wasn't time to uproot and discard herself, nothing of her worth anything if she couldn't produce songs.

Just long enough to find out why being here made her so happy that she felt as if she could sing.

She snuck a guilty peek at Matt. She didn't want to be selfish, she didn't want to hurt him, but music was who she *was*. If she didn't have that, she didn't have *anything*. As long as she was going to let him have it back eventually, surely he could survive sharing part of his valley until she remembered how to sing?

Chapter 11

They parked beneath the old medieval walls of the town of Sainte-Mère that rose above the valleys around it. A short, steep hike led from the parking lot to the great old arch that allowed passage through those thick walls. It cleared the lungs to breathe that deep for every step, to take in the scents of stone and cypress.

Cleared the heart.

Layla put her hands on her hips as they reached the wall and arched her head back to gaze up at it. Nearly a thousand years old. No matter how many places she had been in Europe, it always shook through her, to think of the age here.

She glanced at Matthieu Rosier to find him gazing at her and not the walls. Of course, he would be used to the walls. Her, he must find a very strange creature. Her breath shortened at the look, and she didn't think it was from the climb.

"Why is it yours?" she asked suddenly. "The valley? Out of all the cousins?"

"Technically, most of it is still my grandfather's. He's only deeded part of it over to me. But he rewrote his will right after my father died, and so it's been intended for me since I was five years old. And he's ninety, you know. That doesn't mean he's entirely ready to let go, but mostly I run it and have since I got out of school."

"Like the oldest prince for an aging king?"

The oddest expression crossed his face. "We're really an old peasant family. We've been working the land since the Renaissance. I think *prince* might be a bit of an exaggeration."

His definition of *paysan* might be a little different from her definition of *peasant*, she decided. Little signs of luxury abounded. The nice cars Tristan and Damien drove, the watch on Damien's wrist. Matt himself dressed in worn jeans and T-shirts, with no jewelry, not even a watch, but he was heir to an entire valley off the French Riviera, and he'd just told her what a few small acres of that land were worth.

"Are you the oldest of the cousins, then?" She followed him under the thick arch onto cobblestone streets. An apartment was built into the very wall itself, no wider than her armspan, but with an old wood door and a little window, veiled with a lace curtain, geraniums growing in a pot before it.

"No, Raoul. Then Lucien. But my father was the oldest son. If he'd lived, it would have come to him first, and I might have been a grandfather myself before it came to me. But..." His lips winced downward, and he shook his head, turning onto a steep, shadowed stair-street that ran up along the houses built against and into the old medieval walls. A great, ancient vine, thicker than a man's wrist, ran up the stair-street almost like a banister.

"What happened to him?"

A bleakness settled over his face and then a kind of stoic blankness. "He and my mother went out shopping for my birthday. And they...they were found later at the bottom of one of those cliffs. They don't know if my dad lost control or someone hit their car and knocked it off."

Her stomach tightened at the sudden, horrible vision of a little Matt, tousled black curls around his face, staring uncomprehendingly at some adult in tears, maybe his grandfather, telling him his parents were gone. She reached out and caught his hand before she could even think, holding it tightly. "I'm so sorry."

He looked down at her hand a moment, and then slowly closed his around hers and held on, a little too hard. "It was a blow to my grandfather. No one expected it. And after that, he focused on me. He and my grandmother took over raising me."

It must have been a blow to *him*. Her strong, capable left hand that could play even the most difficult chords, help produce the most amazing sounds, looked too small and inadequate for this task. She squeezed his hand, to try to give him more. "I'm really sorry."

"It was a long time ago."

She kept her hand tight around his. One thing about a guitarist's left hand—she had a very strong squeeze.

"I don't really remember that much," he said finally, low. "Just...the shock of it, you know? Like a bomb had gone off, and you couldn't hear anything or think anything for the longest time. There was just this ringing in your ears that seemed to go on forever and ever. And afterward you try to be...careful, about the other people around you. Not to take it for granted that they'll be there the next day, too."

You, he kept saying, as if he couldn't say *I*. He had to keep that verbal distance, still to this day.

She stared at their hands, feeling very grave. Conscious suddenly of her own transience in his life. She was a wandering minstrel, right? The "wandering" part was as inherent to who she was as the "minstrel"...right? From a family of recent immigrants, war-torn and displaced, to a child of divorce with a father only erratically present in her childhood, to the pressures of touring now. Even that happiest period of her life, traveling around the U.S. in her little van, busking around Europe, she had been footloose and fancy-free. Matt might be all roots, but she was all wings.

But surely nothing about their vacation flirtation mattered in this discussion. There was no way she could possibly even imagine herself having the importance in his life that his own parents would have had when he was five. When she left, it wouldn't matter, as long as she didn't take his land with her.

"And you still feel the consequences today, don't you?" she asked quietly. "That's why you're the one who has to take care of this valley. Your father would have been the one next in line. And you would have had a chance to do something out in the world before it was time for you to take responsibility for the valley from him, if you wanted."

He frowned up the stairs as they climbed them, not answering.

"Your cousins...they don't share in the heritage?"

"French inheritance law requires that all children receive equal parts in a will. Pépé had five sons, and they all had a...son." He hesitated oddly. "Well, in terms of what counts legally."

Her eyebrows went up in confusion.

"One of my cousins, whom you haven't met—I mean, don't talk about this, all right? We don't talk about it *ever*. But it came out about sixteen years ago that Lucien's real father wasn't, in fact, one of our grandfather's sons. His mother had an affair. So that's a bit...complicated. But legally, you can't disinherit someone for that. It's not his fault."

"Did someone *want* to?" Layla asked cautiously. It sounded terrible. To think you were part of this big, powerful clan to whom things like inheritance seemed paramount, and then to find out as a teenager that you weren't.

"No one ever said. My grandfather's never even mentioned the issue, that I know of."

Well, damn. She might have to like that obstreperous old man a bit after all.

"But things felt uneasy. After. His mother should never have told. I guess she just lost it during the separation, so she wanted to hurt my uncle and forgot who would pay the price."

"Will I meet this cousin?" Layla asked, feeling pity for him already.

A downward turn of that sensual lower lip. "He...left. Fourteen years ago. Really left. Joined the Foreign Legion, changed his name, gave us all up, just...left." He grimaced and shook his head. "We can't even reach him. The Foreign Legion never gives up information on legionnaires to anyone who might be looking for them. He's called Raoul a few times."

Layla tried to thread her fingers through his.

One of those quick, brown glances, rather wondering, before he focused ahead as if the uneven stairs might trip him up if he didn't. His hand slowly relaxed enough to give her fingers room between his. "There's a fifteen-year point in the Foreign Legion," he said low, "when a lot of men get out. They've 'done their fifteen years', and can retire. So maybe he...but anyway." Another grimace, his head turning away.

She squeezed his fingers again. After a second, he gently squeezed hers back, and then rubbed his thumb over the callused tips of her fingers.

He stopped on the stairs, and she pivoted toward him, held by his hand, gazing up at that stubborn jaw and high cheekbones, at the sensual mouth his stern upper lip tried so hard to protect, at that black, half-curled hair, at that big, muscled body. He was so much bigger than she was. Despite the strength of her own hand, his engulfed it, his calluses easily outmatching hers. It didn't seem likely, did it, that such a big, rough-edged, growling man could take good care of a heart?

And yet...he seemed to take good care of everything else. She bet he grumbled at that cat the whole time he was stopping his car, picking it up, carrying it safely to its owner.

She sighed. "Women must fall for you all the time." He was worse than a damn drummer. He even had dramatic, brooding wounds in his past.

Actually he had a dramatic wound in his present as well—her.

In fact, he was currently gazing at her as if she'd hit him with something right between the eyes. He even gave his head a shake, as if to clear the ringing. "They, ah, you—"

Glumness settled over her. "They do, don't they?" And now she'd put him on the spot about it and made him all awkward. Obviously he couldn't tell the latest woman about all the others who had fallen for him before her.

He ran his hand through his hair, tousling those glossy half-curls even more. "I mean, not—well—do we have to talk about this?"

She folded her arms across her chest, resting her back against the great old wooden door behind her. Its knocker dug into her back. Maybe it would help dig some sense into her. "I can take it." She scowled. "I'm used to men who have groupies."

He shook his head again. "*Groupies*? You think I have *groupies*?"

She looked him over, up and down the hot, muscled length of him. "Oh, yeah." She glowered a bit herself. What had she been thinking? Flirting with someone like that? As if she didn't know already how men acted when they could have half the women in a room for a wink?

He started to smile, that slow, deep smile, all his brooding fading away. His body angled in over hers, until his good arm braced against the door above her head. That smile, from that position, made hot sensations twirl all through her body. "And what do you have, Bouclettes?" His free hand came up to catch the tip of one curl and tug it gently outward, his gaze following it, fascinated. "How many men am I going to have to fight for you?"

Her scowl disintegrated in pure delight at the flattery. And his words—as if he was willing and ready to fight for her. God, his eyes from this close were gorgeous. They reached deep inside her and melted her middle out. Her breath shortened from his proximity, the angle of his body over hers. "Nobody," she said. "I've been out there on my own for a while."

A ghost of self-pity swept through her, a powerful *hold me, wrap me up so I'm not alone anymore.*

"You must like it, then." He let her curl relax back into its shape and cupped a handful more, squeezing them gently. "Being on your own. If you haven't let someone grab you."

Her self-pity broke under the force of her pleasure. Damn, but he was flattering.

"It's hard to find the person you...you fit with." She pushed one hand into the other to try to illustrate.

After she'd figured out relationships that got started on the tour circuit tended to be very bad for her—too loose, too easy, too fueled by loneliness and performance highs—she'd stopped forming them. But her music career had sucked her in and swallowed her whole, so that it wasn't as if she'd had the emotional energy or even time in one place to find someone outside the industry either.

"Tell me about it," he murmured, sinking his hand more deeply into her curls, fisting them and then releasing them, then fisting again, as if savoring their texture.

The scent of roses reached her from his hand, mixed with the apples of her shampoo, and she closed her eyes against a wave of hunger. It didn't help. Closing her eyes meant that all she could do was feel—his hand shifting in her hair, his breath brushing over her lips, the cool shade of the street after the sun of the fields, and the press of a knocker against her back. The silence of the stone seemed to hold her safe in it. A gentle echo sounded of someone walking down another cobblestone street below. She wanted him to talk again, into her darkness.

"Are you going to kiss me?" she whispered.

"Yes." Just that one deep vibration of his voice through her, while his hand sank deep enough to cup her skull at last, cushioning it from the hard door as his mouth closed over hers.

Pleasure curled like a smile through her body, this sensual happiness that relaxed her lips to his. His mouth was just right. Not too hard, not too grabby. Not too soft, not hesitant. His fingers tightened gently against her skull as he fit himself to her, the silk slide of his lips taking hers, exploring hers. The heat of her own body overwhelmed her so fast, melting her everywhere just at a kiss. Her hands rose up to sink into his hair—oh, yes, those half curls were so silky, exactly like they looked, and her fingers slid through them and found purchase against his head, down over his neck and muscled shoulders, back up to that glossy hair. Every part of him was so enticingly touchable that her hands kept moving up and down, sinking into him, trying to get more of his textures, as their lips met and slid, as the kiss grew deeper and deeper.

She discovered she was climbing up him, pulling herself up and into his body, and finally fell back, breaking the kiss. "Oh, wow," she whispered. Her heart beat so hard it almost scared her, and she ducked her body in against his chest to find refuge there, her head tucked down so they couldn't start that bewilderingly overwhelming kissing again. "Oh, wow." She pressed her cheek against his heart, which thundered against her ear. The gorgeous rhythm of a strong heart beating hard and deep just for her.

One arm still bracing against the door to hold his body off her, he wrapped the wounded arm around her and pulled her in close. His hunger for her pressed against her belly, and she bit her lip against the need to wiggle until it fit into a much better spot. "You'll hurt your arm," she managed.

His arm just tightened around her. "The cut's on the outside of it, Bouclettes." His voice had turned so rough. He squeezed her against him again, and again that pressure of his muscles, that compression of her body, swept arousal all through her. "Besides, a little bit of pain can sometimes help a man keep his head."

What would help her keep her head?

"I'm scared," she confessed into his chest. *Oh, I love this thump of your heart.*

"What?" His arm loosened, and he started to push himself away from her.

She grabbed onto his waist and buried herself tight against him again. "I actually came here to get my life more under control. To find my feet. Not get swept up like a piece of flotsam in a flash flood."

Both his arms closed around her now, one hand rubbing gently through her hair. "You want me to build us a raft?" he finally asked.

She laughed a little and tilted her head back. "I want you to kiss me again. That's all I really want."

He brought a hand to her face, his thumb tugging gently at her lip. His mouth was...tender. Curving gently, as his fingers petted again through that bane of her existence, those corkscrew curls. She wanted to kiss the scar on his chin. No, she wanted to nibble on it. Bite and lick. "It's not all I want. But yeah—let's do it some more."

Oh, yes, that hungry, thorough heat of him as he kissed her again. The energy and gorgeousness of it. The way his mouth shaped and took and gave. That rose-brushed scent of sun-warmed human man. She gasped and fell back again, bringing up her hand to touch her damp lips. "I think I could kiss you like this forever."

An intense kick of pleasure ran through his body and leapt in his eyes. "I couldn't," he admitted, half-laughing. "I'll have to go get in a fight with one of my cousins soon."

That much energy to vent? She petted one of those straining arms, loving that arousal so much. It made her feel hot. Hungry. Happy to be her. Vibrating like her own guitar, as if she'd been turned into pure, eager music.

"But let's not stop yet," he breathed, lowering his head. Tongues tangled, her hands digging into big shoulders, and her body lifting, his hands gripping her butt to help her up, pull her in, and—

The door opened behind her and she fall backward, franticly clutching him as he fell with her.

Matt managed to catch them both, a hand grabbing the doorjamb and the other arm yanking her in tight, before they fell all the way. He righted her in a flustered tangle.

"Tante Colette," he said reproachfully. "You picked a fine time to start answering your door."

Tante Colette? Meaning—? Layla twisted to see an old woman standing straight and tall, in a long skirt, her white hair neatly pinned on the back of her head. She gave no indication that two hot-blooded young people had nearly fallen into her home. This woman was *ninety-six*? Holy crap, this family had good genes.

"It was making unusual noises," the old woman said coolly, even as her eyes flicked over Layla, intense and searching. "After they didn't stop for some time, I thought I should perhaps check on it."

Layla flushed. Her body against the door knocker must have occasionally sent a sound echoing through the house that she hadn't even noticed.

"We were polishing your door knocker." Matt grinned at his aunt, entirely full of himself. "Tante Colette, may I introduce the woman to whom you gave part of my valley?" A little flash of his eyes on that last, a press of his lips together.

For a moment, the old woman just stared at her, eyes widening and searching. Layla held out a hand tentatively. "Layla Dubois."

She felt shy suddenly, before this old Resistance hero who had given her a house, and she found herself easing back toward Matt, so that her free hand grazed the back of his. A little brush of reassurance came with the contact, a kiss of warmth.

Without looking down at her, Matt turned his hand and simply engulfed hers. One big hand. Callused and warm. Fingers linking. *Here. You need my hand? It's right here.*

She looked up at him, on a sparkle of happiness.

"Well, you're certainly in a better mood than the last time I saw you," Colette Delatour told Matt coolly. "Are you resigning yourself to your new neighbor or trying to seduce the property from her?"

Wait, what? Layla turned her head fast to look up at him.

For one second, he just stared at his aunt. Then he dropped Layla's hand and folded his arms across his chest, his jaw thrusting. "Whatever you think the most asshole thing to do is, that's probably what I'm doing. Of course." His arms tightened over his chest, and he angled his head away, his scowl firmly back in place.

"Stop being so touchy," his aunt said, turning to lead the way down the hall to the kitchen, and Layla looked curiously from her as she disappeared to Matt again, as his scowl grew even fiercer and his biceps bulged with the frustration he was compressing. Did people in his family often do that to him? Slap him with something they said, then blame him for being hurt by it?

"Hey," she whispered, wiggling her fingers under his good arm, trying to fit between it and his chest.

He looked down at her, so startled his scowl almost faded.

She wiggled her fingers more, trying to get to his hand. "Let's talk about all the ways you can seduce that property out of me later, all right?" She winked up at him.

The frown disappeared. He stared at her a second, and then a smile grew slowly in his eyes, sheltered by those long lashes of his. "That could be a long conversation." He unfolded his arms to take her insistent hand. And then laughed, a wicked little gleam in his eye. "Or a short one, depending on exactly how much you like my ideas."

Layla grinned, feeling wicked herself and deliciously naughty. "There's nothing wrong with multiple discussions of this issue. Sometimes you have to get things ironed out."

Matt used his hold on her hand to pull her in closer to his body, warmth and arousal and delighted intent filling those brown eyes as he lifted his other hand to her face. "I'd hate to be one of those men who refuse to communicate."

She laughed out loud, starting to go up on tiptoe to kiss him.

"It's a big house," Colette Delatour said sardonically, poking her head back out from the kitchen. "If you need a room."

Matt sighed, dropping his hand from her face and turning to follow his aunt. He had the resigned look of a man who had been putting up with his elders all his life and would just as soon have to keep putting up with them for a long time to come, all things considered.

"You're not going to claim Jean-Jacques didn't tell you to use any means necessary to get that land back?" Colette Delatour challenged, as they stepped into the kitchen and Matt braced big shoulders against the wall by the door...but didn't let go of Layla's hand.

"Maybe," Matt said. "But sometimes, when a man is caught in a war between two people who have been fighting for the past ninety years, he has to use his own judgment about the best way to handle things. Hurting someone who didn't have anything to do with any of this and finds herself in the middle of it by accident doesn't seem like the right choice."

I really like you a lot, Layla thought, squeezing his hand again involuntarily. *They hurt you, but you won't pass that hurt on to me?*

He looked down at her hand, and that firm upper lip eased as he rubbed his thumb over her knuckles.

"You always were a good kid," Colette Delatour said quietly.

From the way Matt's head jerked up, this was the first he'd heard of it. "I thought I was trouble, too stubborn, determined to get my own way, hot-tempered, bossy..."

His aunt's gray eyebrows went up faintly. "I never said any of those things were faults, did I?"

Matt laughed a little. "I guess I misinterpreted your tone at the time."

"You did," his aunt said, with the calm of a woman quite sure who was right in any discussion—herself. "And I never once used the word *too* about any of you kids. Except, sometimes, about how sensitive you are." A firm, chiding look.

Matt tried to fold his arms across his chest again, and Layla's hand got in the way.

It threw him completely off. He couldn't even get his glower right, all fractured, his left arm folding lamely across his chest with nothing to grip, and he finally just ran that hand across his face and through his hair instead, looking lost. But he didn't let go of her hand.

He snuck a glance down at Layla.

You are adorable, she thought up at him.

Color tinged his cheeks.

She brought her other hand to his big one, so that she could squeeze it between hers in its own little hug.

Because her whole body wanted to squeeze him. Her thigh muscles, her inner muscles, *everything* wanted to squeeze him as tight as she could. Maybe she should tell him that, she thought on a surge of mischief. See how the information hit him.

Weren't you going to behave at some point? she reminded herself.

Her ability to forget an audience was really not standing her in good stead here. She focused apologetically on Colette Delatour.

She found the old woman studying her intently, as if a strong enough look could see through to her bones. Layla was pretty sure her bones didn't have the proper density to impress a ninety-six-year-old war hero, and her hand tightened on Matt's for moral support. "I, uh...thank you," she finally remembered to say. "For such an extraordinary gift." *Why did you give it to me? I don't know you.*

"You don't look very much like her," Colette Delatour said quietly. "Your great-grandmother."

"I think I mostly take after my mother." Her mother's hair was even more tightly curly, so her father's genes had had some effect, but it wasn't obvious.

"There's maybe something," Madame Delatour said. "Around the eyes and the jawline."

"You must have known her very well?"

"She died for me," the old woman said simply, and Layla gave a gasp of shock, her fingers tightening hard on Matt's. "Not just for me, but for all of us. To keep what we were doing secret. You don't forget a woman like that."

Tears stung Layla's eyes suddenly. She didn't even know what her great-grandmother looked like. And yet Colette Delatour's words shook her heart.

"Hey." Matt loosed her hand to lay his arm across her shoulders, a heavy, reassuring warmth. "You okay?"

Layla nodded, leaning into him as she blinked, trying not to act ridiculous. "My great-grandmother *died?*" Well, obviously she knew that her great-grandmother had died at some point. But..."*For* somebody? Like...on purpose?"

"Come," Colette Delatour said quietly. "Let me show you a picture of her."

***

Matthieu sat warm and quiet by Layla's side in the kitchen while Colette Delatour showed her the photos. Red pots hung on the walls, brightening the dark wood. A handful of fresh herbs lay on a cutting board on the counter. Colette stood briefly to toss them into a simmering pot, releasing the scents of thyme and rosemary into the air. Taking a copper teakettle off the stove, she poured them both a tea rich with mint. Tea seemed an odd drink for someone as big and grumpily masculine as Matt, but he took his without comment, his hands curling around the cup like a solace.

155

"Here she is." An old hand pressed an age-browned page open and turned it to Layla. Layla stared at the black and white photo of a woman in a slim skirt, her hair twisted at the nape of her neck, smiling for the camera. "That was taken just a few months before Pétain and his like split our country in two and pretended the southern part was free, when he was really a German puppet."

Layla touched the edge of the photo carefully. "How did she die?"

"She was part of our cell."

"The Resistance," Matt murmured to clarify. "They used to ferry kids across the Alps into Switzerland. Among other things."

"But she was always afraid she might not be able to handle the pain if she got caught, so she had cyanide ready. When the SS stormed her house, she managed to take it, so they wouldn't be able to make her reveal the rest of us."

The story was told so simply, and Layla could only stare at its teller with her mouth open in shock. Sometimes her grandparents on her mother's side, who had left Beirut when her mother was a child to escape the war, would mention little, casual things about ducking through streets to avoid snipers, about bombs falling on a house across the street from theirs. They would even laugh over the memory of the whole wedding party dashing madly through the open to get to the church for their wedding, then dashing madly back post ceremony and dancing all night with the music turned up loud while bombs fell. Little revelations of a world nothing like any Layla had ever known.

This was like that. Worse, even. Élise Dubois had *taken cyanide and died* in order to protect herself from torture and her friends from what she might reveal.

That meant she'd had the cyanide ready, in full knowledge that her actions and choices might some day force her to use it. And yet she'd still taken those actions.

Layla's eyes filled, her nose starting to sting, as she stared at the photo of the woman who was her great-grandmother. Tears trembled past her lashes, and she pressed her face into her hands suddenly as she started to cry.

A big, warm arm wrapped around her and pulled her in close, in silence.

"Élise was a schoolteacher," Colette Delatour said. "The first in her family. Her father was a perfume factory worker and her mother picked flowers for us, so it was a big deal at the time for her to have become a teacher. Her husband was one of those who died in the first onslaught, before the surrender, but she had her own child, who was only eight. And there was one child in her class she knew hadn't really left Paris to stay with her grandparents. She knew the child was really a Jewish girl in hiding. So when the Milice started sniffing around and challenging the girl's identity papers, Élise had to do something. She couldn't stand by, not knowing the girl. One of her own son's little friends. That's how Élise first got involved, and it grew from there. Your grandfather and I, we always thought in big, dramatic terms—to save all the kids, to drive the Germans out of the valley, to drive them out of France. But a lot of people helped the individual person. They didn't believe in their ability to change their whole world, the way Jacky and I did, so mostly they wanted to hunker down and ride out the war, and hope someone else would do something about it. They didn't believe in themselves, in their ability to do big things, but they couldn't turn away from a child who needed help. It was hard for Jacky and me to understand people like that at first—people who could feel so small against such a great evil that they could only do tiny things. But tiny things grow and grow. Most people don't set out to save the world, they just can't stand to see one child's tears. Élise was like that. And after she helped one, she had to help all the others."

"Oh, God." Layla cried harder.

Matt made a little rumble and pulled her closer, so that her face was pressed against his chest.

"Your grandfather and I," Colette said to Matt, "we took a lot of risks. We killed people. We saved people. And if we survived, it wasn't always because we were as smart and wily as we thought we were. Sometimes it was the tiny thing someone did to help us, the shepherd who let his flock spill into the path of a car full of SS who might, if they had been five minutes faster on the road, come upon us. The man who spotted a message that had fallen out of someone's pocket and used it to roll a cigarette and smoke it while he told the police he hadn't seen any sign of anyone. Or that tiny, tiny thing—a cyanide capsule that a mother took, abandoning her right to see her own child grow up because it was the only way she could save all those other kids whose parents weren't going to see them grow up either."

Layla fisted both hands into Matt's T-shirt and sobbed.

"When you're as old as I am," Colette said. "You start giving a lot of thought to what parts of your life you want to leave to whom. I thought Élise's great-grandchild deserved something from me. If she hadn't done what she did, we wouldn't have that valley. We wouldn't even have lived long enough for your grandfather to have those five sons of his, of whom he's so proud. We adopted her son and tried to raise him, but we never really managed to heal him from the war and the loss of his parents, and he ran away when he was sixteen. We tried for him, and we failed. But I think we can share a little bit of this valley with his descendants. My adoptive great-grandchild, if you will." She inclined her head to Layla.

Under her cheek and clinging fists, Matt's chest lifted and fell in a great sigh. His arms tightened on Layla. But he didn't say anything.

"Besides, Matthieu, you can't be a valley," Colette said, with a quiet firmness, as if she'd said that the Earth was not the center of the universe. "You've got to be bigger than that. There are more ways of growing bigger than a valley than escaping from it. One way might be to crack it open, so that even while you're here, it has room to let the whole world in."

Layla lifted her head enough to check Matt's expression. His jaw was set, his gaze locked with his great aunt's. She peeked at Colette Delatour, warily, afraid of how much learning more of her family history might hurt.

Colette held Matt's gaze, lifting her two hands closed together in a capsule of age-spotted wrinkles. "Kind of like, oh, a heart," she said. "When you do this." She spread her fingers and let her palms follow, until those tightly-clasped hands were wide open, free to move through the whole world. Then she smoothed them over her skirt and rose.

Matt stared after her for a moment before he lifted a hand to sink it into Layla's hair. "Sorry about that," he murmured to the top of Layla's head. "I forgot to warn you that my aunt has no idea of her own strength."

Colette gave them a curious, perplexed look as she stood sideways by the pot, stirring it. "She's as soft-hearted as you are," she told Matt, as if hearts that soft were an intriguing mystery to her.

Matt stiffened. "I'm not soft-hearted."

"Oh, that's right." Colette ladled the soup into bowls. "I don't know why I keep forgetting that." She carried the bowls to the table to set before them. "Although I'm not sure why you worry about it so much. I thought I was just telling you how soft hearts can be great strength."

Chapter 12

Matt scraped mortar over the crack in the wall, that steady, reassuring scent of cement and earth and gravel mixing with the rosemary that brushed his arms and the lemon thyme he tried to crush as little as possible under his feet while he worked.

At the weatherworn picnic table—he needed to sand that table down and re-stain it—the two women sat over more photo albums from when Tante Colette was young, Layla touching a finger to a page here and there, asking questions. Her exuberantly curly head brushed Tante Colette's shoulder as she bent, her expression giving every evidence of fascination in an old woman's stories.

It twisted his stomach up, how nice she was. This strange, giddy, frantic feeling, like that time he was in the school play when he was nine. He'd been so excited to play the big, bad monster instead of the idiot prince— he *had*, he really had, it was a much funner role—and then he'd looked out from the wings to find what seemed like thousands of faces staring and Raoul and Lucien had had to grab his arms and shove him to get him to go on.

No one could force him to do anything these days— he was too big. He'd done it on purpose, gotten too big to be pushed.

He scooped up more mortar and layered it over the crack. Layla laughed. Either she was genuinely fascinated by these old tales of a time that had reshaped a nation and a world, or she was very patient, because they'd been looking at photos for an hour.

As he glanced across at them, Layla looked up from the album, her eyes sparkling and locking with his.

Oh. The long, swooshing slide of his stomach.

He focused on fixing the wall.

Layla laughed again, that husky, happy sound, and his whole body tightened, yearning. Not as if his cousins were shoving him and his panicked stomach out on stage. As if all those beautiful, bright lights out there had reached a string into his middle and were pulling him toward them.

As if he wasn't supposed to leap out growling and roaring to scare the princess, he was supposed to dance out on stage like the sucker of a classmate who had had to play the idiot prince. Poor Hugo had never lived that down. Much better to be the roaring beast in this world than to try to be the prince.

Really.

It was.

Layla clapped a hand over her mouth, her eyes dancing with delight as she looked at him.

Hey.

Wait a damn minute.

He surged to his feet. "What are you looking at now?"

Layla giggled. Tante Colette smiled.

"Hey!" He strode forward. *Merde*, he recognized that album. "Tata! Did you get out—Tata! *Not the alien photo.*"

Layla grinned at him. "I like the Superman briefs."

"Tata!" Damn it. He tried to cover his nearly naked six-year-old self with a thumb. Painted entirely red, hair tousled in sloppy, paint-streaked curls around his face, he beamed in his Superman briefs there in the middle of his similarly naked cousins, Raoul painted green, Damien blue, Lucien yellow, Tristan—as the youngest and most put-upon at age four—purple. They'd been playing at alien invasion, but all of them had wanted to be the aliens so they'd tried to invade their parents' lazy Sunday afternoon around the table together. All so young and so innocent and so easily abused by their elders that they'd actually posed proudly for the photo, too, and now had to pay for it for all eternity. "*Tante Colette.*"

Damn it, he could never trust his family for a second.

"You're smudging the photo." Tante Colette's old hand lifted his firmly away.

Layla grinned up at him. *Merde.* She had the happiest damn smile. All vivid and merry and eager to play. He was terrible at playing, really he was. He kept wanting to warn her, but then she might stop.

"I had a Wonder Woman outfit once for Halloween," Layla said. "You should have seen my red boots. I wore them to school every day for a year after."

Aww, hell, he could just see her. Cute, happy little girl beaming with delight in her red boots. Trying to be a superhero and stop bullets with her bracelets. Possibly lasso a man up and get him to pour his true heart out to her. "Did you have curls out to here back then?" He touched the tip of one curl, forgetting the Superman briefs.

"Oh, always," Layla said, resigned. "My mother did a movie about it once."

"Your mother makes movies?" He drew the curl out, watching the play of light against the many shades in that honey-brown.

"Just a two-minute short. She's an art professor. She publishes graphic novels. They don't really sell, unfortunately, but she does amazing work and gets invited as a guest to universities all the time. Anyway, she wanted to experiment with animation, so she did a two-minute short once for me about her own childhood, when she used to think of her hair as a sheep's and wish she had someone else's hair. It was just this funny, sweet way of telling me she understood and thought I was beautiful." There was a little sheen of tears in Layla's eyes as she said the phrase "thought I was beautiful", blending with the sparkle of happiness of the memory.

He almost stroked his hand down from her hair to cover her heart. It made him uneasy, her walking around with her heart so vulnerable like that, without any gruff

162

growliness to fend off those who might break it. Made him want to growl a little at everyone he saw looking at her, just to make sure they didn't get any ideas about stepping too close.

"You are beautiful," he said, and then remembered one second too late his Tante Colette watching. A tiny growl of frustration escaped him at such a stupid slip, and he dropped his hand from Layla's curls. Heat pressed at his cheeks as he thought about what he had just said. *Merde*, what was he going to do, offer her another stupid rose next?

But Layla's whole face softened. She reached out a hand and grazed her fingers over the backs of his. "You, too."

Hunh?

He blinked at her. Beyond her, Tante Colette smiled a little and focused on the photo album, stroking the page as if it had gotten unruly on her and tried to wrinkle.

Layla smiled, rested her chin on her hand, and blew him a kiss.

He clapped his hand fast over his heart, but it was too late. He was pretty sure that kiss had gotten to him. He could feel it, the little brush of air from it sinking into his heart, tickling out through the rest of his body. That was a *really* tricky blow. "Stop that," he growled.

She gave him a sweet smile that was just *designed* to mess with him. "Stop what?"

He pressed his feet extra hard into the earth in his efforts not to fold his arms across his chest. "How long are you staying here?" he demanded abruptly. Damn it, had his voice come out all rough and growly *again*?

She blinked, her smile fading. "I have to go to New York in three weeks." Her eyes clung to his in a kind of anxious, questioning way—as if he might know the answer to some problem.

"Of course, one of the things I've noticed about the south of France," Tante Colette murmured, "is that people tend to start out with vacation houses and then end up living here."

Matt stared down at Layla, knowing that he was supposed to be wanting the opposite. He was supposed to want her to get tired of her vacation house quickly and sell it to him.

Not to install herself comfortably here indefinitely. He wasn't supposed to want that.

But she had this look in her eyes and...damn, but he wanted to hand her just one more rose and see if she thought that one was wonderful, too.

"Three weeks." He couldn't help how growly his voice sounded. It rumbled in him, pissed off. He wanted to snatch that phrase *three weeks* out of the air and snap it in two with his teeth.

"That is the most amazing sound," Layla said.

What?

"When you growl like that." She shook her head, her expression strangely dreamy. "It just *vibrates* that way. How do you do that?" Her fingers itched through the air, as if trying to turn that air into an instrument.

Tante Colette bent her head and smoothed her unwrinkled photo album some more, that curve of amusement on her mouth almost timeless on such an old face.

"Sorry." Layla glanced at her and flushed a little, curling her fingers in on themselves to get them to behave. But one second later, her fingers escaped out again, stretching a little toward him.

Matt so much didn't know what to do with himself, he felt explosive. His most powerful instinct, in response to those subtly stretching fingers, was to tackle her, carry her off at a run to some dark cave, and roll over and over with her to see what those hands felt like actually touching his body. It would be a bit like a plunge straight off the edge of a cliff with no hesitation, into the waves, but as anyone who had ever dived off a cliff knew, it was *far* better to just do it, and not freeze too long on the edge.

But still...he was pretty sure tackling her and hauling her off to a cave was not his best move.

Tristan would definitely not approve.

So he rubbed his hand on the back of his neck and realized abruptly that he was speckled with mortar. Damn it. How did these things happen to him? These were not the clothes for a nice restaurant. "Do you like to eat?" he asked abruptly.

Layla gave him a quizzical look, and then her eyes lit, full of this teasing laughter that just kind of tickled over his whole body. "I sometimes even do it three times a day."

He shoved his hand through his hair at the back of his head. "I mean...good food."

"For preference." Those green eyes kept teasing him, but they were so *warm* with it. They tickled at every nerve in his body. If she had any idea how badly he wanted to haul her off to a cave and make that tickling stop, she would probably lock her door the next time he knocked on it.

"I mean...would you like some food *tonight?*"

If his Tante Colette could stop looking so amused, it would be helpful.

"I'm sure I would," Layla said, with that look still in her eyes, the one that made him so antsy in his skin it was all he could do not to thrust parts of his body against her hand like an animal needing to be petted.

He took a deep breath. "Well, good. That's settled then." For some reason, that made Layla's smile deepen. Maybe she liked having things settled, too. He looked down at himself. "I need to borrow some clothes."

Fortunately, his cousin Gabe lived in Sainte-Mère, too, not far from here, and he and Matt wore about the same size tux.

Oh, wait, hadn't he said he was never wearing a tux again? Not for any woman or any reason?

He...he...he...Layla stood up, coming closer to him, and he looked down at that face that seemed so little in the midst of all that hair, at those green eyes that were laughing at him as if her laughter was a warm wash of affection, and he decided he could make an exception.

Chapter 13

Gabe's tux was a little classic for Matt. You could tell Gabe hadn't spent much time at perfume launch parties with the most elite fashion designers in the world and all their models, lucky bastard. Matt rooted through his cousin's drawers a bit to try to find a black T-shirt he could pair with the tux instead of the white shirt, but apparently Gabe had never gone through a black phase in his life.

No surprise there, with Gabe, when he thought about it.

So he left the collar open, because damn but he hated those stupid little ties, and anyway, Damien never wore them, and Damien in a tux made James Bond look like a wannabe awkwardly aping his betters.

The fact that he made Matt look that way too was profoundly annoying, but fortunately Damien wasn't here tonight to make a better impression.

No tie, he thought firmly, staring at himself in the mirror. A man who had vowed to never put on a tux for a woman again had to draw the line somewhere. Besides, they were going to dinner in a three-star restaurant in the south of France, not to a perfume launch in Paris. He didn't have to go overboard here.

He stared a second more, then abruptly started searching through Gabe's bathroom cabinet drawers for fresh blades for his razor.

***

Tante Colette might hate it when he and his cousins knocked instead of coming right in, but Matt figured that if a man got all suited up to take a woman out, he should knock on the door when he came to pick her up. He kind of wished he had a rose in hand to offer her, too, and—

That's enough out of you about the roses. Quit doing that.

Then Layla opened the door with that happy smile on her face, and all his focus zoomed in on it. Damn, she was kissable. He rested his upraised hand against the stone above the door, thinking about going for it—just stepping right in and making this a habit, that he got a kiss whenever she opened her door to him—but then she got a good look at him, and the smile fell off her face.

She looked as if she'd been hit by a truck.

"What?" he demanded uneasily, glancing down at himself.

She pressed fingers to her mouth.

Okay, shit, what? He locked his still upraised arm against the doorframe above her, braced for the worst. Since he stood in the street, one foot on the step that led up to the door, their faces were almost on a level for once.

"Oh, and you shaved," she said in a stunned voice. Her fingers left her mouth to stretch toward his chin, and all the skin on his jaw prickled awake in anticipation. And then she curled her fingers back into her hand and dropped it, which about drove that eager skin mad with frustration.

He bit back a rumble of protest, trying to behave.

Oh, to hell with it. He grabbed her hand and brought it to his jaw. Shit, yes, that felt so good. The warmth of her palm against his skin. The way her fingers shifted in a tiny testing of his texture. The way her eyes dilated, black taking over the green. Oh, yeah. That felt just right.

"You can't keep doing this to me," she murmured in a strange, helpless voice.

He hadn't done anything, had he? Well, he'd stolen that caress of his jaw, but she hadn't objected.

She waved her other hand. "First the no T-shirt thing, and now a tux." She took a deep, shaky breath. "I have a weak nature, you know. There's only so much I can take."

Whoa. His whole body woke up in this hungry wave of delight as he realized what was happening. She *liked* the way he looked. Liked it as in...hungry liked it. And it made his own hot hunger leap even higher.

He pressed his weight into his arm above her, leaning in more. God, but he loved this position. Her in a doorway, him closing her in. "Before you do what?"

"Before I dissolve, I think." Her fingers flexed against his jaw. "Or possibly attack you."

Oh, did he ever like the sound of that. "I'm wide open." He leaned in closer. "I'm not defending myself."

Her eyes widened and ran over him, and she shivered and closed her eyes tight. "No, seriously, you have to stop. You have no idea how sexy you are, do you? You don't know what you're doing to me."

Her words surged through him, a geyser of demanding heat, until he had to lock his other hand against the frame of the door, too, gripping that sharp stone edge with all his might to keep himself in control. "What the hell do you think you're doing to *me*?"

She peeked at him through her lashes, and a little, utterly delighted-in-herself pleasure curled her mouth. All smug and happy to be her and to be driving him crazy.

It was funny, because he'd been manipulated by a woman who thought she was so sexy that sex was her power over him and she could use that power to do anything she wanted. So he should be offended by that smug delight, or at least wary.

And instead he just wanted to kiss her. Give her a little bit more to be delighted about.

Actually, he wished to hell he was standing like this in her doorway back in the valley, instead of out in a sheltered, quiet, but still public street, with neither his bed nor hers anywhere near.

He bent down and bit that little delighted smile— very gently, just a tiny warning graze of his teeth. *You're messing with me. I might know how to mess with you, too.*

She made a little sound that tightened his hands against the doorframe until he thought he might snap stone. So he had to kiss her again, right? Had to show her how he could mess with her with his tongue, too. How he could slip himself into her body. How he could take her over, make her his. Get her to melt and yield and...

One of his hands loosed its hold on the stone to sweep down her body to her butt and pull her into him. He rubbed his hand down to her thigh to lift it to his hip, so his hips could fit better between hers. The bareness of her thigh in her shorts shocked through him, in contrast to his tux. Made her seem practically naked and yielding to all his darkest demands.

Oh, *merde*, yeah, he would like to lay her back on a bed naked to his clothed body. Oh, yeah, he would. Just lay her out there and say, *You are in my bed now, and you are all mine.*

Footsteps sounded against stone, and a child's chattering, and he wrenched his mouth away and locked both hands against the stone again, this time on the walls to either side of her. Layla clutched fistfuls of his white shirt, breathing hard, looking dazed and...oh, yeah, if only he had a bed nearby right this second...

He kept her body framed and as hidden as possible with his, trying not to look at the mother and child who passed, but of course he knew the woman who was discreetly turning her head away, a little smile on her mouth. He knew everyone in Sainte-Mère. Hell, he knew everyone around Grasse. In this case, she owned the inn across from Gabe and Raphaël's place.

"Maman." The child's clear voice sounded back down the stairs. "Why did he have his hand on her bottom?"

"Shh," the mother whispered. "I'll explain later."

Always fun to know he was going to be the prime example in an early lesson on the birds and the bees.

"This is so not a good place for this," he managed, gazing down at Layla, who still looked so dazed and soft, her lips so damp and reddened and her eyes so dark and heavy, that it about killed him.

She blinked up at him in that way that sent every bit of his sex drive into conquering mode. *I've yielded*, that blink said. *Pick me up and carry me off somewhere.*

Damn it. The Rosiers had an unused apartment in this town, too, now that Jolie had moved in with Gabe. If only he had the key on him.

"Okay, I've got to pull myself together," Layla said and covered her face with both arms.

See? What a damn shame, to have all that fallen apartness of hers get sturdied back up into something sensible. He looked down at those slim, tan forearms, pressed together over her face, and couldn't help himself. They were just so much smaller than his, so much more vulnerable, such flimsy and endearing self-protection. He ran his thumb gently up the little gap between them. The size of his own hand against her arms sent unexpected pleasure through him. Yeah, he liked being this much bigger than she was. He liked it when he heard her take a soft breath behind that shield of her arms, and he liked it when he bent his head to rub his jaw over her inner wrist and kiss the palm.

"Please, please stop," Layla whispered. "You're too much. It's too much. I can't handle it."

He hesitated a long second with his face still brushing against her fingertips. Damn it. He closed his eyes. If there was one reason in the world a man didn't want to stop, it had to be that one—that she liked it too much.

Shit.

He wanted to suck one of those fingers into his mouth so damn bad. See how many more things she couldn't handle without falling apart.

He used the wall to leverage himself away from her, and yes, fine, maybe he growled in protest as he stepped back.

She parted her arms just enough to peek out at him from between them. Aww, *hell*, she was so cute. "This is not a raft, Matthieu."

Hell, and her accent around the *ieu* in his name. The only people who ever called him Matthieu were his aunts and, before she died, his grandmother, when he was in trouble, and Layla's reproachful tone suggested he was in some kind of trouble right now, too. But all he wanted to do about it was kiss her again and see what that little tongue that couldn't quite shape the *ieu* right did with his.

"A raft," he said randomly, because she seemed to think he would know what she was talking about.

"That raft you were going to build to help with that being swept up in a flood situation?"

Right. Fuck that raft. "I'll tell you what. You hold onto me as tight as you can, and I'll get us through it."

A little leap of laughter in those eyes peeking at him, and some other emotion, or several more emotions. Fear, maybe, and maybe just a hint of trust. She lowered her arms enough to reveal her whole face. "You will, will you?"

He shrugged a little. In a real life raging river, he would consider it his job to have his strength get them through. So this was kind of like that, right? It was her damn metaphor.

Of course, he'd heard that real life raging rivers overwhelmed strong men all the time. He didn't like to believe it, though. A man had to be strong enough for anything.

"Matthieu." Shit, his name again, in that half-laughing, half-reprimanding tone. "Where exactly were you planning to take us tonight—where I can wear shorts while you wear a tux?"

See? *See?* There was really only one place that would work. His bedroom, with its big white bed, where just about now the lowering sun would be gently sifting light through the windows...

He sighed and thunked his head very gently down to rest on hers. "I guess you'll have to change." Damn it.

She laid a hand on his chest. "God, I love that sound."

He lifted his head enough to look at her again, confused.

That utterly warm laughter of hers leaped again. "You were growling."

He stared down into that laughter. That look of hers, as if even his defaults of character were part of this one big person that she...liked. Just the way he was.

That look was so special that it was utterly terrifying.

His hand lifted, iron to a magnet, to curve over her cheek, one thumb stroking gently over her cheekbone. Yeah, she kept not disappearing, not dissolving back into dreamland, every time he did that. Like she might actually be real or something.

Shit, yes, terrifying. Someone so real and so enticing who was leaving in three weeks. How had she gotten him to act like an idiot so damn fast?

Oh, and she was supposed to be his enemy. Hell. He kept forgetting that.

The enemy who had blithely come into his valley to run off with half its heart as if it was hers by right.

"Matthieu." That half-laughing, accented name rippled through him. "What am I supposed to change into? What am I supposed to wear?"

He was pretty sure no woman, ever, in his whole life, had asked his advice on what to wear. He stared at her blankly a moment. *You look fine to me* was probably not what she would consider a solution to her problem. He cast about rather desperately, past solutions to problems that involved wrenches and grease and machine parts and occasionally hitting someone, to...Tante Colette! She was a woman. She was ninety-six, but Matt had seen photos of her in her twenties. She'd looked like Lauren Bacall or something. "Do you like, you know, those kind of old-fashioned clothes some women like? Like from the thirties or forties?"

That leap of laughter in her eyes. "Vintage?"

Right. That was the word for it. He nodded.

"I *love* vintage."

He gestured upward. "Maybe Tante Colette would let you into her attic."

***

"I feel like a little kid playing dress-up," Layla said ruefully, putting her elbows on the table across from Matt.

Then she remembered the elegance around her and the sudden extreme elegance of the man across from her and shifted her elbows off the table so that only her hands rested there, making sure her back was straight. They sat on the terrace of a restaurant called Aux Anges, the folds of the hills below Sainte-Mère draping in sparkling lights below them to the sea, as if jewels had been sewn carefully into a woman's skirt. Out in the distance some of the lights bobbed, the yachts on the gentle Mediterranean waves floating like the drifting hem of that skirt. Apparently the restaurant belonged to Matt's cousins, one of those rare, precious Michelin three-star restaurants.

Brown eyes smiled at her from what had to be the sexiest face in the world. God, she wanted to seize her chance, just reach across the table and stroke that scar on his chin before it got ward-off-all-comers prickly again. "You also look a little bit like a kid playing dress-up, to tell the truth," he said.

That made her laugh, because it was true. Colette Delatour's attic had been like some treasure trove of wonders for a woman who liked vintage clothes. Alas, Colette Delatour was also six inches taller than Layla herself was. So her dresses from when she was a teenager came down to Layla's ankles—what would have been mid-calf on Colette—and her dresses from the forties came down to Layla's mid-calves. Not to mention the bodice issue.

"Except for that." Matt allowed his gaze to drift to the neckline of her sea-green gown. Designed for someone with a much longer torso, it dipped too far on her.

Well, what Layla considered too far. Matt clearly didn't have any issues with it.

She touched her little flat-brimmed hat, which didn't suit her mass of curls at all, but given how badly the clothes themselves really suited her shorter form, she'd decided to just go with what made her happy.

Hey, she wasn't an indie musician for nothing.

Matt's smile deepened with easy pleasure, as if this whole evening made him happy. "My cousins and I used to love treasure-hunting up in that attic. Some of our family heirlooms disappeared in the war, and Pépé is convinced Tante Colette really stole them, something he believes possibly because he has a guilty conscience. Apparently he said some things about her not being 'real family' at one point and they're both still brooding about it seventy years later."

"What were the heirlooms?"

"Let's see—there was an old perfume box with a wolf on the lid reaching for a rose, which may have come from Niccolò Rosario's mother. Niccolò is the ancestor who came out of Italy to found the Rosier dynasty. His mother's family name was supposed to have been Lupo. There were the gloves his wife Laurianne made for him for their wedding and the ring he gave her. Their old book of perfume recipes—that one about breaks Tristan's heart. And there's Niccolò's seal." Matt fell silent for a moment.

"His seal?" Layla prompted, watching his face. *This is the heirloom that matters most to him,* she thought.

He hesitated. "He probably would have had two made, one for him and one for Laurianne, since they both would have had to sign off on documents and orders regularly. Or maybe she had them made for them—she must have been quite the savvy businesswoman, perhaps the business brain in their couple. But, if there ever really were two, one of them was lost centuries ago. Only one survived until the war. It's supposed to be on a chain, with the entrance to the valley in enamel on one side and a rose, or a rose bush, on the other side, with his motto." Another little pause, and then under his breath he murmured, "*J'y suis, j'y reste.*"

I am here and here I'll stay. It sounded lovely. Oddly, intensely lovely, for someone who had never sought to stay anywhere, who had always been wandering the world in pursuit of the next audience and the next song.

Matt made a little grimace of regret. "We never found any sign of the heirlooms, of course. Probably someone stole them during the war and sold them or traded them to the Germans to get someone released from prison. Those were hard times. And, of course, these days we realize Tante Colette would never have let us 'sneak' up in the attic in the first place all the time if she'd hidden them up there. But we certainly had fun looking. I never realized until now how much more fun some girl cousins would have had, with all those trunks of clothes."

"No girls in your family?"

He waved a hand. "Pépé had all boys who had boys. There are some more distant female cousins like Léa and some on my mother's side. The lack of girls is one of the reasons the aunts are always after my cousins and me to get mar—" He broke off suddenly, clearing his throat and turning his head to stare out over the edge of the terrace. "Nice view," he said abruptly, randomly.

She could have teased him about that broken off M word, but honestly, who needed to talk about scary words like that over the kind of dinner during which a man might actually court a woman seriously? Over the kind of dinner where a man might actually *propose.* So she helped him out.

"I can't believe you have a cousin who has a fountain built for him in honor of his cooking," Layla said, looking down into the *place* below where the stylized angel fountain played.

Matt made a little sound of amusement, seizing on the new subject with relief. "You get used to that kind of thing, in this family. My grandfather and Tante Colette are featured in museum exhibits on the Resistance, and there are far too many Delange and Rosier names on those plaques in all the churches honoring the soldiers and nurses and Resistants who died in the wars. And the Rosiers founded the most important museum in Grasse, which is the most important museum on the history of fragrance in the world. There are a lot of Rosiers featured there. Hell, Tristan's probably going to be in some history books himself, for his work on perfume. He already has two perfumes in the top twenty and he's not even thirty yet."

"Tristan?" Layla blinked. He seemed so...laidback. As if all of life was to be played with.

"Yeah, I know. He fools around more productively than anyone I know." Matt shrugged. Once again, the coat failed to split when he did that.

He'd introduced her to the big, buoyant chef of this restaurant from whom he'd borrowed the tux, Gabriel Delange, and so Layla could see why the tux actually fit his shoulders. Both men were big. But she still kept expecting one of Matt's shrugs to break through the intimidating elegance of that black coat and reveal again the man who got stuck in a T-shirt when she was watching, the man who made her feel as if she could wrap him around her little finger.

This man made her feel as if he could wrap *her* around his little finger. As if he could scoop her up in one palm, eat her up for a midnight snack, and go find someone substantially sexier for breakfast.

As when her music career brought her into contact with the truly famous, the glitzy, glossy über-successes, it made her uneasy. Like maybe she couldn't play in this territory after all. Maybe she needed to go back to her dreaming-of-the-big-time musician friends, the jeans-clad fellow indies who'd worn their jeans out and their fingers, too, strumming their guitars for every bit they climbed. How was she supposed to fulfill the expectations for her next album, when she still felt, and looked like, a bronze-haired Orphan Annie playing dress-up among the millionaires?

She looked down at Matt's hand on the table. Darkly tanned, Mediterranean skin that had been out in a lot of sun. The dark curls of hair, the nicks of a few scars, the kind acquired by a man who worked with his hands. Or occasionally fought with them. She reached across and turned it over, before she could remind herself that hand didn't really belong to her, to do what she wanted with it when she wanted.

Work-toughened palm, calluses all along the fingers and thumb and on the pads of his hand. A little tension of nerves eased out of her, such a sweet release that it raised the hairs on the back of her neck as it ran through her, like coming into warmth out of the cold. It was still the same hand. He was still the same Matthieu Rosier.

He just cleaned up really, really well.

She curled her fingers into his, so that she could keep hold of that earth-bound Matthieu Rosier still, so that she wouldn't forget him under this elegant disguise. Secured by that hold, she could look up into that gorgeous, strong-boned face again, all smooth-shaven as if the prince had come out of hiding. He was gazing down at their hands, those long lashes concealing his eyes, his mouth very serious as his fingers curled slowly but very firmly into hers in response and his thumb stroked over the back of her knuckles.

He lifted his gaze for a quick, sudden look at her, shadowed by his lashes, and then the waiter showed up.

Since they hadn't ordered yet, Layla wasn't expecting the elegant bowl with its tiny mouthful of sorbet, surrounded by fresh rose petals, but Matthieu smiled. "It's a little present from Gabe," he said. "I built a lot of muscle helping restore this old mill when he decided to open his restaurant down here. Good timing—

I was nineteen and always trying to fill out more back then. Tristan and Damien helped, too."

"It must be wonderful to have so much family," she said wistfully. Even though his extensive collection of relatives seemed to drive him crazy, they were *there*. "I'm trying to imagine needing to build something this impressive and being able to call on family who just pitch in and do it, like some great old-time barn-raising."

Matt's eyebrows drew together in puzzlement. "Don't you have family?"

"I have my mom and her parents. My parents divorced when I was two, and then my dad died when I was in college. That was...shitty. I had a tough sophomore year. I almost dropped out, but my mom helped buck me up and get me through. So it's just the four of us."

Matt gazed at her, very obviously trying to wrap his mind around what she had said. "That sounds...light," he said finally.

She smiled and squeezed his fingers. "Does your family feel like a weight on your shoulders sometimes?"

"Y...es," he said slowly. "But your way—you know when you see the astronauts floating outside the shuttle, out in space? That's how light it sounds. Like a kite that doesn't have a string."

She frowned. "I have a string. My mom." She liked that image suddenly—a pretty kite in the sky, held tight by her mother on the ground, the wind pulling her mom's curls out from the scarf with which she would have tried to tie them back, her face beaming as she fed that string out, letting the kite fly as high as she could.

All the sudden it made Layla feel grounded. Not so lost, not so overwhelmed. Her climb as an artist was a happy thing, wasn't it? Her choice and her privilege, not her obligation, and she always, always had someone on the ground who loved her and was watching her with delight.

"My grandparents," she added. Who would have loved to have more kids and more grandchildren, who deeply missed that sense of community in Beirut where they said their whole apartment building was like an extended family, neighbors pulling in closer and closer to each other as the bombardments and snipers continued. Missing all that family, her grandparents had poured all their energy for loving into the only outlets left for it—her mother and her.

Matt's hand turned over and closed entirely around hers, tightening, as if she sounded so alone to him he needed to add more grounding to her life through the sheer strength of his hold.

She looked down at his hand. Again, this shiver of release raised all the hairs on the back of her neck and rippled on down her spine and through her arms, like coming into warmth from the cold. Her lips softened. She felt vulnerable and...okay being vulnerable. Safe, right there, no matter how fragile.

"We can trace our family here back to the Renaissance," Matt said slowly. "When Niccolò Rosario came out of Italy and married a glove-maker named Laurianne, and they founded one of the great perfume families. Fourteen generations of family spreading out in this area. Just in my immediate family, I have four uncles on my father's side and four cousins, and an aunt up in Paris on my mother's side and another in Monaco, and their children. Once you start on second and third cousins..." He shrugged and abandoned the effort to try to count them.

"So you don't exactly feel like a kite flying without a string," Layla said wryly.

He shook his head slowly, as if she was saying words almost impossible to process. "I feel about as much like a kite as five million tons of earth might feel. A valley, and all the hills that shelter it. And four hundred years." He hesitated, rubbing his thumb now over her hand as if it was a worry stone, reassuring to him. And then he confessed, "You know, I like going into churches around here, because they're so much older than I am. Over eight hundred years usually." A rueful smile. "Although if I think about it too much, I know there were probably nameless ancestors of ours hauling and laying stones for some of the village churches around here back in the twelfth century." A little flex of those eyebrows, a press of that firm upper lip down onto the troubled lower one. "Sometimes it's a good feeling, and sometimes I know exactly why Raoul and Lucien left when they were nineteen and didn't come back."

"But you can't do that," she murmured, studying that strong face in the soft lights of the nighttime terrace. "Because you're the valley."

He shrugged a little. This time it did seem as if that tux felt too tight on his shoulders.

She reached across the table and covered his other hand, too. "I don't want you to take this the wrong way," she said slowly. "Because I agree with your aunt, that a human is bigger than a valley, and you have feet, and you can walk out of it if you want to. You even have a brain capable of building wings and flying, if you want to be a kite. But I like that about you, the way four hundred years of history and five million tons of earth were put on your shoulders and you said, 'Yes. I'm strong enough for that.'"

***

Gabe's Rose had gone over well. Matt figured he owed Gabe's fiancée Jolie one for having gotten Gabe to start making that dessert again back when she first met him, because Layla had been thrilled with it. She'd clapped her hands together over the pink-streaked white chocolate petals, and she'd made soft, awed sounds over the secret, melting golden heart until Matt had folded his arms across his chest uneasily, wishing that poor golden heart had some better protection than flimsy white and rose chocolate petals.

Then she'd slipped a bite of that golden heart into her mouth on a little silver spoon and drawn the spoon slowly free, making soft *mmm* sounds, and he'd kind of forgotten how to think. He'd just sat there and tried not to lick his lips.

Merde but she was cute.

She was so cute that his arms kept sliding down, exposing his heart to her. So cute that he did another of those things he had decided never to do with another woman—he took her on a walk through the old part of Sainte-Mère at night. These streets whose beauty he took for granted, and which Nathalie had treated with blasé indifference, as if it was nothing—as if everything of value in his life was nothing...Layla acted as if they were amazing.

Stopping before every view of arches of stone and warm golden lamplight. Breathing in deep when they passed walls covered with jasmine, her head tilting back and her eyes closing. Grabbing his hand to pull him after her as she ducked down little side alleys that he knew by heart, but which to her were some magical labyrinth.

It was astonishing how many good spots there were to kiss a woman in this town, when every time she looked up at him her eyes were wide with wonder and delight. His arms stopped folding across his chest. They started folding her in close to it instead. *Come in here where I can keep you safe and warm, too. God, your mouth tastes so good.*

Pressing her into jasmine, kissing her, her body pliant and responding and drawing him deeper and deeper into her until...footsteps sounded as some other couple passed by, or once even Tante Colette, out for an evening walk, clicked her tongue at him.

So he would walk on, until they came to another dark sheltered corner where jasmine grew or a lamp glowed in just the right way over her face as she turned it up to him, and he'd start kissing her again. Yeah.

Hell, yeah.

Life sang from the old stones, and he couldn't remember the last time it had done that for him. The last time those thousand-year-old walls had played a thousand years of hope to him and not a thousand years of expectations.

The last time the soft, age-dusted colors of the shutters against stone had hit him so vividly and richly, the last time he had breathed in the scents of jasmine and stone blending in the night and taken that second to love it, to really love it. The last time all the old, colored doors and their knockers had offered a hundred possibilities of adventure and not a hundred paths closed against him.

When they came out onto the old town's terrace and stopped beside the *pétanque* courts, the Côte d'Azur stretched out before them, its sparkles crowding toward the sea and spilling over onto the darkness of the water that reached toward Africa.

"I love this view," Layla said wonderingly, squeezing his hand. "You've got all this history and time all around you, and yet it's infinite with possibilities. You could go anywhere, be anyone. Sail to Africa, cross the Atlantic, head into the Orient."

He studied the view for a long moment before he looked down at her. His heart squeezed tight and hard. "I can't," he said. They used to play at that kind of thing as kids—Saracens, or Normans invading England, or Vikings invading France, Marco Polo, Columbus, Resistance heroes like their grandfather. But while his cousins had been able to keep playing, Matt hadn't.

Layla turned her head to smile up at him, this sweet, soft smile of affection that confused his heart so much. It made it feel so damn vulnerable. "Because you're a valley, right," she said, and reached up to touch his jaw.

He might have to start shaving more often, if he was going to get this much petting as his reward.

"Matt," she said. "You can go on vacation, can't you? That's how most people who want to travel and see the world do it. You're not the only person held down day to day by responsibilities and obligations."

He stared down at her a moment. "So I should tough it up, right? No whining." He nodded once, firmly. He hadn't meant to let that weakness slip out to her, and he wouldn't let it happen again. It had just been a stupid moment of vulnerability and intimacy, the effect of the damn evening.

Her eyebrows drew faintly together. Then she smiled almost...*tenderly* and stroked her hand a little against his jaw. "Matthieu." *Merde* but he loved the sound of his full name from her. "That's not what I just said at all."

Sure, right. He tightened his muscles a little, hardening himself against that stupid mushy inside of his. *No more weaknesses. Tough it up.*

She slipped her hand under his tux jacket and pressed it over his heart. His heart thumped once hard in panicked surprised, like a rabbit that had been holding so still it had thought no hawk could ever spot it. "Besides, I like this part of you." Her hand rubbed once, massaging against his chest as if to reach even *deeper.* "I think I like it a lot," she murmured very softly.

Chapter 14

By the time they headed back to the valley, Matt's heart was baffled and starting to panic. *Why is this happening to me? What is she doing?*

But then...she fell asleep.

Quietly, as if she trusted him to get her home.

As her lashes slowly fell and finally stayed down, as her head tucked into her seat with a little sigh, her body still angled toward him, his nerves eased.

The road became his again, the car his to control, everything about him strong, sure, reliable, carrying her back to her home.

He fit behind the wheel of that car, driving her home. He was in the right place, at the right time, doing the right thing.

In the privacy left by her sleep, he brought a hand to the left side of his chest and rubbed the spot she had rubbed earlier. *Calm down. You'll be all right.*

One of us is being an idiot, his heart sighed despairingly.

A cliff drop came up, and he took it, easy and smooth. Layla never even stirred in her sleep. He could handle this road.

Yes, he could.

Layla blinked her eyes open when he parked in front of his house. Probably should have stopped at hers. He smiled at her, relaxed by then enough to tease her again. "Want me to carry you to bed?"

She shook her head. But then she smiled at him. "You can walk me to my door, though."

Merde, yes. He liked having her between him and a door. That had been working out really well for him so far.

"It looks so shorn," she said of the fields, as they walked the couple hundred meters on that upper terrace of rose bushes. "All green, only these dots of pink now ready to come back."

"They seem to have done a decent job," Matt agreed grudgingly, looking out over his valley. He picked a rose that had been missed.

She smiled up at him, this little sparkle of warmth and affection he could *not* get used to. It *tickled* in random spots all over his skin, as if he was being taunted by pixies. "Did you really doubt they would?"

"No," he admitted. Raoul and Damien and Tristan between them, with his grandfather there? No. But then he shrugged. "*Enfin*—" It was *his* valley. He had to make sure.

She laughed, green eyes indulgent, as if it was perfectly reasonable for him to be—unreasonable. Wary. Possessive. All those growly defaults of his character.

Damn, she was cute.

He turned her against her door, tucked under that fuchsia climbing rose, and leaned in over her, so hungry for more of those doorway adventures he could hardly stand himself.

"Dinner was incredible," she breathed, tilting her head back against her door to let those delighted, happy, wondering eyes cling to his in the dimness. It was too dark in front of her door. He needed to install a motion-sensor light for her, didn't he? But right now, it felt just right. "Thank you so much. That rose for dessert...wow. Thank you."

"I didn't make that one," he said, shrugging uncomfortably. And even though he had her locked up by his looming body against a doorway and she was liking it, even from that position of intensely sexual power, even after all that evening with her, he still felt a little stupid and vulnerable to lift the rose he had picked on their walk to her door. And he still...he still wanted to brave the risk and see what she did with that vulnerability. "I made this one." His voice came out rough again.

"Oh." Her soft sound of pleasure rushed through his veins as she reached for it.

He held it away from her, and then pressed his knee into the door beside her so he could still angle his body in close to hers and keep her his as he used both hands to strip it carefully of all its thorns.

"You're so *sweet*," she said wonderingly, reaching for it again.

No, he wasn't, damn it. He wasn't sweet. It made him feel stripped naked in front of a crowd, bare as this poor little rose without its thorns, every time she said something like that.

Only…there was no crowd here. And he really, really wouldn't mind if she reached for the buttons of his shirt and started genuinely stripping him naked.

Oh, no. The whole thought of the morning after, when he'd *wake up* naked, was scary, but right this second…he wouldn't mind at all.

He pulled the rose away from her reaching fingers, watching her expression flicker in confusion and then this kind of trusting question, like she never for a second suspected him of messing with *her.*

She was so damn cute. He touched the rose to her cheek and then trailed the petals down to those rosebud lips.

Which parted, on a little gasp. He smiled, playing the rose over them.

Her eyes drifted closed and her head sank back against the door. Power and pleasure rushed through him. *There you go. Yield yourself to me.*

He stroked the rose down over her chin and then oh-so-gently and thoroughly over her exposed throat. Her breathing started to shatter into this short, fluttery thing, and his own breath grew deep and hot, his body trying to drive him forward. All that need to kiss her, bite her, thrust his hips up against her—he braced one arm over her in the doorway to hold it back. All his strength, his muscles clenching in their fight against each other as he kept that rose easy...so easy...trailing now into the hollow of her throat...down to her neckline.

It dipped so low, that neckline. Wickedly low.

"What does that feel like?" he whispered, as he toyed with the rose deep against her cleavage. "I'll never be able to feel it myself."

Never know what that silk-sweet rose felt like drawing over the breasts that her bra lifted and pressed together. Even if someone ever stroked a rose over his chest, which he couldn't even imagine, his skin was tougher. It had hair to protect it from outside invasion. Her skin, just there, soft, its sun-rich color fading where it rarely saw the sun, was so fine.

Her voice was hushed and fractured. "It feels good."

"Tell me," he insisted, playing the rose all along the dipping neckline.

"Oh." The sound she made shot hungry power through him, made him want to bite and devour. "It's so soft. It makes me feel as if I'm *beautiful*."

"You're gorgeous," he said honestly. Absolutely irresistible, there against her door amid his fields of roses, all curly hair and vulnerability and utter yielding. He hardened his arm still more, keeping himself back.

She gave a tiny laugh of denial.

He bent his head to her ear. "Unzip your dress."

She shivered. "Oh, God, if you growl like that..."

"Unzip it," he growled.

Her eyes closed again, and she turned her head against the door. Her teeth played with her lips, nervous and sensual.

His own rose playing over her breasts hypnotized him. He loved the sight of it. But he wanted to do it more, do it everywhere. He wanted to skip straight past roses and just use his work-roughened hands. *No. Stick with the rose. She'll like it better.* "I'll take good care of you,

Bouclettes," he murmured. "I promise. Don't be nervous." *I'm nervous. I don't know why, but I'm terrified.*

Her eyes caught on his, searching, almost wondering. Slowly, she arched her back to allow her hands room to lower the zipper.

Shit, the hunger that pressed through him at that position, at that act. Nerves were forgotten. His hand hurt against the stone around her door, ground into his palm. "Now lower it."

She bit her lip harder, her breasts rising and falling fast.

"Shrug your shoulders, Bouclettes." His growl grew more insistent. "Let it fall."

She was panting now. But she still hesitated.

He tucked his jaw into the side of her throat, where it would rub when he growled in her ear. "I want to brush this over your nipples, through your bra, until you're clawing at me. Do it, Layla."

She gasped, arching her throat still more to him, and then let the dress slide down her shoulders. Already too big for her, it fell easily when she quit holding it up.

He stared down at that revealed body. Those breasts in black lace that she had just revealed *for* him, to him. Not confident that this would bring him to his knees. Vulnerable and shy, her eyes opening again fast to search his face, to see what he would think or do.

Merde, he wanted to kiss her breasts so bad. The need throbbed in him, throbbed in his lips, made his tongue curl against his teeth. He turned his head and nipped at her shoulder suddenly, under the cruel pressure to let some of that need out.

She made a soft, hungry sound.

He slipped one hand down to pull up the fallen skirt and cover the juncture of her thighs because if he didn't cover it with something, his damn dick was more than ready to drive against it.

A hot dampness was seeping through her panties. He rubbed that dampness, and she made another little whimpering sound.

Her hips pressed into his hand, her body arching, her breasts lifting to beg for him. Some of those corkscrew curls had fallen over her forehead, catching against her lower lip. The angle of her head, a little away and down, her lips parted, made her face look so vulnerable, so *his*.

He brought that rose to one of those begging breasts and twirled it against the lace over her nipple.

All she could do was make little sounds. Her hands lifted to his shoulders, flexing and sliding, pulling at him and then growing weak again, as if he stole all her strength.

"Invite me in," he breathed.

Her eyes flickered open, and then her head ducked. She tucked herself up suddenly against him, burying her face in his chest, and nodded.

Hell, yes. Everything in him surged—that she was shy about this, that she tucked that shyness against him for safe-keeping, and that *she said yes.*

"If you had your key tucked between your breasts, the turnabout from what you did to me for my key would be so much fun." He squeezed her body into his, harder than he meant to.

"It's too big," she murmured, muffled, into his chest. "It's in my purse."

He stroked his hands over her butt anyway, en route to her little purse, found the big iron key easily, and opened her door.

She looked up at him as its solidity left her back, all that space opening behind her into a whole new adventure, a whole new place to get lost and fall without the backing of everything that was familiar. Her expression was nervous and hungry.

He picked her up. *I've got you. Shh. Don't worry.*

God, the light, gorgeous weight of her body in his arms.

She wrapped her arms around his neck. "I'm scared," she whispered.

Oh, her, too? She'd said that before. But why should she be scared? She was the one who had all the power here.

His arms tightened around her, lifting her more snugly against his chest. Strength expanded all through him at her need for it, deep from his center all the way to the tips of his fingers and toes, this deep, sure strength. "Don't be," he said and carried her into the house. "I've got you."

Chapter 15

He was too sexy. It made a woman's whole body want to explode with hunger and eagerness and this scrambling fear at how sexy he was. As if a whole cliff was giving out from under her, and she was going over. What was happening to her?

But he was so damn sexy. The muscles under her cheek, the strength of his arms, the careful, sure way he angled her on the stairs so she didn't bump into a wall. Even through the borrowed tux, Layla could still swear she caught a hint of roses, or maybe it was the lemony, rich scent of the one he still carried in one hand, stem pressed against her skin. Her dress fell down around her waist, so that she was half-debauched already as he carried her, exposed except for those strong arms holding her tight.

He laid her on the bed and paused a second. She followed his gaze to the old jar she'd found in a cupboard and used to hold the rose he'd given her the day before, which sat on the heavy old stand by the side of her bed. "You took care of it." His voice came out even rougher than usual, and he cleared his throat.

She took the fresh rose from his hand and slid it into the makeshift vase beside the first one.

"Hell," he muttered and turned back to her. He gazed down at her a long moment, and then ran his hands down her body in a rush of warmth and calluses, slipping away the dress that was tangling her legs. He stepped away long enough to open her shutters, letting in the light of the full moon. A little laugh escaped him as he came down over her on the bed, having to work to find space for himself. "I'd forgotten how little the bed up here was." He bent that black head to her in the moonlit darkness, with that low, sexy rumble. "We'll have to see if you fit better in mine."

Oh, God, they were going to do this *twice*? She still hadn't survived *once*. She felt as if her skin was going to split with the itchy hunger to be petted and squeezed by hands rough with passion.

"Take off your jacket." She pushed at it. She wanted to feel those muscles, holding his weight off her.

"I kind of like it like this." He slid his clad thigh up between her bare ones.

She shook her head, crossing her arms over her breasts. "I don't want to be all exposed while you're dressed." *I'm always like that. I'm always the one with her heart stripped naked and held up for the crowd that sits on the grass, watching and judging and totally safe.* She pushed at his jacket again. "Take it off."

"You take it off," he ordered, this low roughness that made her want to twist and arch with hunger. "You do it, Bouclettes."

Funny, given how laughing and confident she had felt about threatening to help with his T-shirt out there in public, how shy and clumsy she felt now, to take off his jacket. "No, you." She pressed her hands inside it against his chest. "Please?"

Braced close over her, he lifted a hand to her cheek, his thumb stroking as he searched her face. "All right."

He kissed her once and then knelt back to strip the jacket off, watching her all the time as he worked the cufflinks, as he draped it over the post at the end of the bed. He was going to drive her out of her mind with how hot he was. How could any woman take this?

What the hell had happened to his previous girlfriends, had they just exploded? Their atoms dissipated out to the ether in one great glorious burst of arousal?

He came back over her, lifting her hand to the top button of his shirt. "You do this part." His eyes held hers. "Please?" He gave that *please* back to her as if it was the first time it had ever been formed in his mouth.

So she did it, because no matter how clumsy and exposed it made her feel, she had to get that damn shirt out of her way. And she was definitely clumsy, fighting with those slippery silk-covered buttons. The panels parted slowly to reveal—oh, wow, wow, wow—too much strength and heat and flat hard stomach up so close to her now, where her fingers could touch it.

"I think I'm in over my head," she whispered, her fingers itching, hovering over those muscles as if instinct kept insisting that so much heat, when touched, could really burn.

"I've got you," he said again, and pressed her hand to his skin. A jerk ran through his body. "I've got you, Bouclettes."

"*God*, you're hot." Her fingers spread over those hard muscles, pressing across the ripples of them.

"It's you." He covered one breast with that big hand, its heat crossing instantly through the fine lace of her bra.

It wasn't, though. Her looks were ordinary, she knew that very well. People loved her for her music, and he had never heard her sing. His attraction to her was so confusing and so sweet—as if there was more to her that mattered than whether or not she could perform.

Her hands slid around to that smooth, strong back, and she shivered again at the privilege of touching it. "It's definitely you."

He shook his head a little, thumb hooking in under her bra cup, rubbing. "Allow me to be the judge of how hot you are, okay? I don't think you have any clue."

She arched up into the rub of his thumb involuntarily. "Are you going to take it off?" she whispered.

He bent his head to rub his jaw gently against her cheek until his lips were close to her ear. His thigh slid up between hers, pressing them apart. "I liked when you took off your dress for me," he said, rough and low. His hips replaced his thigh, surging, his erection hard against her panties. "I liked that a lot."

This close, in this intimate and dark a space, the vibrations in his voice were utterly irresistible. She wanted to capture that voice, turn it into a fur coat she could wrap around her body against any chill. She arched again, her hands sliding under her back to the catch of her bra. "I think you could get me to do anything you want when you use that voice."

"Yeah?" His eyes were fixed on her breasts, as her bra cups started to loosen. "I'll keep that in mind. *Merde*, Bouclettes, you're so...you're...you..."

Apparently there wasn't a word for her, there was only a touch. Both his hands, coming to cup her bared breasts, both his callused thumbs, rubbing gently over her nipples.

She couldn't bite back the little moaning sound of pleasure, any more than she could stop herself from reaching for him, pushing at the panels of his shirt that fell to either side of her, finding his bare shoulders, then sliding up his neck to bury her hands in his hair and pull his head down.

"Yeah," he muttered, bending willingly. "I'm on my way." He opened his mouth over one nipple, kissing and sucking, gentle at first, then testing how much she wanted, until she writhed and gripped, until she said no, no, that was too much that almost hurt until she said...

"Yes." Her head pressed back into the pillow, chest lifting up for more of this. "Yes, yes, yes."

"I love that sound in your mouth." He reared back, shrugging out of the white shirt and dropping it, revealing that tan, muscled torso and the white gauze still around his left forearm.

She came after him, his bared torso irresistible, stroking everywhere, testing muscles and smoothness of skin and the texture of his hair across his chest. It was all good. Every single inch of him was touchable. She pressed her ear into his chest and tried to think of a way to make him growl, but her brain was all fogged.

Finally she just pressed her hand down, down, down his stomach, flat and tense under her touch, and curled it over his jutting sex.

He growled.

Her hand squeezed in involuntary delight as she shivered, pressing her ear harder into his chest.

He growled again. She wrapped her other arm around his waist and hugged herself in closer to that strength and that sound and squeezed again. "I like this position," she said mischievously.

"You're asking for trouble." He pulled her hand off him and then lifted it and completely unexpectedly kissed it before he stood free of the bed, reaching for his pants.

She curled her fingers wonderingly into that kiss of her palm, watching him as he unbuttoned his pants. He reached for the waist and froze. "Oh, shit."

"What?" Layla sat up, wrapping her arms around her nakedness, startled and not very concerned. Right about then *everything* seemed fixable, as long as she had Matthieu Rosier in the same room with her, with that muscled torso bare.

"I don't have anything." He thunked his head against the slanted wall. "It's Gabe's tux, and I was right in the middle of a workday when this all started, and I...I can't *believe* I forgot—" Thunk against the wall again. "Usually I would have—" He broke off abruptly.

Layla's eyes narrowed a little. "Eternal optimist? Or are you just used to getting lucky?"

"It's not that." He turned his head, still pressed against the wall, to meet her eyes. "It's just that—it's my responsibility. To take care of you."

She pulled her knees up to her chest and wrapped her arms around them, naked except for her panties. "Of course it is," she said softly. "Everything's your responsibility, isn't it?"

"Will you give me ten minutes? I've got some at my house." He winced. "That spoils everything, doesn't it?" He closed his eyes.

She stood up, baring her naked body suddenly as easily as she sometimes bared her heart. "No, it doesn't," she said quietly and walked to him, sliding in under his bowed body and wrapping her arms around him, pressing her head against his chest. "You taking care doesn't spoil anything at all. I like it." *I actually think I might be doing something way more than "liking" here.*

His body curved around hers as the despair eased off his face into something intense and almost wondering. "Come with me," he murmured, or that growly thing he did that passed for his murmur. "I'll carry you all the way through the roses. You won't even have to put your shoes on."

"*Oh.*" She had been about to propose another solution, and now her original idea wavered. "That sounds incredibly romantic."

"Really?" He looked completely surprised. "Not just desperate?"

She shook her head and went up on tiptoe to whisper a secret. "I have some, though." She halfway wanted to not mention them, so she could get that ride through the roses.

He frowned a little.

She held up a finger. "Are you going to have a double standard?"

"No." But that frown settled into a scowl.

"They were giving these out at a festival I was at in Paris." She left him to dig around the edge of her still-packed suitcase until she found it. "And I thought the package was really funny, so I kept it as a souvenir." She showed him the little packet of three condoms, stamped with the image of a very phallic Eiffel Tower covered with latex. *J'aime à Paris.*

He completely annoyed her by double-checking to see if the package had been opened and smiling when he found the box still sealed.

But he was so damn sexy standing there, with that light heating again in his eyes as he realized this evening could keep going, that her annoyance melted. "So you see," she said. "Maybe once in a while, I know how to take care of things, too."

He hefted the little package. "This wasn't you taking care of things, this was your sense of play. And I got lucky."

She folded her arms across her chest. "All right, if you're going to start complaining about your luck right now—"

He growled and pushed her back on the bed. "No." He came down over her. "No, I'm not going to complain about my luck."

She turned her head away as snootily as she could. "I might be losing my sense of play."

"Oh, no, you sure as hell aren't. Let me fix that problem for you." His hand ran down her body, leaving a path of pleasure and hunger in its wake.

"Maybe you can't fix it," she challenged, holding his eyes in provocation.

"Oh, don't worry." His eyes gleamed as his thumb taunted its way over that ticklish crease of her thigh, making her hips twist and jerk a little, half toward that tickle and half away. "I can fix anything."

"Maybe," she said haughtily, "you'll get lost and need directions."

Laughter and arousal leapt in his eyes in equal proportions. She loved the blend of it. "I never get lost." His hand slid unerringly to exactly where she wanted it to go, proving his claim, a firm cup of her panties and a press of the heel of his palm against her clitoris through them.

She turned her head away, a resigned princess. "Well, I suppose if you do, we can always find an app for this on your phone."

He laughed out loud, this great shout of happiness and desire, and she turned her head back to him, grinning with triumph. His eyes were alight with humor and arousal as he lowered his head to her. "You're going to pay for that, you know," he growled, removing his hand from between her thighs. Uh-oh.

"God, your voice should be illegal." She hugged him hard, trying to crush his body to hers or hers to his.

"Don't talk to me." He began to drag his body down hers. "I'm concentrating on the road."

"Hey." She grabbed for him, her fingers sliding through those glossy half-curls as he paused above her chest.

"*Merde*, I don't know," he said, with the most ridiculous semblance of anxiousness on that big and dominant a man. One large finger touched just above her breastbone and hesitated. "Should I go here?" His fingers walked their way up one breast, and then, just as he was about to reach the aureole of her nipples, his upraised index finger paused...and he turned and retraced his steps. "Or here?" He walked them up the other breast.

"Hey." She tried to grab his hands and press them fully to her breasts, but he dragged them down her ribs as easily as if she hadn't been resisting him at all, leaving her poor abandoned nipples quite desperate for that failed contact.

"I am so confused," he said. "I definitely need a damn phone about now to tell me what to do. I mean, what the hell is this?" One flat palm paused dramatically just at the edge of her panties. "A road block? Where do I go from here?"

"Matt!"

He raised his head, his eyebrows drawn together in pseudo-worry as his fingers trailed uncertainly back and forth along the line of her panties in the most maddening way. "I don't know." His eyes gleamed. "Do you want me to pull over and let you drive this thing?"

"You're a *beast*!" she said incredulously. She might have made a mistake waking up this man's sense of play.

"Well, I mean..." His fingers slid strong and hot and oh-so-charily a half centimeter under the line of her panties into her curls. "If you can do it better..."

"I'll show you what I can do!" She twisted, trying to reach down toward his own sex, far past her arm's length at this point. "You're so going to pay."

He caught both her wrists and surged up her body to pin them with one of his hands above her head. She twisted them to try to break free, and his eyes gleamed as he didn't let go. "It must be hell to be a puny girl right about now."

"*Matthieu Rosier.*"

"God, I love the way you say my name." He kissed her, hot and deep, until she was gasping, her hips twisting and bucking against that entirely uncooperative hand of his down there.

"You let go of my wrists right this second!"

His grin was so wicked. "What are you going to do if I don't?" His free hand stroked down farther, until the long, strong middle finger was just shy of exactly where she wanted it to go so badly. "Tell me to stop the car?"

"You, you, you—oh, God." As that callused finger rested quite gently on her clitoris and very, very gently stirred.

"Yes, Bouclettes?" His hand slid farther, his thumb taking the place of his finger as those long fingers slid through the slick lips of her sex. "You were saying?" His thumb began a gentle, unhurried rhythm.

"Hush." She turned her head into the pillow, her eyes closing. "Let me concentrate."

"But I'm having so much fun," he complained. "I mean, wow..." A finger probed deeper into her slickness. "I wonder where this goes?"

200

"I'm going to kill you," she promised, wetting her lips, her hips bucking up to his finger.

"Yeah, I know. But still..." That finger began its sure slide deep into her. "Let's find out."

All her inner muscles tightened on his slide, first at the foreignness of his entrance into her body and then at the desire to have more of it, bigger, harder, faster.

"That's going to feel so damned good on me in a minute," he said hoarsely. "Shit, Bouclettes."

"Hurry up!" she begged, trying again to break her wrists free so she could grab for his hips.

"Isn't that just like a woman?" His thumb moved over her clitoris again as he slipped a second finger inside her. "I'm the one waiting on you."

"Ma-tt." The word broke and shattered out of her, in little lost huffs.

His thumb kept moving in such sweet strokes, firming just barely. "Think I'm going to have to wait much longer?"

"Matt." She couldn't keep her eyes open. She wanted to cover her face with her arms and hide what she looked like right then, shut out everything but the sensation of his hand, but she couldn't, because he wouldn't let go of her wrists.

"You look so damn beautiful," he said incredulously, and pressed his thumb down just...just...right as the waves of pleasure mounted in her, as they swept over her, as that raging river caught her up and bore her away. As she fell apart.

***

She came back to herself almost ready to cry, from that beautiful shattering feeling, from how exposed she had been during it, all her heart laid out there once again.

His hand cupped her face a second, stroking her curls out of her eyes, and that threat of tears eased into the security of his hand. His thumb stroked her cheek again, that way she was growing to love so much. Then he twisted away a second, tearing open the little box of condoms.

"I ripped your little Paris souvenir," he said, as he came back over her. "I never did get along with that city."

"Come here." She reached for him and this time he didn't stop her, as she gripped his bare butt. God. "*Nice* butt," she said involuntarily, her fingers trying to sink in and meeting muscled resistance.

"*Merde*, you're generous," he said roughly. "You just *say* things. Do things. You're just about to let me right in, aren't you?"

She nodded, gripping his butt and pulling.

"In here." He rubbed her still over-sensitized sex. "Where you're all soft and vulnerable."

She was more than a little afraid that she'd already let him into a much more vulnerable part of her than her body, but she just gripped him and arched her hips up, twisting to try to fit herself onto him since he was still bracing himself off.

"Hell." He surged into her, hard and deep.

"Oh." She went very still, taking deep breaths.

He did, too, braced off her, his chest moving in great pants. "Okay?"

"I think I need to just—" She shifted her hips a little, and pleasure relaxed all through her as they found their fit. "Oh. Yeah. That...yeah."

"You let me know." He held her eyes. It about killed her, how tense his body was and how deep his breathing, and the way he took time to make sure he was taking care of her, still. "I've got you, *chérie*."

"Actually, that is factually incorrect." She squeezed him as hard as she could with all her inner muscles and grinned up at him. "I've got you."

His body jerked a little in her. He caught it, all his muscles rigid, still trying so hard for control. "Easy for you to be full of yourself. You already came."

"Again I have to correct your word choice here." She shook her head chidingly. And squeezed again. "I'm full of you."

Breath rushed through his body, and his hips surged. "You're still messing with me," he said incredulously.

"I know," she agreed mournfully. "I can't seem to help myself." And she winked at him. "Besides, admit it. You like it."

"You really are going to kill me," he muttered.

She liked killing him. She liked driving him crazy. It made her feel giddily, hungrily powerful. She gripped him hard, pulling herself into his body, pressing her lips into his shoulder, kissing and nipping. The roses on his skin had entirely faded. He'd showered when he changed into that tux, hadn't he? But even though he came from a fragrance family, it hadn't occurred to him to put on any scent, to be anyone but him. His life was the fragrance.

"You know what I would like?" she whispered fiercely into that strong joining of his neck and shoulder. "To make love to you when you've just left the rose fields, when you smell of them all over and I can follow the scent all over your body."

His eyes closed, his expression strained, as he moved inside her in one long thrust.

"And then you could leave the scent of them all over *my* body," she breathed, enraptured with this vision.

"Oh, *bordel*," he said. "You're—you—be quiet. Let me concentrate."

"On this?" she asked innocently, arching her body and squeezing. "Or this?" She slipped under her legs to cup him.

His breath hissed. His eyes opened, and he stared down at her, as he pulled slowly almost out and slid deep again. "On all of it. On every single second."

That intense gaze speared her, held her, almost as deeply as his body did. She stared back up at him, caught—by that sensual lower lip, by the upper one that couldn't get the lower one to behave, by those long lashes that so passionately defied the strong, stubborn bones of his face, by those dark eyebrows drawn together. By the hard, bronze body, by the gauze that showed that he could be hurt, too, by the dark hair on his chest and the way his stomach muscles flexed with each movement of his hips. The way that movement into her body rippled out all through her. "You are so gorgeous," she breathed wonderingly.

"Bouclettes." His eyes tightened closed again and he turned his head away, hips surging. "Please don't—not now."

"I can't help it," she whispered. "You really are."

"Hell," he muttered, cupping one hand under her butt to pull her in tighter to him as he braced with his wounded arm.

"And you feel so good inside me," she confessed. "Can we do this again sometime?"

"Oh, *merde*." His hand hardened on her butt, his movements growing stronger, faster. "Bouclettes. *Yes*. Now will you please shut up and let me get it right this time?"

"You already got it right." She rubbed him, flexing her hand gently as she tightened all her inner muscles as hard as she could. "Now you should just focus on having fun."

He opened his eyes again and gazed down at her, shaking his head wonderingly. "Fun?"

She flopped back on the bed, arms spread wide. "Fun. Yes. Here I am. I dare you. Have all the fun with me that you can."

"Oh, *bon sang*." His body shuddered. "You don't know what that *does* to me. You look so—so—"

"Do it," she whispered. She cupped her own breasts, pressing them together and up, an offering. "Do it. *Do it*."

"*Merde*." He bent and kissed her as his body began to move faster and harder.

"Yeah," she breathed wickedly and bit his lip. "Oh, yeah. Like that."

"*Merde*, Layla, please—"

"Yeah." She squeezed. "Harder. Faster."

"Shut *up*—" He was losing himself in his own movement, his eyes going blind.

"Oh, yeah. *I love the way you feel.*"

"Oh, *bordel.*" Big arms engulfed her, wrapped her in tight, tight, tight, into his body, into his strength and darkness, as he growled hard and low as he came.

Layla wrapped her arms tight around him and held on, so pleased with herself that the only thing she could do was grin like a cat in cream. She was still beaming later when he came back from the bathroom and slipped into bed beside her. He tried his best not to take over the narrow space, but the whole mattress dipped toward his weight, tumbling her body against him. He propped himself on his side to gaze down at her, his face oddly solemn, one hand framing her face, stroking back curls. She smiled and curled on top of his body to leave room for him on the mattress, draping her arm over his chest as he tucked her in close. Still smiling, she nuzzled her face into his chest, falling gently into a dream of roses.

Chapter 16

Calm down. Matt rubbed a grimy hand on his T-shirt, over the left side of his chest. *You'll be all right.*

In the quiet gray of early dawn, his hands sank again into dirt, digging up the old fountain's pump. He might have to follow the old buried wood pipes up into the hills to solve this particular problem, but he was hoping the failure of the fountain really lay in the modern pump someone had installed in the fifties or sixties to add a decorative lion fountain here to the old system for bringing water to the houses above the valley.

The moist, old scent of fountain earth rose around him, and a little movement in the doorway onto the patio lifted his head.

Layla leaned sleepily against the doorjamb, barefoot, in soft knit yoga pants and a gray hoodie, her hands in her pockets, her head resting against the doorjamb, too, as if those curls were too heavy at this hour for her to hold them up.

And his heart did ease, at the sight of her, as if something as soft as her bare footfalls had brushed across it. He sat back on his heels, rubbing his dirty hands against his jeans automatically. Maybe his hands wanted to make themselves a little more eligible to touch someone if the opportunity arose.

"It's official," she murmured. "Our sleep schedules are not compatible."

"Is that a big deal?" Matt asked warily. His last girlfriend had made everything a big deal. Casual friendliness to another woman. Not noticing if she painted her toenails. Taking a deep breath. Of course, she'd been famous, and famous women obviously weren't for him. He couldn't handle the narcissism. Layla, in contrast, was so down-to-earth and human, his girl next door.

Layla gave a dreamy shrug, as if she was barely awake, and smiled at him. "Thanks for the rose." Her voice was almost a whisper, this husky blend with the softness of dawn.

He flushed a little. Him and his stupid roses. Why he had to go leave one on the pillow beside her, he did not know.

"I put it in the vase," she said.

Had she? Taken care of it just like the others? He bent his head, trying to focus on the pump while his mouth kept wanting to curve ridiculously.

"What are you doing?"

"I've been meaning to fix this fountain," he said.

That smile she sometimes had for him made him feel so confusedly and vulnerably happy, as if he was a teddy-bear she was about to pick up and squeeze. He had never in his life felt very squeezable before.

"And that's the only thing you could think to do at— what is it, five in the morning?" she said.

"I was afraid working on your showerhead or your car would wake you up." He rubbed his hands on his jeans again, really wishing he could get more of that dirt off. "And I didn't want to get too far away."

Her sleepy smile made him feel as if she was stroking him everywhere—long, generous strokes. He looked down at the pump again, scared to take a deep breath in case it accidentally overfilled his body and all those emotions pressing up in him exploded. "And nothing other than fixing something occurred to you, at this hour of the morning?"

He shoved a dirty hand through his hair, confused about what she wanted from him. "It's my valley," he tried to explain.

Her smile broke into something radiant.

He stared at it. "And...I don't really fit in your bed. I was making you uncomfortable." He'd been afraid to fall asleep, in case he rolled over and knocked her out of bed.

Or snored. Or sweated, with her hot body smashed up against his like that. Or did, really, anything a big male body in a tiny bed could come up with to do to make the woman in it crinkle her nose and wish he was elsewhere.

She rubbed her shoulder, still smiling. "I do have a crick in my neck."

His gaze zeroed in on her rubbing. His palms itched. He could rub there better than she could. He rose, then remembered how dirty his hands were.

"I bet your bed is a lot bigger."

It was, yes. And it was *his* bed. She'd fit perfectly in it.

She blinked heavy, smiling eyes up at him. "I don't suppose that offer's still open?"

He couldn't remember what she was talking about, so he played it safe. "All my offers to you are still open." To take care of her, to make sure she didn't get lost, to fix her shower...oh, shit, as long as she didn't mean that offer to buy this house back. Could they not talk about kicking her out of this valley this morning?

"To carry me," she whispered, lifting her arms to him. "Through the roses to your house. I'd like that so much."

Of all his offers, it seemed by far the least practical. But then again, she *was* a musician. He lifted her, and her weight felt just right in his arms—something he could carry, but heavy enough that he knew she was worth the effort.

"Sorry," he muttered, as he saw his hands against her gray hoodie and yoga pants. "I'm getting you dirty."

"They'll wash." She wrapped her arms around his neck. "Am I hurting your arm?"

He shook his head. Nobody ever worried about whether he could take a little pain. With the five wild cousins, all of their elders had assumed they would tough it up when they got hurt. Sometimes, he had vague, sweet memories of his own mother's tenderness, but it was so long ago, and he'd been so young, that maybe he'd just dreamed those memories up.

"I'm pretty tough," he mentioned. He didn't usually have to point that out to people.

Her arms tightened around his neck as she tried to lift her weight off his arms. "Oh, no, I am?"

He tightened his hold. "The cut's on the outside, Bouclettes. I told you. I'm fine."

She searched his face, her arms still holding her weight off his.

He jostled her body gently. "I'm fine."

She relaxed slowly, watching his face, and as he failed to flinch, she slowly curled back into his chest, easing back toward that dreamy, sleepy state.

So he carried her between those last two rows of roses, from the house she'd stolen from him to his, in the soft dawn. She mostly snuggled into him, but once she stretched out an arm and let it trail over the rose petals, still wet with dew. When she brought her hand back, she drew the dew droplets down his cheek, a cool freshness against his morning stubble.

And she did fit absolutely perfectly in his bed. By the time he came back from washing his hands, she was already nearly asleep again, all the honey shades of her nestled into his white sheets. He sat on the edge of the bed, sneaking a caress of her hair and shoulder. Her eyes blinked open, and she reached for him, pulling him down with her and kissing his chest, her hands running with this dreamy softness over his arms, down to his wrists.

"I think you're in my dreams," she whispered.

He leaned over her, on a surge of hungry pleasure at the way his body now caged hers in his big bed. "What do you want me to do in your dreams?"

A sleepy, sleepy smile, as her lashes fell against her cheeks and her face lifted to him. "Growl like that," she murmured. "And do whatever you want."

So...he did.

***

It was going to be a tough day. Having to deal with rough men, and machines, and his grandfather, and probably his cousins, with all his shields torn wide open like that, so that anyone could see all his vulnerable spots at the slightest glance. Matt had to dig his hands into his back pockets to keep from folding his arms over those vulnerable spots so that he could at least cover them with *something*.

"I've got to go," he told Layla. "I need to get the crews started."

She nodded, dipping her Nutella-spread baguette in her milk and nibbling on it, a little chocolate smear on her upper lip.

"Are you coming down later?"

"I think I'll go see Tante Colette," she said, maybe adopting the use of "aunt" because she didn't know quite what else she should be calling her adoptive great-grandmother. "I'd like to get to know her better."

A smile eased his mouth involuntarily, and all his exposed insides felt just a little safer to be revealed like that. She really was just a profoundly nice, decent person, wasn't she? Interested in and respectful of her elders and kind to rough men who growled at her.

"Don't lock up," he said. And, in case that needed further explanation: "It's, ah, my valley."

Her smile lit her eyes and the whole kitchen, making those slate counters shine. "Nobody would dare steal from you?"

His fingers flexed against his back pockets. "Well. Except for you."

Her eyes laughed at him. It wasn't so bad having your heart all exposed with that kind of shimmering laughter falling down over it. That laughter felt so soft and sparkly it was like it belonged in some other life, some magic fairy tale life. It felt soft as rose petals. "You did manage to get me out of that house, didn't you? First step toward getting it back?"

Oh. She'd misunderstood what he thought she'd stolen. "You're, ah...welcome to stay here." *I...I might not mind so much letting you have a piece of my heart, if you'll take care of it.*

She gave him a searching look and then looked back at her baguette and Nutella, and...was she blushing a little bit?

God, it would help so much to fold his arms across his chest right now. But it would shut her out. He dug into his back pockets hard and offered her solid reasons. The things he was good at. "Here, I mean. In this house. My place is a lot more comfortable than Tante Colette's old house. Fully equipped. Everything works well."

A little smile on her face and a mischievous sideways glance that skimmed over his torso and lingered on his—crotch?—as if she almost made a joke, but she bit it back, whatever it was, and took a sip of milk.

His arms were going to break in two if he couldn't fold them across his chest soon. *No,* he snapped at himself. *I'm not going to do it. I'm not growling her away.*

Is this all a joke to her? All a game? Did she not understand what I just offered? Or did it just not have that much value to her? She wouldn't be the first woman who hadn't valued who he actually was. "Okay, I've got to go."

She got up suddenly from the stool and crossed to wrap her arms around his middle and press her face against his chest.

His own arms wrapped around her automatically in response.

Oh. Now that felt perfect. His arms folded, his heart shielded, but her shielded with it. Soft and sweet, this cushion of female body and curly hair. He stared down at those honey-brown curls.

"Can I tell you something?" she whispered.

A man had to be careful about what a woman might say to him, when she'd snuck her way into such a vulnerable spot close to his heart. But he couldn't say no, so he made a low sound that passed as yes.

"Promise you won't tell anybody," she whispered. "Please?"

"I won't tell." He petted a heavy hand over her hair.

She stood on tiptoe still, to bring her mouth closer to his ear, just to make sure no one else in this empty room could catch the breath of words. "I think I'm falling really hard for you."

He fell—just this strange, internal trip of his soul right over a rock it hadn't expected and then, *flip*, sailing, falling, down toward this great, great space that opened out below.

He didn't fall really hard, that was the strange thing. So big and so used to the solid hardness of the earth— he fell like floating.

Chapter 17

"Maybe I need therapy," Layla said, letting a few notes float from her fingers questioningly into the kitchen in which Colette Delatour, Allegra, and a previously unknown woman, Jolie, had gathered. It was nuts how much she felt like playing her guitar today. As if she had so many notes vibrating inside her, they'd drive her crazy with their buzzing if she didn't let them leak out.

"Okay. I'll make some dal," Jolie said. Newly married to Gabriel Delange, the famous chef at whose restaurant Layla and Matt had eaten the night before, she looked and even smelled like something sweet and buttery fresh out of the oven, her golden-brown hair pulled up in a ponytail.

"The soup's almost ready," Tante Colette said. Its scents of herbs and chicken broth filled the kitchen.

"The cookies are coming," Allegra said, busy blending butter and sugar with a wooden spoon. "Those are good therapy." She gave Layla a brightly inquisitive glance. "Why do you need therapy? I love pretending I'm a therapist."

"You can take some of the soup back with you for Matthieu, in case he needs therapy, too, right about now. He responds very well to being fed," Colette said, double-checking it on the stove.

"Does he?" Propped against the wall in one of the kitchen chairs, Layla smiled down at her guitar strings, sliding her fingers lower for a deep, deep bass, trying to nurse a growl out of that guitar. "You know, I've seen all kinds of homegrown therapy in my line of work—from mushrooms and marijuana to incense and yoga—and I think chocolate chip cookies and soup is my favorite. Reminds me of my mom and grandparents." With her grandmother, it had been more baklava and ma'amoul, but her mother had loved making chocolate chip cookies with her. Maybe Layla could get a phone today and call her mom. She hadn't talked to her since she'd drowned her own phone. Maybe Matt had WiFi she could hook up to and Skype.

If he didn't, he'd probably figure out a way to fix that for her. She smiled, caressing that deep bass sound.

"Your own choice of therapy seems like a good one, too." Colette nodded to her guitar.

Now it was Layla's turn to snort. "This isn't therapy, this is the *problem*. I'm always sticking my heart out there, bare-assed naked for everyone else to spank. I *hate* it."

"Oh, so that's why you do it," Colette said thoughtfully. "I've known some people like that. Who always do what they hate the most. It's a powerful force, masochism."

Okay, now she sounded as if she really did need therapy. "I don't hate it all the time," Layla admitted. "I mean, I love it when I'm doing it—writing the song, performing the song. It's afterward, when I realize how damn naked I am among a crowd of clothed people passing judgments on me, that I always...I don't know...wish I was better at keeping covered up." Maybe that was why she had started feeling so dried up, unable to produce.

Maybe you're just not getting enough fertilizer, the thought whispered through her brain. *Not giving yourself time to pull in enough nutrients and life between blooming periods.*

Like...those plants of Matt's. There's all this other stuff to them besides their blooms. Whole bushes of existence. If they tried to be all bloom, all year, they wouldn't be anything at all.

"Yes," Colette agreed matter-of-factly, stirring her soup. "The people who don't do things and don't take risks are always much safer than those who do."

Layla looked a moment at the old, old woman who had fought against terrible evil and snuck children across the Alps, and who had probably known plenty of people who ducked their heads and let it happen while they tried to keep safe.

It was kind of...strengthening, to know that this old Résistance hero identified her as one of the people who was willing to take risks. Although Layla strongly suspected that if she herself had had to live in this country during World War II, she would have crawled into a cave and curled up in a fetal position until it was all over. There was courage, and then there was...*courage.*

She wondered if there was any song in the world that could ever capture her great-grandmother and her adoptive great-grandmother and *that* kind of heart.

"Have you thought about stopping?" Jolie asked.

"Well...I came here to take a break," Layla said. To escape from pressure, but she was kind of embarrassed to say that in front of the adoptive great-grandmother whose idea of pressure was the Gestapo. "Sheltered by a valley, far from any media, no Internet—even surrounded by medieval walls." She gestured to the stone of the house to suggest the walls beyond. "And I still found a way to stick my heart out there naked." She frowned down at her guitar and slid her fingers back up to higher notes. "That's what I mean—I have a problem. Who does that to herself?"

Allegra tasted some of her own cookie dough. "Maybe you felt safe."

"Acting like a complete idiot over a guy I met three days ago?" Layla asked dryly. "That's safe?"

Allegra shrugged. "I hooked up with Raoul in less than an hour. I just had an instinct with him. I felt just right. And I went with it. And the two of them are kind of alike, you know. I mean, Matt's more a big grouchy bear while Raoul's a feral wolf, but they both have that big wannabe-the-strongest-toughest-most-invulnerable thing going on, and are all mushy inside it."

"I'm very fond of Matthieu," Colette agreed.

"You've got a funny way of showing it," Layla blurted out.

Everyone in the kitchen froze for a tiny second. Oops. Probably she wasn't supposed to challenge the ninety-six-year-old Resistance war hero.

"You gave part of his *valley* away," Layla said. "That's the most important thing in the world to him."

"It was my land," Colette said coolly and firmly, "given to me by *my* father. And I gave it to *my* great-granddaughter. Jacky might have a vision of family that excludes those of us who are step-children or adopted, but *I don't*."

Layla blinked a moment. The old woman had a way of speaking that made her want to shut her mouth and nod obediently.

"I get that," she finally said. Colette and Jean-Jacques Rosier must have had one hell of a fight once upon a time. "But...you hurt him."

"Nobody ever said life was painless," Colette said, faintly exasperated, as if the Greatest Generation was having a hard time with the later ones, yet again. But then a very faint smile curved Colette's lips. "Besides, I think I did him good."

Layla was beginning to see why Matt got that tear-his-hair-out look around the elders in this family sometimes.

"I really am very fond of Matthieu," Colette repeated. "He's got a very tender heart."

"I noticed." Layla smiled a little, with a hint of wistfulness. "That's why he keeps it covered all the time." She wished she knew how to keep her heart covered like that. When he let her put her head on his chest and closed his arms around her, she felt sheltered from all the fame in all the world. He hadn't said anything, when she whispered that she was falling for him. But his arms had tightened so strongly that a woman really felt he'd catch her before she got hurt.

216

"Well, you know. Four rough-and-tumble cousins and his grandfather and his crew to impress with his strength all the time," Allegra said, chopping chocolate into bits with a big butcher knife. She chattered on, apparently eager to distract the conversation from the head-butting between Colette and Layla: "And then he got really burned by that Nathalie Leclair. But—"

"Who's Nathalie Leclair?" Layla asked, sitting up.

"He dated her last year. Don't worry, it's been over for a while, but—"

"What, was she named after a supermodel?" Layla demanded, feeling just a tad acidic toward the other, unknown woman.

Allegra hesitated, searching her face. As if she was starting to realize she should have kept her mouth shut. "Nooo. The actual supermodel."

Layla gaped at her.

"It's the perfume industry," Allegra said. "These guys meet all kinds of famously beautiful and profoundly narcissistic people. It's very bad for them."

"Holy crap." Layla put a hand to her forehead, the guitar going silent in her lap. "*Nathalie Leclair?*"

Allegra grimaced apologetically.

"I've been throwing myself at a man who can have *Nathalie Leclair?*" All smugly confident, as if she could wind him around her little finger?

Oh, hell, and she'd felt so damn beautiful last night. Like the most beautiful woman in his world.

God, she'd told him she was falling for him. She'd petted his heart like it was *hers*.

"He didn't *want* Nathalie Leclair," Allegra said hastily. "He's the one who broke up with her."

"She was bad news," Jolie explained. "Gabe *hated* her. She wouldn't eat his desserts."

Allegra and Colette gave Jolie ironic looks.

"What?" Jolie flung out her hands. "It shows a very unhealthy attitude toward life!"

217

Allegra and Colette gave that some thought and then nodded judiciously, acknowledging Jolie's wisdom.

"Jesus." Layla dropped her hand from her forehead to press the fist of it against her mouth. "He could take her or leave her? *Nathalie Leclair?*"

She touched her own uncontrollably curly hair, and a vision of herself in her publicity photos flashed through her—that quirky face and the funky clothes that did just fine on the indie folk rock scene, but could hardly be called beautiful, except by her mother.

Well...and Matt. He had said she was gorgeous. Several times. As if he really meant it, too.

"She liked the idea of having a man who would do anything to solve her problems at her beck and call," Colette said with stern disapproval.

"But she likes messing with men, too," Jolie said. "I guess it reassures her to know she can. Not so good for the men, though."

"But...*I've* been messing with Matt," Layla said, both guilty and wounded. It had felt innocent and fun...and yes, empowering. Teasing him and seeing if she could make him blush.

Allegra shook her head, stirring her chocolate chips into the cookie batter. "You mess with him as if you like him and want to get him to come out and play with you. It's not the same thing at all."

"Does *he* know that, though?" Layla asked uneasily.

Colette lifted one old eyebrow, dishing up soup. "He seems to."

Yeah, she bet. Her own teasing must have looked so clumsy and unsophisticated, compared to what he was used to. "Who else has he dated?" she asked gloomily. "Gisele Bündchen? Angelina Jolie?"

"You know, I think you're taking this the wrong way," Allegra said. "We're not talking about possible rivals to you. We're just trying to let you know that Matt has layers and layers of reasons for trying to be the tough guy nobody messes with. It's still pretty obvious to anyone who knows him that Matt is falling like a brick for you."

Layla clutched her guitar to her torso. "It is?"

Allegra gave a sudden shout of laughter. "Oh, trust me. I *told* you it was going to be so cute to watch."

Colette gave a slow, slightly wicked, deeply approving smile as she set the bowl of soup on the table beside Layla. "I have to agree with that," she told Allegra. "It is rather *mignon*."

"He doesn't even seem to care that you're a musician," Allegra said. "And I could have sworn he would stay well away from anyone who spent her life performing for an audience, after Nathalie. Maybe it's only famous performers he wants to stay away from. You know, people caught up in what everyone else thinks of them."

"Famous?" Layla said uneasily. She snuck a glance at Tante Colette, whose lawyer had surely told her Layla's stage name. Not that her fame had even begun to approach Nathalie Leclair's. She only had the one big album. Semi-big. Indie folk rock big. One Grammy. That was nothing, compared to a supermodel of Nathalie's stature. She was hardly Lady Gaga.

Obviously if she were *that* famous, she'd have to tell Matt, give him a head's up, before she got more involved with him. But as it was…it wasn't that big a deal, was it? She'd told him she was a musician. The rest of it, this sudden focus of fans and media…it wasn't who she *was*.

So why would anyone else need to know about it? Particularly not *him*, the man who seemed to wind that kite slowly down until it could fold itself up and rest a little in the shelter of a valley, of a man, of…okay the kite metaphor was breaking down here. But…the man who let her just *be*, with no hint of fame to color what he thought of her or even what she thought of herself.

"Nathalie." Allegra shook her head. "I mean, trust me, she was bad news. You should get Damien talking about her sometime. He saw a lot of it."

"Damien gossips?" Layla asked, startled. Granted, he was the cousin she had the least read on, but that was because he was always so cool, contained, and saturnine. Kind of like James Bond. Or maybe Bagheera.

"It involves a lot of alcohol," Allegra said. "Whenever a few of them get together and get a little drunk, they like to try to solve the problems of the one who's missing. I believe Damien was starting to consider assassination as a possible method of solving Nathalie."

"She made Matt out to be the bad guy," Jolie said. "As a publicity stunt. To the whole freaking world."

"Before *that*, she would try to make him jealous for the slightest thing," Allegra said. "I was here researching while all this was going on. Like, say he relaxed enough at one of her fashion industry parties to actually have a conversation with someone, and in the group of people he was talking to, there was a female...in the next week, she'd make sure photographs of her with another man were all over the media, with captions like, 'Is Nat tired of slumming? Looking for a new man?'"

"Slumming?" Layla asked incredulously.

"Oh, yeah, she'd play up the farmer-peasant to her fragile, exquisite princess role all the time. And then, when he called it quits—broke it off with her—she started confronting him in public, and whatever photo the paparazzi caught that showed him looking the most frustrated or angry—that would be the photo they published. With her hinting at abuse like you wouldn't believe. It drove his family *livid*. And Matt, too, of course, but he couldn't do anything about it. The angrier it made him, the more it would play into media hands. You know how growly he is, how easy it would be to catch photos of him looking all big and out of temper."

"Rosier SA nearly lost the contracts for his roses over it," Colette said. "Since that spoiled brat is the face of the main Abbaye perfume that uses the absolute from those roses. That contract accounts for half the revenue those roses bring in."

"What a *bitch*," Layla said, furiously.

"And it hit him close to home here in terms of what people thought of him, too," Jolie said. "I mean, most people around here know him too well, you know? And they know the perfume industry, too, and how anything is good for a media blitz. But there are still people who look at him suspiciously, wondering if anything she hinted at might be true. It did *wonderful* things for her, of course—her name was everywhere, beautiful and brave, exactly the way she likes it. But Matt was always one of the pillars of the community here, the next Rosier patriarch, and it shook that."

"Don't get us wrong," Colette said. "Matthieu has always tried to play the tough, growling man and make sure nobody, most particularly not his cousins, tries to mess with him. But now he tries even harder to keep his heart covered."

Allegra smiled. "Until you. Of course, I guess you're not famous enough to draw more media down on him."

Layla pressed her fingers over her mouth. "Oh, my God," she said. "I've got to tell him."

***

"You know, of all your cousins, you're the last one I would have thought would choose the seduction method," Pépé said thoughtfully as Matt paused to flex his shoulders, toward the end of the afternoon. Pépé was back, refreshed from the nap he didn't like admitting he took after lunch. "But as long as it's working for you..."

This was one of those times when Matt liked to fold his arms across his chest when dealing with his family, but for some reason, his arms didn't want to cooperate. It was as if his muscles had gone all floppy. Or as if his heart was taking over, and that insane suicidal organ didn't *want* to hide behind a strong line of defenses.

It wanted to come out and play.

"I'm not trying to seduce that property out of her, Pépé." They stood near the truck by the fields, watching the field workers, the trailer bed filling with the sacks from the harvest. It was a good harvest this year. A

221

harvest that a family could have depended on, back in the old days, when this valley was truly the center of the family wealth and power and not just the symbol of it.

"It backfires, you know," Pépé warned. "If you seduce a woman and something goes wrong and she gets mad, she'll do the thing that will hurt you the most."

Matt thought about those slim, strong arms of hers trying to hold her weight off his, in case she was applying pressure to his wound. He looked down at the line of stitches that she'd insisted on re-wrapping with gauze even though, twenty-four hours out, there was really no need to keep them covered. "No, she won't."

"You don't think so?" That assessing blue gaze.

"She won't," Matt said quietly. It wasn't a question of his opinion. She just wouldn't.

His grandfather gave him a disgusted look. "So you didn't learn any lessons about women from that last girlfriend of yours?"

"Not any lessons that apply to Layla."

Sometimes his grandfather had a way of looking at him that made him feel as if he had an apple on his head, and his grandfather was deciding whether his aim was good enough to shoot it off to protect his valley. "You're sure about that?"

"Look, I know better than to get involved with someone famous now, Pépé. Layla...she's human, you know. Fame hasn't gotten into her brain and messed with who she is and how she relates to people the way it did Nathalie."

Pépé gave a frustrated shake of his head. "You're willing to risk the heart of this valley on some girl you like? How are you going to feel when one of her descendants sells that land to a hotel?"

"Maybe the same as I'd feel if one of my descendants sold some of this land to a hotel."

Pépé sent him a sharp, searching glance. Matt wished his arm muscles would start working. But instead of locking over his chest against that glance the way they were supposed to, his hands stayed in his back pockets, his chest wide-open and exposed to everyone around him.

It felt—big like that, his chest. It felt broad. It felt as if he could breathe deeply.

"I still say," Pépé said slowly, eyes keen on Matt, "that the land needs to be kept in the family. Of course, there *is* more than one way of doing that."

Oh, for God's sake. That's what a man got for letting his family get a glimpse of his heart: invasive curiosity and pressure about the most delicate and powerful feelings it held.

"I've only known her for four days, Pépé," Matt growled, turning away as Raoul came up through the fields. After fourteen years of harvests without Raoul, it was still strange to have him there so much. To be able to see how deeply Raoul wanted to be a part of this land again.

To have Matt's own heart feel open enough to allow him back in.

Matt took a deep breath. "I see you did a decent job without me yesterday," he allowed.

No sense getting effusive with praise, after all. There was "opening up" and then there was acting like an idiot. He wasn't some damn oyster on a half shell.

Raoul slanted him a dry glance. All Raoul's glances had a slightly feral gleam to them, ever since he'd headed off to Africa. A wildness that had gotten in him that could maybe never be entirely appeased, unless Allegra was there. "You don't know how relieved I am to hear that you approve."

Matt bit back a grin. See? At least *Raoul* didn't go forcing a man to expose his soft insides recklessly. He knew how to keep up a tough front. Knew the importance of it.

He sighed in relaxation, oddly reassured. Glad that to this day, all he and his cousins had to do to mend a rift was some version of punching each other on the shoulder.

Damien's car pulled in from the main road, and he got out and came up to them. Matt knew right away that something was wrong, maybe with some business deal for Rosier SA. Damien had that look on his face that he got whenever he might have to assassinate someone. Metaphorically speaking, of course.

At least, he was pretty sure Damien hadn't ever literally assassinated anyone.

Damien looked at them all for a moment, squinted briefly at the sky, and then handed Matt his phone.

Raoul made a sudden movement, as if to grab for it, before he stopped himself. "Damn it, Damien," he snapped. "I *told* you—" The supreme frustration of the eldest cousin whose younger cousins *still* weren't doing what he told them to do.

Matt looked down at the screen. It showed a celebrity website that was all too familiar to him after his stint with Nathalie Leclair. The photo was of him kissing Layla in jasmine the night before in Sainte-Mère, edited so that it looked as if a tragically beautiful victimized Nathalie was looking on. His mouth tightened. Was his stupidity in dating Nathalie going to taint his life forever? Were those damn sites still obsessed with his private life, even when he was dating a perfectly ordinary girl next door?

He looked at the caption: "Did the Beast find his Belle?"

Bastards. He glanced down at the article despite himself. "Seems as if Belle Woods has replaced Nathalie Leclair in her peasant's heart. We'll have to see if she handles the beast better..."

Matt lifted his head. Something began to ring in his ears, all the air in the valley pressing in tight to his head, squeezing his brain. "Who's Belle Woods?"

Damien sighed sharply, sent a reluctant glance toward Raoul who was frowning at Damien in stern disapproval, and then reached to swipe a thumb across the phone screen. Another web page appeared, this one of Layla in an elegant evening dress, clutching a little purse in front of her, and posing for the camera. *Belle Woods arrives for the Grammys.*

The valley was going to crush Matt's head. What the hell was going on?

"I thought—I thought she gave guitar lessons and bartended and played little gigs wherever she could find them." The words tasted all funny on his tongue, as if he'd been to the dentist and half his mouth was still numb. He'd thought she *needed* him. Hell, when she'd talked about bartending, he'd had to bite his tongue not to rush ahead and say, *I'll keep a roof over your head for you. I know how to do that.*

"Maybe she used to," Raoul said. "Damn it, Damien, I thought we agreed—"

"Somebody was going to tell him today," Damien said. "With those photos all over the web. I preferred to control the circumstances."

"She's been *lying* to me?" When he had thought she was trusting her whole self to him? That sweet, incredible trust, as if she knew he would be worthy of it?

She hadn't even thought he was good enough to know who she really was. She'd just been...what? Fooling around with the farmer boy for a few days? Getting her groove back?

"Maybe she's not mentioning the parts she doesn't want to talk about," Raoul said. "That's not the same as lying."

"In her defense," Damien pointed out, "I certainly don't tell people any truths about me when I've known them less than three days. Or thirty years."

The phone's screen cracked in Matt's hand.

"I'm sorry," Damien said low. His mouth was very grim. "I thought you needed to know, now that the media have found out."

Matt's head whipped up. "Wait. You knew before this?"

Damien grimaced, glanced at Raoul again, and looked away.

So Matt had been a fucking idiot, too, and all his cousins had known it.

Betrayal rushed at him, straight at that over-exposed heart, raking claws through that vulnerable organ. Rage soared up in defense, calling for back-up, trying to muster a defense before the betrayal ripped his heart out.

"Isn't that just like Colette to give a piece of this valley, the heart of this family, to some star as a toy?" Pépé said bitterly. He turned his dry, dark irony on Matt: "Still think you can trust it to a woman who's lying to you?"

"God damn it." Matt threw the damn phone across the field and strode off.

Chapter 18

Layla slowed her little van as she saw the dark-haired man waiting in front of the door of her little stone house, confused. That wasn't the right dark-haired man.

She got out and walked slowly toward Damien, lean and long and watching her quite grimly, as if he was gauging the best way to take her out.

"Can I help you?" she asked cautiously.

"I want to buy back this land," he said abruptly.

Oh. "I'm sorry," she said. "I think if I sell it, it needs to be to Matt."

Damien made a slashing motion of his hand. "It comes to the same thing."

"I don't think it does," Layla said slowly. "I mean, I wish it did, but it sounds as if you all haven't gotten that worked out yet."

"Better me than a hotel chain," Damien said. "Or some actor or rock star."

Layla frowned at his tone at the word "rock star" and searched his face. He looked back at her, face inscrutable.

"I wouldn't do that," Layla said. "I'm...I like Matthieu."

Gray-green eyes searched her face. "Do you." He didn't make it a question, as if he was too cool and acerbic to use the interrogative. He had to know all the answers without asking.

But she nodded anyway.

"The thing about Matt is, he's got a very soft heart," Damien said.

Happiness sparked in Layla. "It's funny how all of you seem to realize that, except for him."

"I don't have a soft heart," Damien said evenly, holding her eyes with his merciless gray-green ones. "I'm the mean one."

Hunh. Layla tilted her head. He certainly didn't *look* soft-hearted, all lean and cool and elegant, like some Hollywood embodiment of an assassin. But his lips pressed together exactly like Matt's did when he denied his own soft heart. "You guys are hilarious," she decided. "I bet you *all* try to say you're the mean one."

Damien's expression flickered. Just for a second, before he got that cool control over it, he looked completely taken aback. "I *am*," he insisted.

"No offense, but I'm pretty sure your great-aunt and your grandfather are the mean ones. I mean, they play *hard*. It must have been one hell of a crucible, the war."

Damien frowned at her.

She smiled at him.

"I know Creed," he said, of one of her producers.

"Oh, crap." She took a step back. "You're not going to tell him where to find me, are you? That *is* mean." Wait, to mention Creed, he definitely knew her performance name.

"And you know that contract Abbaye is negotiating with you to use your Grammy hit for their new perfume? I could change their mind about that."

Damn it, why did men always try to push the little female around? You'd think she hadn't been standing up for herself to strangers for pretty much her entire adolescence and adulthood. She channeled Matt and folded her arms. "Well, you *could*," she said. "If you want to be a bastard. I was a little worried about going too commercial anyway. But I'm still not selling this land to you instead of to Matt."

"How much do you want for it?"

She sighed. "Why do the money people always think they can put a price on people's hearts? How *do* your brains work?" She peered at Damien, trying to turn her eyes into an MRI scan and figure out what lobes lit up in his head that didn't light in hers. Or vice versa.

"I'd rather count on being able to outbid someone than on her heart," Damien said dryly.

"Oh." Layla's mouth drooped for him. "That's kind of sad."

Damien frowned at her.

"Well, it *is*. You need to work on that."

Damien ran a hand through his perfectly coiffed hair, looking just a little frazzled. Which was kind of a good look on him, to be honest. He should try it more often over the lean, elegant assassin look. "Look," he snapped. "If you sell this land out from under Matt, you're going to break his heart."

"Isn't that what you're asking me to do?" she asked, confused.

"I'm his *cousin*. It's not the same thing at all."

Layla peered at him. "Because he trusts you with it?"

"I wouldn't go that far," Damien said sardonically. "I'm not sure Matt trusts anyone with his heart. That's what he gets for having such a damn mushy one."

"Oh, yeah, right, I was forgetting yours was so adamantine," Layla said mildly.

Damien raised an eyebrow at her, lethal and saturnine.

"You know, the next time they need a new James Bond, have you thought about trying out?"

His eyes narrowed in exasperation, but the corners of his lips twitched before he could catch them, and a little leap of laughter gleamed green in his eyes.

"Look, don't worry," Layla said quietly. "I'm happy here, but...I know I need to give it back to him, okay? I promise it's safe with me. I know you guys have his back, but I'll try to take care of his...front." She rested her hand over her own front, right over her heart, before she realized it.

"Will you?" Damien asked, and for once he let it be an actual question. His eyes searched her face.

Layla nodded solemnly. "I promise," she said. "I really will."

"What if the two of you have a fight?" Damien asked. "What if he yells at you, and breaks up with you, and you want to hurt him back?"

Layla hesitated. "You say that as if you're expecting it to happen."

Damien grimaced. "You probably should have told him who you were."

Her arms folded back over her chest, her heart sinking. "I gather you took care of that little oversight for me?"

"Oversight?"

She hunched into her arms, not answering. *Break up with her? Like he'd broken up so easily with his top model when things went wrong?*

"He's pretty pissed off," Damien said. "He's not going to handle this well, Layla."

"All right," Layla said, but her heart sank more and more. "I don't expect him to be perfect." But she'd felt...safe with him. Emotionally. Not like he would *dump* her, even if he got pissed off.

Damien held out his hand to her, handshake style. "You promise you won't sell it out from under him in a temper?"

Right. Whatever happened, even if it hurt, she did understand at least right this moment that she couldn't do that. Good idea to commit to it, while her feelings were still unhurt and less likely to lead her off the ethical path. Layla put her hand in his. "I promise."

Damien shook it once, firmly. "This is important, Layla. Belle."

"Yes." Layla looked wistfully at her little house with its roses climbing over the door. Too important for her to play with, no matter how much she liked it here and no matter how much it filled her with song. It sounded as if Matt would never be able to relax, deep down, and trust her, as long as she could steal away his heart like this— sell it to someone else. "I've got it."

When Damien left, she picked up her guitar and walked down the long rows of roses to Matt's house to wait for him on his doorstep.

***

The later the evening grew, the more anxious Layla grew. How mad was Matt, exactly? Was Damien right, that he might break up with her? Was everything really shattered by her own efforts to be someone other than a fulfillment of expectations?

I think I'm falling really hard for you. The last words she'd spoken to him, in some kind of blithe, arrogant dream that he must feel the same for her. That this evening was going to be like last evening, and tomorrow was going to be more of the same.

She should have told him the truth.

It hadn't really felt like telling him a lie, though. It had just felt like...being herself. Taking time away from everything people wanted her to be and...being her.

Her stomach knotted more and more, the longer she had to wait, and she got out her guitar and sat on the stone step in front of his house, playing the guitar the same way a child might hold a silkie for reassurance.

Wish for me
On a falling star
No matter where you are
Look for me

It soothed her a little, to try to make a song out of this. She brooded over the guitar.

Wish for me
On a four leaf clover
Don't think it over

Just come and find me

Darkness was settling over the valley, shadows creeping toward her like anxieties that had snuck out of holes in the ground and out from behind trees, prowling towards her.

Wish for me
Just blow out your candles
I'm not too much to handle
Be a hero for me

The shadows nibbled at her toes and caressed fingers through her hair.

Wish for me
Toss your coin in the fountain
Come climb the glass mountain
Take three apples from me.

The shadows climbed up her legs, crawled down her arms, and he still hadn't come.

Wish for me
It's not too much to ask for
A man who will last for
Ever, dreaming of me

The notes died away. She bent her head.

That was...was that actually a halfway decent song? Did it have potential? She needed to record the rough version before she forgot it. If she had a phone, she could do that right now. If she had a phone, of course, she could have called Matt.

What did it mean, that he still wasn't here?

***

Matt went rock climbing. Up the limestone cliffs at the end of the valley, where he and his cousins had climbed so many times before, where they went when they needed to get away and needed to burn up a lot of frustration, to strive against a rock face into the blue above.

You couldn't stay enraged, rock climbing. You had to focus on the rock, on the next grip, on the muscles flexing you up, working that hurt and rage out. It was a good thing to make yourself do, before you faced the person you might lash out at with that rage.

He climbed to the top of the cliff and sat for a long time, gazing down at his valley. A few yards away, invisible from almost every angle, was the gap in the rock where Niccolò Rosario's heirlooms had once been hidden during the war. Pépé insisted Colette had stolen them, but Matt had a hard time imagining his aunt climbing up that face. Even with all those old photo albums to help him, his brain kept failing to envision her that fit and young.

His hand stroked over the phrase his grandfather had carved into the limestone, Niccolò Rosario's motto, adopted when Niccolò laid claim to this valley. *J'y suis, j'y reste.*

I am here and here I'll stay.

My valley, Niccolò had said, on behalf of all his descendants. Mine. We will hold this land against all comers: French kings, Italian mercenaries, German soldiers, perfume house accountants, time. We definitely, definitely won't weaken and give up part of it to some rock star who can't even tell the truth about who she is and clearly just came here to leave a great gaping hole in a man's heart when she ran back to New York.

Where he couldn't follow her to get it back, obviously, because...he was a valley.

I am here and here I'll stay.

I think I'm falling really hard for you.

With her head pressed against his chest, she had said that, so that nothing protected his heart from the words.

The sun was setting over his valley. He was going to have to have it out with her sometime, wasn't he? Face her again, with her betrayal like a knife right there where he'd lowered his arms to let her at his heart.

And he didn't want to. He didn't want to have this fight. He didn't want to defend his territory. He didn't want to drive her back and leave everything that mattered to him safe.

He didn't want to need to.

He'd wanted her to be a safe person to let in. A person he could trust.

He wished he could stay up here all night, but he couldn't. From the full moon above, a vague blur of his mother frowned down at him. *Matthieu Michel Laurent Rosier, what are you doing rock climbing in the dark?*

He always imagined how his mother would react based on the ways his cousins' mothers had acted when they got in trouble. He blurred it with memories of his grandmother's chiding of him to be safer, and with photos, and with a child's almost-memories of a lap and hugs, to try to come up with an approximation of a mother-in-the-moon. But he'd never really had that—the person who kissed his skinned knees. Who was tender with him.

He looked down at the stitches on his arm, remembering the graze of callused fingers as Layla re-wrapped it in gauze, remembering the strength of her arms around his neck, holding her weight off it to make sure it didn't hurt.

In the valley below, where his house was, a light clicked on as if someone had made herself at home inside it.

He stared at that light a long time, and then grimaced and reluctantly started to abseil down.

***

In the end, Layla was just a coward. She couldn't face the dark anymore, or her fear that Matt was going to leave her alone in it. She couldn't stand it, so she just took what she wanted.

Light and warmth and welcome.

She just went through that door he had left unlocked, to that space where he had said she was welcome to stay, and sought refuge there, locking the door against the dark outside.

Chapter 19

Not only was Matt's own door locked against him—that strange, alien gesture that kind of pierced his heart with how vulnerable and small Layla must feel in this world, compared to him—but an empty bowl of cereal sat in his sink, her guitar leaned against his biggest leather armchair, and she was sleeping in his bed.

Now how the hell was that fair?

He folded his arms over his chest.

That was just—that was outrageous, that was what that was.

She lied to him about who she was, she lured him in under false pretenses, she stole his heart—his *valley's* heart, he meant. His valley. And now, when a man had spent four hours climbing rocks to try to work his mad out and not yell at her, he came home to find her curled up in his bed, with his light on in his bathroom as if she'd been scared without it, and her arm over his pillow, as if it had substituted for a teddy-bear, and all that curly hair mushed and tangled across her face, and her lips faintly parted in sleep, and...

That was just cheating.

He growled about it, very softly, experimentally, but she didn't wake up, and he felt instantly guilty for adding any possible fear factors for a woman who had clearly gotten scared of the dark.

He felt guilty for not having *been* there, so she hadn't been scared of the dark.

She'd told him flat out that she'd been on her own in strange situations for a long time.

He was good at handling the kind of fears that came after a woman when she was alone in the dark. Those were the kind of fears he could punch in the nose. When he got done with those kind of fears, they whimpered back where they came from and never, ever messed with what was his to protect again.

He eased closer to the bed. It was late. She was very obviously sleepy. Maybe he could just skip this whole confrontation-over-lying part and, and...what? His heart winced at the options. Pretend she was telling him the truth? Pretend she was here forever?

She looked really good in his bed, damn it. She looked as if she should be there forever.

A curl had gotten caught against her parted lips. One of his hands worked its own way free of the protective fold of his arms and eased that curl away. Then the other curls, stroking them back, freeing her face. Her hair was so damn intensely curly that it felt a bit like parting the bramble bushes to get to the princess when he did that.

He glanced around, but there was definitely no one to see him be such a complete idiot, and because he *was* an idiot, clearly, he bent and snuck a little kiss of the sleeping princess.

She screamed, coming awake in a clawing, fighting roil.

"It's me!" He jumped back. Damn it. The whole damn prince thing never did work out for him. "Layla! It's me!"

"Oh, God." She stilled, blinking around in confusion. "Oh, I'm—here."

"Where did you think you were?" He made his voice gentle. Well, what? A man couldn't yell at a woman for lying to him when he'd just terrified her out of her mind. He was *not* being a softie or a pushover. It could wait one minute, until she calmed down.

"I don't know." She pushed a hand across her face as if to clear her vision. "My old room back at my mom's, maybe. You know how you wake so disoriented when you're in a new place and your mind still expects to wake up in an old place."

No. He wasn't that familiar with that sensation, in fact. He mostly woke up right here. "You still live with your mom?" he asked, distracted by his own curiosity.

"When I'm not touring. I used to not be able to afford my own place. Impractical musician," she added wryly.

Anger flicked him again. He opened his mouth to bring up the lying—and she launched herself abruptly across the bed into his arms.

They folded around her automatically.

She clutched his shirt and tried to bury herself in him, shivering. "You scared the hell out of me," she whispered.

Yeah, he did seem to have a knack for doing that. He spread his hand wide over her bare arms, rubbing gently. Hell, she was sleeping in one of his T-shirts.

Aww, *hell.*

That made him feel so damn...mushy.

Also, to be honest, rather aroused.

Damn it, it was not fair for her to be that cute. How the hell was a man supposed to deal with that?

"I think you gave me a bloody nose," he said.

She looked up at him quickly, in credulous guilt. "I did not!" she realized in instant relief. And then, "Oh, crap, I did scratch you, though." Her fingers stroked over his cheek.

The touch, gentle and apologetic, eased through him somehow, from that burning streak across his cheek down toward his chest and into his heart. "It's okay," he said softly. "You didn't mean to hurt me, did you?"

"Of course not!" she said, horrified at the idea.

No. Of course not.

"I was just scared," she said. "I didn't know who you were yet."

"Right." He stroked his hands up and down her arms.

"Just some stranger in the dark when I was out here all alone, you know?"

"No." He didn't know. He'd never been afraid of strangers in the dark. But with her in his arms like this, their size difference was so obvious that he could kind of understand. He sure as hell wouldn't like to be the small one in this scenario, with nothing to keep her safe but the morals and decency of a stranger she couldn't control. He wouldn't like to be the one exposed to the world's mercy or lack of it.

"Bouclettes," he said very gently, adjusting his arms to cradle her as completely as he could. "Is there something you should tell me about your music career?"

She went very still. And then her head slumped. Right against his chest. She didn't say anything at all, but she wrapped her arms around him and held on, like she didn't mean for him to let her go.

He liked that so much that instead of growling at her, he found himself petting her hair. This was pathetic. How could a man expect to protect himself if he couldn't even stay properly mad over being lied to? "Damien told me. There are pictures of us all over the web."

She lifted her head, blinking. "Of *us*?"

"'Did Belle Find Her Beast?' You know, the usual." He shrugged as if he didn't give a crap about that kind of thing. Which he almost didn't. Obviously, he wouldn't mind punching a few people who wrote copy for those sites or possibly some paparazzi, but that didn't count as giving a crap, did it?

"The usual?" she said blankly. "I've never been on a celebrity gossip site before except once when there was a red carpet shot of me for the Grammys."

"Well, there you go," he said very dryly. "I've upped your visibility."

"Because you dated *Nathalie Leclair*." She sat abruptly away from his body, shaking his arms loose to scowl at him. "You could have warned me about that!"

His jaw dropped. "Now how the hell was I supposed to warn you when I didn't even know who you really were? It wouldn't have been an issue if you were just *Layla Dubois*. Besides, when was I supposed to mention it? 'God, it's so much nicer eating in this restaurant with you than with her'? That would have gone over well."

She shoved away from him so hard she hit the headboard and made him wince at the impact on her. "You took her to the same restaurant?"

"See?" He opened his palms. "I *told* you it wouldn't go over well." And he was a damn idiot for proving his own point, too. He should have kept his mouth shut on that one. "It's the best restaurant in the area," he said. "One of the best in the world. *She* wouldn't put up with anything less, and *you* deserved the best I could give you."

Her lips parted. She hugged her knees to her chest. "Oh," she said very softly, as if he'd said something right.

Wait a damn minute. How had he ended up being the person in the wrong here, trying to work his way back into being in the right? She'd *lied* to him. "You—"

"Did you make love to her in the same place, too?" Her mouth had gone very sulky. She tightened her hold on her knees.

Well...he glanced down at his bed and back up at her. She looked like a woman who was never going to let him get her naked again. Damn it. Date one damn supermodel in your life and the consequences pursued you forever. "This is a *really* terrible subject of conversation. Let's talk about you lying to me instead." *Let's talk about this trip to New York you have in three weeks, and whether you're coming back here after it.*

"I didn't lie to you!"

His teeth snapped together. "Layla. You didn't even tell me who you really are."

"Yes, I did. I didn't tell you the name I use when I perform, but I definitely told you who I really am. That's who you make me feel like—me."

Well...hell.

His heart had gone so mushy it was pretty much liquid, dripping in some stupid mess through his fingers, impossible to keep together. This was completely and utterly unfair. "Layla," he said helplessly.

"Does she make love better than me?" she asked mutinously.

Oh, for God's sake. He shoved up from the bed. "Layla," he said between his teeth.

"I can't believe I told you I was falling for you." She dragged her hands through her hair until fistfuls of it were clenched over her face, hiding it while she yanked at her own curls. "I'm such an *idiot*."

"No." He came back to her immediately, sitting on the edge of the bed and putting his arm around that balled-up body. "Don't say that, Bouclettes. Not—not for that."

She peeked through her hands, wistful and uncertain.

Damn it. He wasn't even entirely sure he had any heart left in him, it had gotten so mushy. He quite suspected it was being crushed in two strong guitarist's fists along with handfuls of curls. Why couldn't he defend himself against her? Growl her back? Stand his ground? Keep his heart safe? Point out, at the very least, that the last thing he needed was crap over someone he had dated six months before he even met her?

"Not for that," he repeated softly, stroking her hair, trying to ease some of the poor curls free of her fists. She had one hell of a grip.

Her mouth trembled. Subtly, with the shifting of a couple of centimeters, she snuck a little deeper into the hold of his arm. "I'm sorry I didn't tell you," she whispered. "I just...wanted to pretend it wasn't true. That there were no expectations, nothing for me to fail, nobody wanting anything from me. That I was just me again. Just me and you. And that it wasn't a *just*, you know? That *me,* without music, was still a huge, wonderful thing to be."

Hell. He cuddled her. His heart lacked backbone, that was its problem. It couldn't stand up for itself against this kind of treatment. *You make me feel huge and wonderful, too,* he wanted to say to her, with his squeezing arms.

She looked up at him again, something sparkly shimmering in her lashes. "You made me feel as if I wasn't pretending. As if I really was...me."

Damn it, he gave up. No, seriously, he just flat out surrendered. A man couldn't fight this kind of battle. She won.

He kissed her, having no arguments left in him at all, just that need to part her lips with his, to blur that intimate space of their bodies together, gently at first, and then with more hunger.

He eased her back on the bed as her body softened to him, her guard lowering.

She turned her head into his throat. "You smell of roses," she whispered. "And..." This delicate searching breath against his skin as she tried to figure it out.

"Limestone," he said. "Dirt. Sweat."

"All these you smells. I like them."

He drew a breath of pure wonder, stroking his hand down over her body in his T-shirt. All the shapes of her— slimness and curves, muscles and softness. It made his body seem kind of boringly, stubbornly just-plain-hard in contrast.

It made his body feel really, really strong.

"Belle." He found one of her wrists and rubbed his calluses very delicately against the inside of it, watching her face as she shivered and her eyes closed. "I like it. It suits you." He could imagine her as a dream-filled, clueless teenager wanting to be *Belle* and taking the name of a fairy-tale princess to perform.

"It's what Layla means," she explained, a little embarrassed. "And with the French language from both sides, I thought...well. I mean, I had to use something besides my real name when I first started posting covers on YouTube, back when I was sixteen."

"Of course, now the media are having a field day with the Belle and the Beast thing."

"The media never get anything right." She sighed. "Although I guess a big, grumpy bear is a kind of beast."

Hey. "A big, grumpy bear?"

She smiled at him.

So he kissed her again, lowering his body so that he could slide his length against hers, feel her breasts rub against his chest, his thigh flex against her leg, his erection rub against the inside of her thigh.

"So in that story about when that bear found that curly-haired girl in his bed, which version of the fairy tale are we doing?" he asked, threading his fingers through her curls on his pillow as he braced his forearms to either side of her. "The one where he eats her all up, or the one where she runs away?"

"Definitely not the one where she runs away," Layla whispered, wrapping her arms around his shoulders. "Please?"

So he had a say in that? Whether she ran away? That wasn't somehow a given, an aspect to her career and growing fame? His breathing grew deeper as his chest eased, as his hunger felt freer and freer to grow big and play. "So I get to eat you all up?"

She bit her own smile. In the light from the bathroom, her eyes glimmered with excitement and arousal and maybe a last hint of the tears that had almost fallen a moment before. "I might be hungry, too," she murmured. "I only had cereal for supper, after all."

"Yeah?" He dragged his body gently up and down hers, a few centimeters back and forth, rocking himself against all the right places. "Something you want to bite, Bouclettes?"

"Oh, maybe...this." She curled a hand over his upper arm, running her thumb over the curve of his biceps.

"Mmm." The sound vibrated deep in his throat. "Go ahead."

"Or...definitely this." She lifted her other hand to his face, tugging on his lower lip. He caught her thumb, sucking it into his mouth, holding it with his teeth as he teased the tip of it with his tongue.

Her eyes grew dreamy, and her hips rocked up against his in slow, almost sleepy motion. Desire surged through him.

"Making love to you is like...like swimming in gold, or something," he said. "You're just so damn sexy."

Her face crinkled with pleasure. "Gold is sexy?" she challenged, despite that pleasure, a natural word-splitter.

"You're the songwriter. You find a better comparison."

"It's like swimming in rose petals," she murmured, stroking both her hands down his arms. "It's better. It's like being lost in you."

Damn, she had a way of finding words that reached right to his heart. The way the calluses of her left hand scraping over his right arm sank into his heart, too, and the way she teased him and the way she smiled at him and...

He took her left hand from his arm, holding it against the bed so that he could run his thumb over the calluses on the tips of her fingers. "You worked your hand to death to get it this strong, didn't you?" he murmured, and lifted it to run her calluses over his lips.

"You like them?" She sounded puzzled.

"They're sexy as hell."

"Well, *yours* are, but..." She trailed off, confused by her own statement perhaps.

"Yeah," he said. "Yours are, too."

The sexiness of someone who tried hard for what she wanted, who kept at that work every day no matter how much her fingers ached, who gave it her all.

He kissed her again, wanting that persistence and that dedication for himself, too. *Don't leave. Stick with me, too. I know I'm a pain, but...persist with me.* She made a little humming sound and dragged her hands down over his back. He flexed into the touch. "Harder," he whispered. "Give me more of what you can do."

Her eyes glinted, and she slid her hands all the way to his butt and dug those fingers in.

Ow. Yeah. "Yeah," he said out loud, guttural. "Yes, just like that."

"I bet I can grip something else hard," she murmured, with that glint of sexy mischief. "And maybe play some calluses over it. See what sounds I can get out of you."

"Oh, holy fuck," he whispered. "Yeah. Please."

She found the button of his jeans and undid it, and his breath hissed between his teeth.

"We'd better slow down." He grabbed her hands, pressing them to his stomach. "I was making love to you."

She laughed. "We can do it at the same time. Make love to each other."

"I'll lose my concentration." He touched his forehead to her cleavage and then rubbed his face sideways until he could press a kiss to her nipple through the shirt and bra. "Or rather, I'll only be able to concentrate on that one spot. We can't have that, can we?"

He'd much rather give her the kind of experience in his bed that kept her coming back for more.

Persisting.

Giving it her all.

She took advantage of his loosened jeans to slide her hands over his back and slip them in under his briefs. And squeeze again with those strong fingers.

"Shit, that feels good." He found the catch of her bra under her shirt and pushed both bra and shirt off together. He loved getting her clothes off. When her breasts were revealed, it was like discovering buried treasure. Again. Coming back to his special treasure spot and discovering it was all still there, all for him. He cupped one breast with delight, rubbing his thumb over her nipple, which perked up for him immediately. Damn, that was beautiful. Her arousal, her response.

His own arousal wasn't so beautiful. It was hard and greedy. But he enjoyed it with everything in him.

Stroking her, kissing her, feeling the hunger in his body, watching her grow more and more yielding, more and more wanting, even as her hands pulled at his body, fighting him for more.

Oh, yeah. Yeah. He let the weight of his hips press into her, capturing her mouth again with his, sinking into the scent and texture of her. Yeah. This was a far better way to spend the night than arguing.

Also, if a man was falling, the curves of her body felt like a really nice, soft place to land.

Chapter 20

"Layla!" Her mom's delighted voice on Matt's borrowed cell phone made Layla's whole body relax with comfort and happiness.

She felt young again when she talked to her mom. Safe. Happy. Like the old days, when being a fluttering yellow kite high up on the end of a string was a little girl's dream come true.

In some ways, it was like talking to Matt—the sense of security and the happiness. And in some ways it was completely different. Matt made her feel...adult. Like she should plant her feet against the ground and stand, let her roots sink in. Grow. It was time to grow.

"I was wondering when you were going to call, sweetheart. Didn't your tour end last week? Did you go check out that land?"

Layla sat on a great flat rock tucked under a cypress on the hill behind her little house and Matt's, reached by a ten-minute walk up a root-ridden trail through the pines. From it, she could see all the valley: the stretch of roses, the rooftops of the little village and the steeple of the church at the far end, the limestone cliffs rising at the other end, and the slopes patched with lavender fields and small vineyards and silvery olives rising on the other side. "It's beautiful here, Mama. It's like...it's like living in a song. Or a painting. You'd love it."

"Maybe I can come join you there for a couple of weeks!" her mother exclaimed happily. "Wouldn't that be fun, sweetheart? A vacation in the south of France together? I turned in my final exam grades yesterday, and I've got the usual round of end-of-semester meetings and workshops this week, but after that..."

Layla pulled her grip exerciser out of her pocket and worked it absently, with restless fingers. "I don't know if I can stay."

"More concerts?" her mother asked, her voice somewhere between happy for her daughter's success and concerned. She'd been the one person in whom Layla had confided how stressed she was getting over the touring and pressure, how she couldn't find a song anywhere in her, how she was starting to break down.

I can't do this, Layla had sobbed to her on the phone only a month ago, in a moment of crisis. *I think I've slept twenty hours in the past week. Concerts and interviews and always on to the next town and I CAN'T WRITE. I don't have any more songs, Mama. I think maybe I killed them.*

"Nooo. I'm due in the studio in two and a half weeks."

"So you've got some material?" her mother said, delighted. And then a little sad: "I miss hearing you around the house, working on your songs. I don't even know what you're doing on this next album. But I know it will be fantastic, sweetie."

"I've got...the beginnings of material," Layla said. Her stomach knotted at the thought of trying to turn it into a full-fledged album in only two and a half weeks. All her joy and excitement in the burgeoning of new songs got crushed like a shiny sheet of aluminum in a tight fist. She took a deep breath, using the stress relief techniques that she'd been trying to acquire in the past year, ever since her career had turned from this happy, dreaming thing into this ambitious, successful monster that ate her up like a juicy peach and forgot to spit the stone out so she had even a hope of re-growing. "This is a great place to work," she said.

And it was. Remembering that made her smile a little, despite the visceral force of the memory of all those expectations.

It was a good place to work, but it wasn't a good place to be temporary. As if the water and the nutrients were buried deep in the soil. You had to sink your roots in properly, to get it all.

The thought of sinking roots in deep again eased that crumpled aluminum ball of stress even more, made it feel less permanently crumpled, less metallic...maybe more like crumpled silk that could eventually be smoothed out again. If she let it. If she gave it enough time to relax.

"Then maybe you should stay and work there," her mother said quietly. "Layla, sweetie. There's no point reaching your dreams if you yourself are no longer around to enjoy them. If you can't be happy, if you're losing who you are..."

"I want to be able to write, Mama," she whispered. "It's like if I can't, then...I'm not me."

Except...it was exactly as she had told Matt: when she was flirting with him, when she was sinking her hands into the incredible sensory overload of those sacks of roses, she rarely thought about whether or not she was producing songs at all. That absence of pressure to produce was so...innocent. Like she had been only a year ago, writing so many songs because her life was so full, and that was the only way she knew how to process it. Not as if writing songs was her *only reason for being*, but more as if it was just her *way* of being. Pulling life into her and letting it come back out as song.

"Then stay there longer," her mother said firmly. "Call your producers. Postpone. If you can't produce well under this kind of pressure, with this kind of deadline, then *drop the deadline*."

"Mom. I was lucky to land Creed and Sonny. If they decide I'm an unreliable one-hit wonder, trust me, they have other people lined up begging them to produce them."

"Well, you know what, honey? There are other producers out there, too."

Maybe. But Creed and Sonny were the best, and everyone knew it, too. It would make an enormous difference to the potential success of her next album to have them behind her, as opposed to a lesser-known producer. And her *songs* would be better, too. Creed and Sonny knew how to respect what she was trying to do, her own artistic integrity, and yet catch what would enhance that music, make it stronger, more impactful, more compelling to the listener. A producer who could do all that, who could *really* do all that and do it superbly, was very hard to find.

Still...she gazed out over that beautiful valley. Her fingers eased off the grip exerciser and she ran them instead over the grain of the rock. Took a deep breath of the scent of pines. Spotted a dark head among the roses, heard maybe the faintest distant rumble of a bass call over the fields.

"The thing is, Mama," she said slowly, reluctantly. "I don't think I can keep this place here. I think I'm being a bad person, not to give it back."

"Why is that, honey?"

Layla tried to stay discreet, but maybe she ended up telling her perceptive mom more than she realized, as she explained—about the Rosiers, and Matt, and Colette Delatour, and this valley. How it was the heart of a family. How it was his heart. And that heart wasn't hers to *take*. Wasn't hers to *steal*. It was only hers if it was given.

"It was given," her mother said. Her voice had tightened a little. "It's a heritage that came to you through your father, clearly."

"No, but...by the person it *belongs* to." How to explain? That her having part of this valley left this worry in Matt's heart, and he couldn't trust her, he couldn't entirely let his guard down, because her owning this land made him feel so vulnerable in who he was.

"That's not the way the law works, Layla. The person it *belongs to* did give it to you. Everything else is someone else's delusions."

Layla frowned. It wasn't like her mother not to understand her.

Except, of course, when they were talking about men. Her mother had *never* approved of Layla giving anything up for a man.

Divorced with a two-year-old, her cheerful, determined mother had been glad of her career and of her parents' support, perhaps, and never inclined to depend on a man again.

"Mama. It *matters* to him more than it does to me."

"A few acres of land matter more to him than your *music* does to you? Than being able to write songs again?"

Layla rubbed her fingers over the rock uneasily.

"Don't give yourself up for a man, sweetie. Don't do that. Your heart and your dreams and your success are not less important than his."

She flexed her fingers one by one into her palm, until her whole fist had tightened. "It's not like that, Mama. It's who he *is*."

Flat silence on the other end. Her mother didn't have to say a word.

Layla scrubbed her hand over her jeans now, retracting it from the rock. Jeans she could take with her, wherever she went. A rock stayed in the valley. "I can write my music anywhere."

"Clearly you can't, Layla. That's what you've been telling me for the past six months."

Layla spread her fingers on her knee and stared at them. "I always used to be able to."

"Maybe you've been wandering too long, and you need to take root," her mother said.

Suddenly, inexplicably, Layla's eyes filled with tears. It was that word *root*. It made her want to sink and sink long reaching strands of her soul down into the ground and go as deep as she could. It made her want to come down out of those high winds, battering her kite. It made her want Matthieu. Just to press herself up against that big body and close her eyes while his arms folded around her, until the world was all gone.

"Mama, you're not helping."

"Just because I don't agree with a choice you want to make doesn't mean I'm not helping, sweetheart. Remember when you wanted to tattoo your first boyfriend's name on your arm when you were thirteen? Do you remember his name now?"

That was a low blow. "We only went out a few weeks!" Then the "boyfriend" had started wanting to get too hot and heavy, and Layla had not felt in the least ready, and she'd stopped seeing him and written one of her early experiments in heart-broken lyrics. A song that sounded absolutely ridiculous to her now.

It ought to be illegal for a mother's silence to be so expressive through a trans-Atlantic cell phone connection.

"I'm trying to do the right thing!"

"Do the right thing by you," her mother said unequivocally. "First."

Layla knuckled her hand into her knee.

"Let me put it this way, honey. If any man other than this Matthieu wanted you to give up that land—if, say, he was some short, balding Frenchman in his sixties with a taste for wearing berets—would you be tempted?"

Well...no. Layla frowned at her mother through the phone.

"I saw the pictures on the web," her mother said.

"Mom! I told you to take that Google Alert off my name!"

"Somebody emailed me a link. I know he's a hot guy. I know you like him enough to kiss him out in public and not even notice someone with a camera. But, honey...put your music first. That's who you are."

Layla flexed her toes, trying to grip the rock through her shoes.

Her mother's voice softened. "Well, that and my daughter. Your grandparents' granddaughter. You. We miss you, sweetie. If you decide to give it all up and become an astronaut instead, like you wanted to be when you were nine, or a gymnast, or a schoolteacher, or a pet sitter, or even a cat, like you wanted to be when you were three...any of those other yous you ever dreamed of...we'll still love you. And you'll still be you."

So that Layla was hugging her knees, crying a little from an overfull heart, when she hung up.

She might not have the roots Matthieu did, but thank God she had a mom.

***

"You planned this, didn't you?" Matt asked Tante Colette, setting the dusty chest from the attic down on her parlor floor with something of a huff. The thing was heavy, even for him, after the attic ladder and three flights of stairs.

She smiled at him. "Plan to ask you to get that chest down for me? I wouldn't say you specifically. Any of you boys would have done."

"Layla," Matt said. "Me. You took one look at her photo or something and said, 'There's someone who can wrap him around her little finger.'"

And to be honest, he still felt kind of ridiculous to be wrapped around a little finger. Not ridiculous enough to unwrap himself, but still...

That secret, deep smile of Tante Colette's that meant she was never going to tell him everything. "I was worried about her," Tante Colette said. "I'm responsible for Élise's descendants. It's for my sake she's not around to look out for them herself. And Layla seemed so...out there. No grounding at all. Did you listen to that album of hers? All wandering and rootlessness and 'I'm footless and fancy free'? What way is that to live? Next thing you know, she would have been doing drugs like all those other rock stars."

"So what am I supposed to do, hold her down?" Matt asked grimly. Put all the weight of the valley onto that pretty kite's string and trap her the same way it trapped him?

Colette just gave him one of her gentler smiles, struggling with the lock on the chest. "Give her roots. Look how hungry she is for them. She started trying to sink herself into the earth—into *you*—the second she got here."

Matt frowned at his aunt. "Did you give her my land as some kind of planting soil? Thanks a lot."

"First of all, Matthieu, it was *my* land. To give to whom I chose. And second of all, she's single, and there are five of you boys the right age for her, and four of you have persistently failed to find the right woman up until now." Matt liked the way his Tante Colette always used the number five, as if Lucien was still there. "I thought the odds were good that *one* of you would be her type."

Hey. Matt scowled. "Damien or Tristan?"

"If it worked out that way. I hadn't met her yet, Matthieu. Or seen how you reacted to her."

Heat touched his cheeks. But he said, "Damien or Tristan would probably be a better fit for her. They'd be able to fit in that world of celebrities and performers. Be better able to travel with her on tour." Well...actually Damien and Tristan both had a lot of responsibilities, themselves. Maybe the need to tour was a challenge for any couple to figure out.

Colette made that little moue of hers that said, *Kids these days. They have no brains but I'll try to be patient.* "Interesting, then, that she went for you. Almost as if she felt *you* fit best with her."

Matt smiled and gently brushed his aunt's hands aside to open the lock for her and lift the lid, revealing layers of women's clothes, laces and silks. So many old scents came off it—dust and cedar and hints of lavender water. The essence of a long life. He wanted to be like Tristan, and bury his head in that scent, take deep breaths of his aunt before she was gone from his life.

"Layla would love this," Matt said. And he thought, *She really would.* She wouldn't dismiss it or be impatient with it. She'd be delighted. Tante Colette was right. Layla had embraced everything he showed her, everything about his land, his family, himself, as if all of it was exactly the nutrient-rich earth she needed, in order to bloom.

Hey. That was...an interesting way to think about it.

She needed him? In order to flourish?

It was probably utterly ridiculous to actually like the idea of being planting soil, but...he'd always been good at that. Solidity. Dirt. Growing things. It made it seem as if she needed him for exactly who he was.

"I do have something I think Layla would like," Colette murmured, reaching into the folds of clothes. "A good thing to pass on to a great-granddaughter."

"Is it something of Élise Dubois's? You made her cry with those stories."

"She's got a soft heart." Colette focused on the chest. "She might need someone else to take care of it for her."

Matt smiled involuntarily. People rarely remembered this about him, but he was actually pretty good at taking care of soft, delicate things.

Colette glanced up at him, her smile a touch ironic but not in a mean way. "You like it? When she buries her head in your chest?"

"Yeah," Matt said, embarrassed. It made him feel...strong. As if he could fix her problems just by existing. As if she trusted him with her weaknesses.

Colette shook her head, a little amused, a little rueful, and focused back on the chest. "I do have some things of Élise's to pass on to her descendants."

Wait—what? Descendants? Had she just used the plural?

"Humble things, really, that were precious to her. Sentimental value only. Remember, Élise's father worked in our factories and her mother worked our fields, so hers wasn't a family of means. She was the first in her family to become a schoolteacher, to 'make it', so she didn't have the kind of accumulation of things and land the Rosiers did."

"Layla will like them," Matt said quietly. He knew that about her already. She respected what others offered her. She challenged his grandfather because his grandfather loved the challenge, and she bent her head over photos with Tante Colette, and when a man handed her a rose, she almost cried.

A man could trust a woman like that with what he had to offer. Himself.

It was funny, because she told this story about herself as the wanderer who was hard to hold, who didn't want any demands on her, and it wasn't even true. That story was more like her defense mechanism. Her response, maybe, to being the daughter of a father who had wandered off on her when she was two and a mother who had herself fled a war-torn country when she was nine with only what she and her parents could fit in a small suitcase. Hell, maybe her "I am a wandering minstrel" story was like the way he folded his arms and growled so people would quit the hell telling him he had a damn mushy heart.

Which he totally didn't.

But Layla did. She cared, and she needed someone to hold her—to give her roots. Maybe she was almost starting to trust him for that job.

"But this is something from my side of the family." Colette withdrew a pair of stockings from the chest—the kind of thing that would have been precious back in the war, when women had had to paint on fake stockings. She unrolled one of the stockings and shook it. Something metal slid out, followed by a chain that slithered down into her palm.

Matt gazed at it. The gold chain had curled on top of some kind of pendant. Through the chain, he could make out enamel on an oval about the size of a small coin. Enamel that seemed to depict a...his breath caught. "Tante Colette. Is that...the seal?" The family seal, the

256

patriarchal seal, the symbol of power over his valley, of the head of the family. "*J'y suis, j'y reste?*"

"Niccolò didn't put *J'y suis, j'y reste* on his seal," Tante Colette said and slid the pendant into his palm.

"What?" Her words made so little sense that Matt couldn't even look at the precious pendant yet. He had to stare at her to make sure she wasn't finally going into dementia.

"Your grandfather really took to that motto, when we were fighting the Germans. Carved it on those cliffs. *I am here and here I'll stay.* 'You can't budge *me.*' But the only place Niccolò himself ever used it, that we know of, was here."

She shook another stocking, and a gold ring slid into her palm. Real gold, but simple, no jewels, only a twining rose symbol. *The wedding ring,* Matt thought with a shock. That simple ring that must have been all Niccolò could afford, when he first married Laurianne. "Tante Colette, you *did* take all those heirlooms. Pépé was right."

"They're mine as much as his," Colette said flatly. She angled the ring so that he could make out the inscription on the inside. *J'y suis, j'y reste.*

Matt took it from her. Everything inside him hushed. Four hundred years ago, his rough, dangerous, mercenary ancestor out of Italy had sworn his fate to such a little, little hand. He could barely squeeze it on the tip of his pinky.

"He was talking to her," Colette said quietly. "When he said that. Not making a vow on behalf of all his descendants to tie them to some chunk of land. *He* was making a promise to *her,* his ring on her finger: *I am here and here I'll stay.*"

It moved him so much, so suddenly, that his eyes stung, and he took a quick breath to get *that* under control, since he would never live it down if he let it show.

Colette watched him a moment, letting him look at the ring, and then eased it out of his hand. "This one's not for you, Matthieu," she said quietly. "I hope you understand. I think one of your cousins will need it more."

He wished they could give it to Lucien. Just hand it to their long-lost cousin like a weight, like a vow, like a thing that reeled him home and anchored him here: *J'y suis, j'y reste. It's the person that matters, not who your father was.*

Niccolò had been illegitimate, too.

"The seal Niccolò created," Colette said, after she'd hidden the ring away again, "says something completely different."

Matt looked down at it again in his left palm. With his thumb, he stroked the chain away, to reveal that exquisite enamel, so clearly his valley, although empty of roses—just the shape of the hills, the river running through it.

He turned it over to show the gold seal on the other side. Two rose bushes growing out of the ground, twining together, reaching higher and higher, escaping the mountains that framed them, up into the symbolic heavens of the edge of the seal. They twined together to make one bloom, in the center of the upper half of the oval. Along the bottom edge, where the bushes grew out of the ground, curved the words: *Quivi s'incomincia.*

As exposed as he'd been to Latin, through all the old-fashioned Masses his grandmother took them to, and Italian, through their own proximity to the border, and Provençal, with its roots sunk deep into both languages, and of course, French, it was easy enough to make out the translation, however archaic the wording: *It all starts here.*

He could only stare at it, as the words seemed to expand and expand inside him until they pressed against the hills that framed the valley, until they pressed against the outermost limits of his heart and still kept trying to make it expand even bigger.

It all starts here.

Not where he was bound, but where he began.

I'll give my family roots, Niccolò's seal said. *And from them, they'll grow as big as they can.*

He ran his thumb over the words, over the roses rising out of the ground, up to the bloom, pressing that smooth enamel of the valley on the other side more deeply into his skin.

"I'd like to give it to her, but now I think I can't," Tante Colette said softly. "I think if she ever receives a gift like that, it will have to come from you."

He looked from the pendant to his old aunt, trying so hard not to flush, trying so hard not to let his eyes sting.

Colette reached out an old, old hand and closed his big, young, strong fist around the seal. "Because it's your valley," she said quietly. "And it's you."

"Aww, hell." Matt bent his head into his hands, the seal and chain pressing against his forehead. "Tante Colette."

She patted his shoulder, this rare, precious touch from a woman who was not that emotive. "It's all right, Matthieu. You're strong enough to be a valley and to be bigger than a valley, and I've always been very proud of you, that inside that much strength, you keep such a tender heart."

Chapter 21

Peace pressed up against Layla from the ancient village. Matt had brought her to the top of the world. They strolled through little cobblestone streets. A wall of ivy framed pale blue shutters. A sundial was painted dusty gold against an ochre wall, with some saying in Provençal she couldn't understand. Flowers grew up the walls between old painted doors and in pots on balconies and on the edge of fountains. Children ran through streets with *cartables*, those square French book bags, as they came home from school, stopping to play in a playground set in the middle of a garden off the central *place*. A sign over a shuttered shop proclaimed *Huiles d'olive de région.*

She and Matt reached a little church at the top of the town, surrounded by an old cemetery, and stood on a stone terrace beyond the cemetery, gazing over the Côte d'Azur.

Ageless stone quiet brushed against her with the soft wind, the air so clean of everything but stone and cedar that the light up here seemed to work its way into every stress-darkened part of her soul and breathe it clean. The slope plunged steeply away below the stone terrace, giving a view of the Mediterranean, its azure deepened by distance.

Matt stood beside her, gazing out at the view. His valley lay below them to the right, the river through it a fine thread, the limestone cliffs through which it cut to enter the valley a thumbnail-size patch of gray. He had showered after he finished with the harvest work for the day, before he took her on this date, so that if a woman wanted to seek refuge from all that clean, pure air and find a more intimate scent of roses, she would have to nuzzle her nose in a quest for it all over his body.

She smiled, reassured by the thought. Reassured by how, every day, after he finished up, he took her to some new amazing spot in his world and offered it to her like the special gift that it was. Ancient hill towns, and Roman bridges, and hikes through the *maquis*. And this view right now.

"It's beautiful here," she whispered.

He gave her a curious, marveling look. "You always do that," he murmured. "It's as if you take everything I know, wrap it up in wonder, and hand it back to me like this bright, shiny new present. It's like my whole life is Christmas when you're looking at it."

"Well, it's just that...it's so beautiful," Layla said helplessly, a little confused. How odd to have such an extraordinary life, to be part of, lord of, such incredible beauty, and take it for granted.

"He would have stood right here, once," Matt said low. "This church would already have been four hundred years old. He would have stood here, looking down into that valley, deciding he would make it his."

"Your first patriarch?" Layla guessed. "Niccolò Rosario?" What an incredible feeling, to know that you stood in the same spot your ancestor once had when he founded a dynasty. And that even though it had been four hundred years, the place where you stood would have felt old to that ancestor, too, when he was here.

Matt's hand shifted in his pocket, as if he was rubbing change or something.

Her mother was wrong, she thought. She had to give that land back. It was a hole in him, for her to have it. You couldn't leave a hole in a man's heart and ask him to trust you with it.

And if she needed this place to write music, then maybe she also had to trust that he would let her stay.

"I worked on a new song today," she said. *Does my world matter to you, too? Do you understand how important this is to me?*

"Yeah?" He abandoned the change in his pocket to take her hand, rubbing his thumb over her fingertips as if he could still catch the tingles from her guitar strings. "You going to sing it for me?"

She shrugged, embarrassed in that way she was never embarrassed when standing on a stage. "It's not ready yet."

He smiled a little. "I'll just pretend to be asleep tomorrow morning and listen to you toying with it."

"Hey! Have you been pretending this whole week?" She often woke up in a dreamy mood beside him, pulling her guitar to her and propping herself against the headboard while he slept, testing chords and lyrics softly, trying to catch that dreaming.

He shrugged, his smile deepening.

"I should have suspected something, when you started sleeping in late." But it felt kind of...sweet, too, to know she'd given him that pleasure of lingering in bed, listening to music, as if he, too, had other facets to his being than fixing problems and making things work. It felt sweet to know he pretended so he could listen to her, as if that was something special to him.

"That's not the only reason I like to 'sleep' in late now." He rubbed his thumb up the edge of her palm, the curve of his lips a little wicked.

"Shh." She ducked away to push open the door of the little twelfth-century church, pointing up at the solemn saints carved above it. "Behave."

He smiled, following her into the church's profound quiet. Nothing moved inside but time and their own hushed footsteps.

Simplicity greeted them: bare stone walls, almost no decoration at all but a cross and a statue of Mary behind the altar. Worn wood pews led to that altar, under the simple barrel nave above them and the old round columns that supported its arches. Layla stopped in front of a marble sarcophagus. Fourth-century Roman, a little bronze sign proclaimed. She crouched down to trace the forms of the Latin letters that covered the marble and read their translation. An inscription from parents to their eighteen-year-old son, dead on the day he was due to start his military career for Rome.

She straightened, her throat tightening suddenly for those parents seventeen centuries ago. "One of your ancestors?"

"Well, probably not on Niccolò's side. But on Laurianne's, who knows?"

"Hey." Such a strange, intense thought struck Layla that she had to reach out and grab Matt's hand again. "He might be one of *my* ancestors."

"Well, probably not him," Matt admitted. "Since he died when he was eighteen, and the inscription doesn't mention a wife and kids. But...yeah." He reached out and took her other hand, too, holding her face to face with him, his eyes warm and his body so solid in front of her. "You have ancestors around here. We could probably track them down, the Dubois gravestones. Élise's name must be on some of the plaques to World War II heroes. And on the lists of the 'Righteous Among the Nations', if she died saving children. I think I remember now seeing her photo in the Musée de la Résistance."

Layla stood very still, her hand over her lips, shaky suddenly with this sense of time. Of weight. As if she was part of this great sweep of existence that made her mortal and immortal both, as if she had existed before she ever played a note, and she would exist after those notes stopped.

Which was what her music did—made immortality out of her mortal human experience, turned it into something that would outlast her life. But...she'd always had to rely entirely on that music to anchor her into human history. She'd never been able to be a part of it just by being herself.

"And then, of course, you have the Rosiers and the Delatours." Matt curled the tips of his fingers into hers for a gentle squeeze. "By adoption. So yeah...you have roots here."

Her eyes stung a little. She bent her head.

Matt loosed her hand to reach into his pocket again.

She took a deep breath of that peace and time. "I'll give it back. Your land. I don't need it."

Matt froze. "You...don't?"

She shrugged, trying to do this lightly, so that he didn't see how much it cost her to give it up to him. "It's not important to me like it is to you."

Matt rocked back a step, almost as if she'd hit him.

Was she saying something wrong? Maybe he just didn't understand. "I can write my music anywhere. The land doesn't matter."

He took another step back. Why did he keep looking like that? She was doing the right thing, wasn't she? Healing the hole in his heart, no matter what it cost her?

"It doesn't really," she repeated, insistently. "All of this"—her hand waved to encompass the church with its time, the views outside of the Côte and the valley, this whole world of his that was so beautiful—"is secondary."

"It's *what?*"

She shook her head, trying to get at what she meant. "None of that is the *heart* of things."

"You don't care about it?" His voice sounded so flat, so numb.

Her words were coming out all wrong. Maybe she should have written this in a song first. With rewrites. "Not as much as I care about—"

"You." His accusation cut her off. "And your music. And your fans. And your touring, and whether people are clapping for you. Not as much as you care about that, right?"

What? She stared at him, as shocked and hurt as if he'd slapped her. Even though she hadn't been going to say any of those things at all, temper touched her at his tone, and she argued against the wrong thing: "Well, that's my *career*, Matt. It's okay if I value my career, isn't it? That clapping you're so contemptuous of is how I know if I did a good job."

"And that's more important?" His hand had come free of his pocket, fisted tight around something. The other hand flexed and closed. "You're just going to dump this? All of this? Like some toy you got tired of?"

"I don't—" She scrubbed her hands across her face. How had this gone so wrong? Wasn't he supposed to be overjoyed and relieved right now? Feel whole again? Trust her? Wasn't he supposed to be showing her that even if she gave up her legal claim to part of his heart he would still keep her safe in it? "That's not what I meant."

"You weighed them up, and you figured it out, right? Between your music and this. What really mattered."

"It's not supposed to be an either/or choice," she snapped, anger growing. This was the man who hadn't even gotten properly mad at her for lying to him, and now, just when she was making herself the most vulnerable, he was acting like this? "And you shouldn't make it one. If who I am and want to be really matters to *you*."

He stared down at the hand he had fisted around something and then at her. "I can't believe you would *give this up*. I—God damn it, I thought it meant something to you."

He shoved hard at the nearest pew and turned and strode down the aisle.

***

God, Matt hated churches. They dotted this country so ubiquitously, and everything bad in the world happened in them. His parents' funeral. His grandmother's. Raoul's mother's.

A sulky, brooding child, being dragged there by his grandmother every Sunday, being made to go to Confession as he got older, when he wanted to punch the screen between him and the priest. *You stole my parents!* he'd wanted to shout. *All I did was sneak out of the house at midnight to build a bonfire with my cousins. So Tristan*

265

melted the bottom of his shoe! Why am I the one apologizing to You?

He reached the back of the church. All those backs of churches. All those funerals and, yes, weddings and baptisms, at which he and the men in his family had stood, biceps pressed against each other as they squeezed in, leaving the pews to the women because they couldn't all fit. That mass of heat and strength that they made when they stood together.

He stopped. The echo of his strides died away.

He reached out and rested his hand against the stone, pressing Niccolò's seal against the same wall where his and his cousins' backs always pressed when they were here for weddings. Or funerals. Always, a restless peace would settle over them as they prepared themselves to be patient and respectful and stand still for an hour of prayers and singing and, half the time, Latin. They'd done it so many, many times, to keep their grandmother happy, or to do their duty by the family and honor someone's wedding or the new life being born into the family, or, yes, to grieve together, to press their shoulders together to bear up an unbearable weight. He could half hear the echoes of those Latin chants now, as if the stone held so many of them they sifted down over anyone present like dust motes dancing in soft light.

In this old church, the quiet sifted off the stone, centuries of pleading and gratitude, of grief and joy, of guilt and promises, all of that absorbed and cleansed from the air, released back out in this long, soft hush.

A hush that said: Even when hurt to the deepest part of his heart, a man could still be strong.

He looked back at Layla.

Her face had crumpled. She was hugging her middle as if he had hit her in it, and trying not to cry.

Oh, hell.

"I'm sorry," he said uneasily.

Her face crumpled more as she stared at him, and then she did start to cry, covering her face with her hands.

Hell. He came back to her, pulling her into his arms. "I'm sorry, Bouclettes. I'm sorry."

But you just...you want to throw me away? Give me back? You don't want to keep me?

I'd do about anything to keep you.

His special present of himself. That she didn't need. That didn't matter. That wasn't the heart of things. She was going to take it back to the store and exchange it for something more practical.

"I was trying to say something," she cried. "I think I must not have said it right."

Oh, hell, he was such a bastard. Such a grumpy, stupid, touchy bastard. "Come here," he said, drawing her out of the church and away from the statue of Mary looking down at him with a maternal forgiveness that made him feel as if he'd just killed a damn kitten.

He drew her to the great rock that interrupted the wall of the terrace looking out over the valley. An old cypress shaded it, so old that Niccolò must have sought its shade once, too.

He leaned back against the rock and drew her weight against him. "I'm sorry," he said yet again. "Tell me what you were trying to say."

"I don't want to anymore." She tried to push a glare through her tears, but it got all blurred, and her mouth trembled over her attempt to scowl. "I don't trust you with it!"

Ouch. That really hurt. "Okay, I'm sorry. Shh." He rubbed her back, tightening her into him. "Shh. I'm so crazy about you, Bouclettes. I just...I thought you loved this valley, too."

She slapped her hand hard against his chest. "I love *you*. That's all I was trying to say. I do love your valley, but not as much as *you*. You jerk." And she burst into tears again.

267

Shit.

And...oh, wow, really?

Really?

"Shh, shh, shh," he murmured, easing her into him, soul lighting up with this strange, scared wonder. Did she mean that? And had he just broken it?

"I wanted *you* to be happy," she told his chest accusingly. "I wanted *you* to feel whole. I wanted *you* to feel safe with me. I thought for sure that I was safe with *you.*"

That hurt so much. "It's just a fight," he said anxiously. He was one of five male cousins. They had fights all the time. Most of the time they didn't even bother to make up but shrugged and went on as if it had never happened. Once the dust settled, it was settled, after all. No sense stirring it up again. If any extra calming of the waters needed to happen, someone made a joke or someone shoved the other in the shoulder, and it was all good.

But she was an only child. Almost as bad, she was a *girl.*

Maybe she didn't know how to make up after fights by going on as if they'd never happened.

Maybe she didn't know how to forgive a man for acting like a jerk.

"I just misunderstood." He rubbed her back more and more coaxingly. "I thought—you know, for a songwriter, you really need to work on your word choice."

"Hey!" She lifted her head and glared at him. Her eyes were still wet, but at least the tears stopped actually falling.

So the pushing-her-buttons had worked, a little bit like that would work with his cousins. He gazed at her helplessly, not quite sure of his next move to smooth things over. Probably not punching her in the shoulder and saying something rude.

"You certainly seemed to have some nasty assumptions about me ready to pop out at the least misunderstanding." She scowled at him.

"I had a crappy experience with my last celebrity girlfriend." He kissed her forehead. "I'm sorry, Layla."

"Okay, quit saying that," she said as her eyes filled again. "It makes me cry."

Saying he was sorry made her cry? So...did that mean it was a good thing she was crying? It would be so helpful if he had had a little more exposure to women growing up and could actually figure one out.

"Well, I am sorry," he said firmly, and scooted them back on the rock, until he was sitting against the cypress and she was tucked between his upraised knees. The position anchored them into the very solidity of the earth and at the same time hovered them on the edge of the whole vast world, falling away below them and rising blue above them to the heavens. "Tell me what you meant?"

"No." She scowled at him, very stubborn. But she wasn't crying anymore.

He sighed. This was what he got for trying to defend his heart when he was supposed to be opening it. He kissed her hairline, and a little part of him still could focus on the pleasure of the texture of her curls against his lips. "Layla. I don't want you to give me back the land, all right?"

"You don't make any sense whatsoever!"

Well, at least it was mutual. "I want you to have it," he said, and loosed his hand from her back to show her what he held.

"*What?*" She jerked her head up to stare at him, not even seeing what he offered.

He nudged it at her again, making her look down at what he held in his palm. A small, enameled gold oval depicting the valley, exactly as it looked from where they sat. The hills that framed it. The fine thread of the river.

The tiny patch of limestone cliffs the river cut through to enter the valley.

"That's beautiful," Layla said, instantly distracted from anger and hurt by her own wonder. She was so generous she couldn't stay wounded and mad worth a damn, could she? She stroked her fingers over the smooth enamel. "Is it a copy of the old seal you were telling me about? The one your ancestor had made...Niccolò?"

"It's not a copy."

It took her a second. And then she gasped. "You *found* it?" That fast, she had forgotten all about their fight. "Matt! That's *wonderful.*" She hugged him.

"You're a really nice person, aren't you?" he said softly.

A sulky frown hinted its way back. "I thought I was the kind of person who cared more about whether people were clapping for me than anything else."

He sighed and rested his forehead against the top of her head. "I was stupid," he said. "Sometimes I'm a little sensitive." That idiot soft heart of his. She'd slipped in under all its shields, and it made his heart a little jumpy to have someone in so close where it could get hurt.

She tightened her hug enough to rest her head against his chest. So maybe this was the way he made up with her. Not a punch on the arm or a rough joke, but a touch of her hair or a kiss of the top of her head.

Well, then. He could definitely do that, too.

It made him feel a lot more vulnerable than punching somebody's arm, but he was going to try to handle it.

"Tante Colette had it all this time. She gave it to me."

"Well, I'm glad she finally did the right thing," Layla said approvingly. "It's your valley." She stroked his chest. Look at that, she was already petting him. She was *lousy* at grudges. "You are here and here you'll stay."

He took a breath. "Turn it over."

She did, with the care of someone who had never touched a piece of jewelry four hundred years old in her life, and stilled at the gold seal revealed on the other side. Her finger felt the shape of the gold very carefully. The roses growing up out of the ground. The gold bloom at the top. The words...her finger hesitated over them. "I thought you said the motto was..."

"I guess we changed it, over time," he said. "Apparently what Niccolò said was 'It all starts here'."

"I like that. Not a resting place, but a starting place. A place to help you bloom." She stroked it again, her face wondering and a little wistful. "That's incredible, roots like that."

"Yeah," he said softly. "I thought you might like it." What an idiot he'd been in the church.

"It's amazing. It's even a rose. It's perfect for you."

He took the chain and slipped it over her head, settling the seal over her breastbone. "It's perfect for you."

Her hand covered it. "*What?*"

"I want you to have it."

"Matt, you can't—"

He put his hand over her mouth before she could throw his heart back at him again. "Because I thought," he said carefully, "that it didn't have to be an either/or choice. That maybe you could stay here *and* bloom. And pursue your career. Maybe you, you know...needed me. And...I can give you that. Me."

"Your valley is not you, Matt. I mean—"

"It is," he finished for her. "It really is. And I want you to keep that, too. But I also meant...me. I can give you me."

"*Oh.*" Her loose fist rose to her lips, and she bit into the side of her index finger, staring at him.

"Don't give it back," he said anxiously, gesturing to himself.

271

"But—but—" She looked from him down to her chest and back. "You can't give me something so *old.*"

A little smile ghosted through him. "It's a bit younger than the valley."

She gave a tiny, indignant shove to his chest. "I was trying to give that back! And anyway, someone else gave it to me. You know what I mean. This should stay in the family."

His smile grew inside him, even while his cheeks heated a little. It felt good, though, that heat in his cheeks. Like warmth escaping his heart to expand all through him. "I know." He rubbed his thumb over the seal, resting the heel of his palm against the swell of her breasts. "But I bet if you let me, I could figure out a way to fix that problem."

Her breath caught. She stared at him, her eyes such a beautiful green. Just like rose leaves in the early gray morning.

"I, ah..." He touched his chest, his cheeks heating more to try to say these words. He *meant* them, that wasn't the problem. They just sounded so untough, so soft-hearted, so exposed. "You know I'm crazy about you."

There. He could say that. It wasn't so...raw. It wasn't so open.

And she liked it. Her cheeks flushed a little, and she bit her lip, staring up at him in pleasure.

But...yeah. She deserved the rawness. The openness. He bent his head to slide his face into her curls until his lips were by the lobe of her ear. "I love you," he said, and his cheeks flamed like fire. Because it was true, and saying something so true could sometimes take all a man's courage. "*Moi aussi, je t'aime.*"

It was worth the courage, though, for the way she wrapped her arms around him and held on tight, as if she would never let go.

She fit in his arms just right.

Chapter 22

"She's really good, isn't she?" Tristan said, stopping beside him at the side of the stage, their shoulders brushing.

Matt beamed with pride, his arms folded to try to contain his chest before it swelled so much it exploded. "She's fantastic."

Layla was chatting with her audience, teasing them by playing bars of "La Vie en Rose."

She had ended up calling her producers and stating flat out that she needed to delay the album. Her producers had said, "Better a delay than crappy music."

I told you so, Matt had said. Layla had gotten indignant with him about that, but her relief had been enormous. She'd actually gone out on a blanket on the hillside and slept the whole morning in the shadow of the pines after that phone conversation, her face so relaxed and peaceful. Her joy in her music grew back from that point like a plant taken out of a dark closet and given some sun, her energy and pleasure more and more vibrant. He'd loved it, how excited she grew to share with him something she'd been working on, when they met for lunch, or she came down to the fields to sit on the back of the truck and play a while, or in the evening. When she was no longer under pressure, when she was in the shelter of his valley, when she had all kinds of things that gave her life and worth besides her music, it was amazing how attached she was to that guitar.

But then, of course, the Rose Festival committee, half of whom were related to Matt and all of whom had seen the photos, came down on him like a ton of bricks to try to get Belle Woods to perform at the festival.

Matt didn't give a crap about the committee pressure, of course—would-be-dominant other family members were the main reason he'd had to grow up so growly and tough in the first place—but Layla laughed and said, "Sure. No problem."

Which was pretty damn annoying, actually. No wonder she was so stressed and overworked if she didn't know how to say no.

Of course, the only consequence *he'd* gotten for pointing that out and arguing with her over her acceptance had been this incredibly maddening and yet intimately delicious evening in which Layla teased him with all the ways and times she could say *no*.

So here she was, on stage in Grasse, across from the great fountain with its huge, stylized jasmine and rose flowers.

One side of the stage reached nearly to the wall of the esplanade, the valleys below Grasse spilling below it. Once those valleys, too, would have been full of flowers, the entire region so dense with them you breathed perfume. These days, all the land he could see from here was full of houses and buildings, all the way to the sea.

One day, the Rosier valley would be the last valley of flowers in France. The land's production would no longer suffice to justify its existence, and it would become just a show-piece of the larger Rosier SA. Kept for sentimental value, because they could afford it.

The great, underlying grief of his position as patriarch was that it was probably going to be in his lifetime, actually, if he lived to be as old as his grandfather.

His grandfather stopped beside him. Matt waited for some comment on the need to not let a rock star get a chunk of their valley.

But his grandfather was quiet.

Il me dit des mots d'amour, Layla sang on stage, that beautiful, rose and burlap voice of hers caught by the microphone and carried out to the whole crowd. *He speaks words of love to me.*

Rose and burlap. *That's* what her voice sounded like. The rough and the silk. The sweet and the tough.

His grandfather gave a soft sigh.

Matt slid a glance at him, braced.

"I remember," Pépé said softly. "Hiding in the shadows with Colette, listening to that song."

After all these years, Matt knew the rare, precious tone of a war memory. He went quiet, focusing, one ear for Layla, one for his grandfather.

"She had a song order that would let us know if she had information she needed to pass on. And if she did, she'd take her break after this song. The Germans loved her so much she could get away with anything. A couple of times, she'd give a concert just to keep them occupied on a certain evening and less likely to notice what we were up to."

"Edith Piaf?" Matt guessed.

"Of course," his grandfather said. "This was her home, too."

Matt nodded. His grandfather, and others, had shared memories of Edith Piaf with him many times before this. But still, it was always something of a wonder to Matt to hear some of these stories.

"You can tell a lot about a woman by the way she sings," Pépé said quietly. Hands crossed behind his back, he walked that aged but still straight walk of his over to one of the tables set up under the trees at the edge of the esplanade. Tante Colette sat there watching the performance.

Pépé sat down in the shade across from her and leaned back in his chair, not speaking, as far as Matt could tell from here.

They rarely spoke to each other these days except to bicker. But there were other tables Pépé could have sat at.

Matt looked back at Layla.

She looked quite radiant, completely in her element.

Funny how well she and he fit together, when she was so different from him. There was no way in hell anyone would get him up on a stage like that, in front of this mass of people, half of whom already liked to remind him of seeing him in diapers.

"Damn, she's good," Raoul said, stopping beside him with Damien.

Matt grinned. "I know."

"Her tour schedule is going to be a bitch, though. How are you two going to handle that?"

Matt slowly loosened his arms from his chest and shoved his hands into his pockets. He took a long breath, and that breath felt...just right. Big enough. "I thought I'd ask you."

Raoul stilled. For a long moment, he didn't look at Matt at all. Then he turned his head at just enough of an angle to see Matt's face. "How to handle it?"

Matt cleared his throat. "To help. With the land." He flexed his fingers in his pockets, keeping hold of the denim so he didn't cross his arms back over his chest. Tristan had turned and was looking at him, too, alert and astonished. Damien, past Raoul, took a step forward so he could see Matt, too. Matt cleared his throat again. "I'm not in any rush about this, but I wonder sometimes if, eventually, we should set it up as a trust. So that, you know, we can all have it, and...none of us can lose it."

There was a dead silence. All his cousins were staring at him.

"A trust with me in charge of it, of course," he said firmly.

A sharp, wry grin from Raoul. "We guessed that part."

"Hell, Matt," Tristan said low, wonderingly. And then, "You *really* like her, don't you?"

Matt flushed hot. That was just rude, to point that out like that. He glared at Tristan.

Tristan grinned and punched him in the shoulder.

"This one's a new one," Layla said up on stage. "My producers haven't got hold of it yet, so I'm testing it out on you all."

The crowd cheered excitedly.

"I wrote it for somebody here," Layla said, and Matt got caught by curiosity, focusing on her again.

She was grinning down at him. "Matt, can you come up here?"

Wait, what?

What the hell?

Layla beckoned coaxingly. Her crowd cheered, everyone craning to try to see the man she was talking to.

Hell, no. He took a step back, and firm hands gripped his arms.

"No!" he growled. "Tristan. Raoul. Let the hell go of me. Don't you dare."

Damien ducked behind him and shoved him hard between the shoulders as Tristan and Raoul dragged him forward.

"Damn it! You bastards! I'm going to—"

He tripped over the first step as they shoved him up it. The crowd was cheering more and more as they spotted him, and Layla beamed down at him.

Oh, hell. Now what was he supposed to do? Disappoint that face?

He came on up the stairs.

Below the stage, his cousins were grinning, Allegra and Léa had appeared and were clapping and cheering, and pretty much the entire half of the audience who knew him personally were staring at him with their mouths open.

"Layla," he tried to hiss, but her mic was on, and he didn't know how much of his voice it could pick up, so he had to bite back the protest.

277

She wrapped her arm around him, her guitar bumping against his ribs, and turned toward the crowd. "See?" she said, and everyone cheered again. "Wouldn't you write a song for this man?"

Oh, hell. He felt like he was on fire. He started to glare at all his relatives in the crowd and then remembered that a glare probably wasn't the best look on stage.

"He's pretty cute, isn't he?" Layla said to the crowd, squeezing his waist affectionately. "I'll tell you a secret— he's pretty sweet, too."

He was going to kill her. It was official. In the crowd, his cousins were laughing their heads off and cheering her louder than anyone. He clenched his fist as tightly as he could to stop himself from at least giving them a little *doigt d'honneur*.

"I am not sweet," he said to her between his teeth. Shit, that seemed to have gotten picked up by the nearest microphone, because the crowd cheered again. He was going to kill the festival sound crew, too, while he was at it. Wasn't one of his Delange cousins on that crew?

"Here we go," Layla called to the crowd, stepping away from him to free up her arms to play. And to Matt: "This one's for you."

Her first chords were quiet, brooding, this sweet, wistful call:

Lonely
Lost looking and lonely
Doing everything solely
Cause I hadn't found you

His heart felt so vulnerable and funny, and he wished to hell she wasn't telling him this in front of the crowd. But...that was so...*sweet*. And, and...well, she was wide open, too, wasn't she? Just laying herself out there, the way she always did.

278

Lonely
Wandering lonely
Footsore and only
Wishing for you

Aww. Damn it. She was killing him. *Bouclettes, no wonder you need to hide in my valley, when you're always sticking your heart out like this in front of a crowd.* And, *Really? You really feel that?*

Her chords grew stronger, braver, truer with each verse, like the energy that surged through a weary traveler when she spotted the light of home.

Lonely
Always everywhere lonely
Seeking everywhere only
In hopes of you.

His hand reached for her. *Bouclettes. Me, too.*

Her chords softened again, growing quiet, sure, true. This profound simplicity to them.

Lonely
No longer lonely
No longer only
Because my wish came true.

Aww, *hell.* His eyes felt damp. This was *terrible.*

And everybody was cheering, and she was gazing up at him with this soft look in her eyes like he was *amazing*, like he was...her wish come true, and, and...

"I love you," she said, with her *mic still on so that the whole freaking world could hear.* The audience went *crazy.*

And she didn't even seem to notice them. She was all focused on him, like her hero, and—

"You make me happy," she said softly.

Damn it. "Me, too," he said gruffly, and he could hear his own voice echoing out over the crowd. The damn sound crew must have turned on the main mic right beside him. But what the hell else was he supposed to do? Leave her hanging out there on her own? "I love you, too," he said simply.

While the crowd cheered, he bent to her ear. "And don't you ever do this to me again," he growled.

She turned her head and kissed him.

Something hit him on the shoulder softly, then several somethings. People were pelting them with...no, not rotten tomatoes. Roses. People were throwing the roses that had been handed out during the festival.

He took a step back and then another, eyeing his escape route. Petals fluttered around his face. He could leap over the edge there, shove through his cousins like their old rugby games, duck behind that post—"Hey." He turned suddenly as he thought of something and glowered at Layla. "You'd damn well better marry me after all this."

She grinned. "That is *so* sweet of you to ask."

Shit, had he just said that for the whole world to hear? He didn't fold his arms across his chest, though. He put his hands on his hips and gave her his bossiest glare. *You'd better do what I said.*

"Okay," she said and picked up one of the thrown roses to kiss it. "I will."

Oh, thank God.

He leapt off the stage, going for the rugby shove-dive through his cousins, and—they'd caught him, damn it. And they were...

...hugging him.

Pounding him on the back. Hugging him again in congratulations. More distant relatives and friends were pressing in beyond them, trying to join in the celebration.

"I've got it all on video!" Allegra was exclaiming cheerfully as she tried to force her way in to hug him, too. "This one's going to go down in family history! It might even beat the alien photo!"

"Well," Layla said with a deep breath through her mic. Over his cousins' shoulders, he saw her standing there with her cheeks all flushed, too, and her eyes starry, and her hand pressed to her chest, over her heart. "Isn't he a prince? What do you want me to play after *that?*"

And he finally relaxed into his cousins' embrace, grinning and flushing at the congratulations and teasing that poured in and watching his happiness up on stage as she played.

She'd come back to him in a little while, and they would be able to take this somewhere quiet and private, the quiet and private she needed, too. It fit together, those two needs.

He was her roots. And she was his wings.

FIN

THANK YOU!

Thank you so much for reading! I hope you enjoyed Matt and Layla's story, the first in the Vie en Roses series. And don't miss Tristan's story, coming next in this series.

Before Tristan, though, I've got some other stories coming. Next up, for those of you who love the Amour et Chocolat series, is *Once a Hero*, a novel that takes us back to Dom Richard's chocolate shop in Paris for the story of his chocolatier Célie and her older brother's best friend, home from the Foreign Legion. Keep reading for a glimpse.

And I'm working on a (free) short story that involves Dom and sandcastles and the night before his wedding, but alas, I can't share it with you until after *Once a Hero* is out for chronological reasons. But sign up at www.lauraflorand.com to be emailed your copy when it's ready, as well as to be alerted when these other books are released.

Meanwhile, make sure to catch the books that first introduce us to the world of the Roses series. You'll find Gabriel and Jolie's story in *The Chocolate Rose*, a prequel to the Vie en Roses series that bridges with the Amour et Chocolat stories. Daniel and Léa's story is in the novella *Turning Up the Heat*, and Raoul and Allegra's in the anthology *No Place Like Home*. Keep reading for a glimpse of *The Chocolate Rose* as well as a complete book list.

Thank you so much for sharing in this new world with me! For some behind-the-scenes glimpses of the research in the south of France, check out my website and Facebook page. I hope to meet up with you there!

Thank you and all the best,

Laura Florand

ONCE UPON A ROSE

OTHER BOOKS BY LAURA FLORAND

Amour et Chocolat Series

All's Fair in Love and Chocolate, a novella in *Kiss the Bride*

The Chocolate Thief

The Chocolate Kiss

The Chocolate Rose (also a prequel to La Vie en Roses series)

The Chocolate Touch

The Chocolate Heart

The Chocolate Temptation

Sun-Kissed (also a sequel to *Snow-Kissed*)

Shadowed Heart (a sequel to *The Chocolate Heart*)

La Vie en Roses Series

Turning Up the Heat (a novella prequel)

The Chocolate Rose (also part of the Amour et Chocolat series)

A Rose in Winter, a novella in *No Place Like Home*

Once Upon a Rose

LAURA FLORAND

Snow Queen Duology

Snow-Kissed (a novella)

Sun-Kissed (also part of the Amour et Chocolat series)

Memoir

Blame It on Paris

ONCE UPON A ROSE

ONCE A HERO, EXCERPT

An Amour et Chocolat novel

He left her for the Foreign Legion. And now he's back.

Oh, hell. Célie tried to pull herself together. "Joss. What are you doing here?"

He just looked up at her with those hazel green eyes and that stillness he had, emphasized even more by five years of military discipline. "Would you rather I wait outside?"

It was all she could do not to just shove that little table aside and climb into his lap, bury her head in his chest and hold on tight. *Why did you leave me, you bastard? Oh, thank God you're home.*

Yeah, and that would be insane.

Plus she'd already done it once.

"Joss, you know I love you—"

A little jerk ran through his body. And hers, as the echo of her own words ran through her.

"Like a brother," she hastened to add.

"Fuck, Célie." He turned his head away, his jaw setting. "Like *Ludo?*"

Okay, well, maybe not like her actual brother. Or like any other male she'd ever known either. But, but... "But I'm not your person to come home to here." Oh, hell, had she just said that? *Yes, I am. Yes, I am.* "I've moved on."

"Moved on from what?" Joss asked.

She stared at him.

"We never dated, Célie. I wasn't Sophie's boyfriend, but I was never your boyfriend either. I was saving you for later."

Her jaw dropped. Fury sizzled once deep in her stomach and then just flared all through her. "You son of a bitch."

"For when you were *older*." He tried to regroup. "And I deserved you."

"I'm going to *kill you!*" Célie pressed her hands into his table and her weight into them as she leaned her body over his.

"Okay," Joss said, and just lifted the table to the side to expose his body to her, shifting the table as if neither it nor her pressure on it weighed anything. "You can do that."

Once a Hero, coming 2015! Sign up to be emailed when it's released at www.lauraflorand.com.

THE CHOCOLATE ROSE EXCERPT

Gabriel straightened and moved to the wall of the terrace, almost positive he heard a frustrated puff of breath behind him. Looking down over the fountain Sainte-Mère had built in his honor when the town's tourism economy quintupled after he got his third star, he took a moment to stretch. Hands locked high over his head, he arched his back into it, rolling his neck, his shoulders. What started as a deliberate calculation was such a relief after the past seven hours without a break that he sank into it, taking his time, muscles easing. *Putain,* but that felt good. It would feel even better if slim little hands added their pressure.

He glanced back at Jolie Manon, who had her knees pulled up so he couldn't even see her chest, staring at him. Her fingers rubbed slowly back and forth over her jeans-clad knees, as if she needed texture.

Don't hold back, chaton. I'm happy to be your texture.

He sat on the edge of the terrace wall, stretching out his legs, bracing his hands against its edge so that his torso was long, lean, fully exposed, the muscles of his arms and shoulders flexing a little.

Merde, but he liked it, when she had to bite on her lower lip.

He had so many things he could do with that mouth of hers. Make her lose not only her worries but her entire mind, tangling with him desperately in a—

A beast, though.

A *beast.* Was he really that bad?

Would one of those civilized men who paid a fortune to eat at his tables sit here in front of that slim, vulnerable, adorably delicious little body, those eyes so wide and dark on him, and not do anything about it?

And just because some men were *des putains d'idiots,* did that mean *he* had to be? In order to live up to their standards? Something was screwed up, there.

"About that *other* idea," he said firmly, because, well—he would *like* to be a prince. If it was remotely possible and didn't require him to ignore her screaming body language indefinitely. "I think you should give me fifteen percent of the royalties. Since fifteen percent of the recipes are mine. Of your father's royalties," he added, as he saw her eyes flicker in calculation.

She bit her lip. Wait, had that not been a princely thing to say? Damn it.

"*Not* yours. You did the same amount of writing, whether you knew you were writing up my work or not."

She worried at her lip.

Would she *quit doing that?* It appealed to every heroic instinct he had—and he had a lot more of them than she gave him credit for—the thought of swooping in and protecting that lip from her cruelty. Offering himself to her teeth in its place. . . .

He shifted, wondering what her head was doing with his increasingly obvious arousal. Anyone would think she would like it, *since he aroused her*, but apparently it couldn't be that easy.

"And I want subsequent editions to acknowledge me under each recipe that's mine. *Created by Gabriel Delange* works fine. For the remaining print run of this first edition, you can just insert one of those slips of paper that corrects errors. It's not ideal, but it's either that or make you destroy the entire run."

That lower lip got more punishment. Her physical awareness of him faded as her worry rose. *Merde. You're not the knight in shining armor, you're the beast, remember? She's never in a million years going to think of you as the hero.* Women never did. "I'm just starting out as a food writer," she said, low. "If I have to get my publishing house to do all that, they probably won't ever work with me again."

Gabriel sat still for a moment, his fingers pressing into that rough stone. He tilted his head back, closing his eyes, concentrating on the distant sound of his fountain, below in the square. "I'm never going to get any damn justice, am I?"

She said nothing. When he opened his eyes again, she had her arms wrapped even more tightly around her knees, and she was watching him with a mixture of worry and apology.

Bordel. "It is so like that *salaud* to have a stroke just before that cookbook came out."

"As if he did it on purpose!"

Yes, all right, she loved her father. *Le connard.* He got three daughters to love him, even though he didn't deserve it, while Gabriel lost his girlfriend of six years—sixteen to twenty-two—and had had a really lousy success rate when it came to long-term relationships ever since.

How did Pierre Manon always manage to manipulate his situation to get everyone else to give him their all, so much more than he deserved?

"Forget it," he said roughly, shoving to his feet. "Don't mess up your career with your publishing house. I'll think of something else."

He headed back toward the hotel door and paused in front of her. Her eyes ate him up, making him very conscious of his naked upper body, of the way his shoulders blocked out her moonlight. *Chaton, you don't have to just look. I know what I make might mislead you, but I myself am more than happy to be devoured like junk food.* "Do you have a boyfriend or something? Fiancé? Married?"

Her eyes went enormous. She tightened her computer over her breasts, a defensive shield, but he saw her throat work again. "No," she whispered.

He shook his head, feeling heavy, puzzled. Like some damn *beast* who had wondered out of the woods and gotten lost, baffled, in society. "Then I don't understand why, when you want me to kiss you so damn badly, you'll get so mad if I do."

He strode out before he could crack and try it anyway and heard her tablet smack onto the stone terrace behind him.

Fallen out of her lap as she lost herself in dazed arousal? Or just poorly aimed at his head?

Why was he so bad at this? Surely no other man had to sue a woman just so he could make her put up with him long enough that he had a chance to figure out how to talk to her.

Available now!

ONCE UPON A ROSE

ACKNOWLEDGEMENTS

I owe a huge debt of gratitude to the wonderful Virginia Kantra, whose insight into story really helped me find the right track again on this book, after some unexpected events derailed it in the summer. She is not only a fantastic author, whose feedback is invaluable, but a true friend. Many, many other authors and readers offered to beta read, too, and I want to thank all of them for the impulse to help. I know how hard it is to take time from your own obligations to help someone else, and it's truly appreciated.

And thanks also to my daughter Mia, for all the straightforward advice!

In the research for this book, I owe a huge thanks to Joseph Mul, who has one of the real last great valleys of roses in France, and who allowed me to come "help" with the harvest, play in his roses, and interrogate him relentlessly as to the career and life of a rose-grower in the south of France. I am deeply grateful also to Jean-François Vieille, who answered all my often-clueless questions about the extraction process for roses. Carole Biancalana, of the Domaine de Manon Plascassier, also graciously allowed me to visit her domaine and answered my many questions.

And these thanks would not be complete without mentioning the wonderful Lynne de R., the artisan perfumer who, in partnership with Guy Bouchara, has a shop in the old streets of Grasse and who spoke to my and my toddler from a doorway one hot Provençal afternoon, when I was finding all other doorways into the close-guarded perfume world of Grasse quite closed. Not only did she prove a fount of information about perfumery—research that will come out in another book—but she is the one who put me in touch with M. Mul and finally made the setting of this book possible.

And I want to give a shout-out to the wonderful graphic novelist Zeina Abirached, whose work and conversations with me inspired the backstory for Layla's mother. (And who did, indeed, make a video about her "sheep hair" which you can find on YouTube.) While any other resemblance is completely accidental, her beautiful curly hair did inspire Layla's. For a beautiful and vivid look at the civil war in Beirut through the eyes of a child, I strongly recommend her work.

And a huge thank you, of course, goes to all my readers for your patience in waiting for this book and for all your support. I hope you enjoy this world, too!

ONCE UPON A ROSE

ABOUT LAURA FLORAND

Laura Florand burst on the contemporary romance scene in 2012 with her award-winning Amour et Chocolat series. Her international bestselling books have appeared in ten languages, been named among the Best Books of the Year by *Romantic Times* and Barnes & Noble, received the RT Seal of Excellence and starred reviews from *Publishers Weekly, Library Journal,* and *Booklist,* and been recommended by NPR, *USA Today,* and *The Wall Street Journal,* among others.

After a Fulbright year in Tahiti and backpacking everywhere from New Zealand to Greece, and several years living in Madrid and Paris, Laura now teaches Romance Studies at Duke University. Contrary to what the "Romance Studies" may imply, this means she primarily teaches French language and culture and does a great deal of research on French gastronomy, particularly chocolate.

Website: www.lauraflorand.com
Twitter: @LauraFlorand
Facebook: www.facebook.com/LauraFlorandAuthor
Newsletter: www.lauraflorand.com/newsletter/

LAURA FLORAND

COPYRIGHT

Copyright 2015, Laura Florand

Cover by Sébastien Florand

ISBN-13: 978-0-9885065-9-6

CPSIA information can be obtained at www.ICGtesting.com
Printed in the USA
LVOW11s0252120815

449697LV00008BC/681/P